NO ROOM FOR TWO GUARDIANS

When Steve parked on Megan's side of the street, he noticed another vehicle parked across the way with a man sitting calmly in it. The car was positioned so it wasn't in the direct illumination of the streetlight. Once in a while, the driver was on a cell phone, but it was clear to Steve that his attention was on Megan's house.

"Son of a bitch," he muttered. "The bastard's gone and hired someone to watch her." He waited a while longer and then drove away and circled the area. When he returned, the vehicle was still there.

He noticed the driver had his window open. Perfect, he thought. He put on his work gloves, got out of his truck, went to the rear and found his small sledgehammer. . . .

Other *Leisure* books by Andrew Neiderman:

THE MAGIC BULLET

Guardian
Angel

ANDREW
NEIDERMAN

LEISURE BOOKS NEW YORK CITY

For our grandson Dustin, another
graduation gift.

A LEISURE BOOK®

January 2010

Published by

Dorchester Publishing Co., Inc.
200 Madison Avenue
New York, NY 10016

ISBN 10: 0-8439-6285-2
ISBN 13: 978-0-8439-6285-7
E-ISBN: 978-1-4285-0790-6

Visit us online at www.dorchesterpub.com.

Guardian
Angel

PROLOGUE

Scott Lester's Beverly Hills street was dazzling under the glow of the streetlights. The lawns of houses were veritable carpets of rich green, the driveways immaculate, many with rich textured tiles that looked too expensive and too good for mere car tires to ride over. Everywhere he turned, he saw Mercedes, Rolls, Lexus, and Jaguar. You could smell the money here, he thought, and imagined the combined net worth of the people on any one block would equal the budget of a number of Third World countries.

And what was wrong with that? Nothing. The purpose of wealth is to insulate you from the ugly, the ordinary, the pedestrian. The richer you were, the thicker and higher became your walls and the more you could protect your family and yourself. His father and so many wealthy people he knew took it all for granted after a while, maybe in most cases from the very beginning, but not him. Oh, no. If he had one good quality, he thought, it was his appreciation of his money, not for its own sake, but for what it could provide and how hard he had to work to get it.

Almost every night he rode back from work, he

had these arguments with himself . . . or with his wife Megan, to be more exact. These objections and doubts, these challenges to his way of thinking and living were hers, not his. He couldn't ignore them, however.

So he was obsessed with making more. So what? It was a good fault to have. If his intentions for making it were admirable, how could his pursuit of it ever be incorrect? He just happened to be married to a woman who didn't quite get it yet, despite how many years they'd been together. They were looking toward their tenth anniversary, in fact.

She'll appreciate what I'm doing eventually, he thought. She would look around her and see how others lived, how other husbands were lackadaisical and satisfied with being average. He was confident about it. Eventually, she would understand and see what he was saying.

Most important, she would stop nagging him about all the time he spent away from her and their daughter. He'd told her from the beginning that he was not a nine-to-five, five-days-a-week kind of guy, hadn't he? She'd known what she was getting into when she married him. He wasn't dishonest about it. He'd made it as clear as possible. His and his father's investment business was what they call 24-7. It was how his father had built this large financial empire and Scott, as the obvious prince to inherit it all, could do no less than live up to his father's expectations, despite Megan's constantly urging him to be his own man.

What did that mean anyway? Be your own man. What if he wanted to be just like his father? It was his choice, wasn't it? Lately, she was making him feel as though it weren't. She was trying to convince him he was not only working in his father's shadow, but was wearing it.

He put Megan out of mind quickly when he heard the Wall Street report come on the radio. He had been too busy all day to check his portfolio, but there were five stocks he was hoping would take off finally. His father never stopped mocking him for investing so heavily in the market. The old man had made his fortune and built his company on smart real-estate deals and nothing else.

"Property, Scott, that's a sensible place to put your money. It's something tangible, something you can see, feel, smell, if you have to and know you've got something that won't let you down, if you just have the patience."

Was there a day that passed when his father didn't lecture him about something, especially his marriage? Right from the beginning, his father had known what Megan thought of men like him, men consumed with their work and with the power that came from great wealth. He did his best to sugarcoat it, but there was no denying what his father saw in Megan's face—not only a lack of respect, but defiance and disdain.

"The reason you're having trouble now, boy, is you chose a woman who was simply too pedestrian," his father had told him just recently. "She didn't have, and I'm afraid will never have, the vision to see what is important and what is not. Now, your mother . . . There was a woman who knew on which side the bread was buttered. That woman never once stood in my way or discouraged me. If I told her I couldn't make a date or an event, she didn't whine about it. She went alone if she was so inclined, or just nodded and understood. She knew I wasn't doing anything to hurt her. On the contrary, I was building something for us all. She took that attitude to the grave, and I always appreciated her for it."

Scott had simply nodded. He'd wanted to say, *But what about me, Dad? What about all the ball games I was in that you missed? You even missed my graduation ceremony because you had what you called a major acquisition to make in Texas.*

He didn't say or ask about these things. More and more he was feeling like the son in Harry Chapin's "Cat's in the Cradle" song. He was or had become just like his father. That was Megan's complaint when she talked about the shadow. He hated to admit it, even for a second, but maybe she was right.

This moment of self-doubt was short-lived, however. He heard some good news on one of the stocks and turned up the radio. Then he cried out his joy, slapped the dash and flipped to his CD to hear some music. He was so into his moment of happiness that he almost drove past his own large Tudor home. It was one of the bigger houses in Beverly Hills, valued at more than twelve million. He loved bringing prospective clients to it and watching their eyes widen at the sight of his property.

A familiar car coming out of his driveway slowed him down. He saw another come out, and then another, and hit his brakes. Why so many visitors?

"Holy shit!" he exclaimed and sat back when the realization hit him.

He had forgotten.

Today was his daughter Jennifer's ninth birthday party and he had sworn to both Megan and Jennifer at breakfast that he would be there.

Megan settled Jennifer in her room with her new toys, dolls, games and clothes, and went down to the family room, where she had staged the party for a dozen of Jennifer's classmates and their mothers. Even two fathers had attended, coming directly from their work. One of them was Ernie Cornbleau, a major criminal attorney with some high-profile cases. He was always in the news or on local television. How could he find the time? But he had for his daughter, Jennifer's best friend. How many times had both Megan and Ernie remarked that the two girls were more like sisters? Scott, on the other hand, always forgot Ernie's daughter's name.

"If she were a stock," Megan had told him, "you'd remember."

She stood looking at the decorations and then settled in the corner red leather chair. The January afternoons were shorter, and with their house facing the east, shadows came flooding in the picture windows, darkening the room that earlier had been bursting with light and the laughter of children. She conjured Jennifer's face when the cake had been brought in. Jennifer had been taking piano lessons for three years now and was doing really well. What was most important was that she loved it and didn't see it as some dreary interruption of playtime.

This was her father's influence, Megan thought.

Although he had become an insurance-company executive, rising rapidly on the corporate ladder, her father had had a wonderful musical ear and was actually self-taught on the piano. He'd never been able to read music, yet he was always the one entertaining at family parties. It brought a smile to her face, remembering those days when she and her older sister, Clare, would harmonize behind him and their mother would brighten with pride. Their dad's death in his early fifties had been like an earthquake that would not stop. The aftershock lasted until this day.

Their mother lived with Clare in Akron. Clare was married with three children, all girls— Dawn, fourteen; Terri, sixteen; and Steffi, now eighteen and in her first year at college. Megan and Clare spoke often, so Clare knew of her marital unhappiness, but she was more like their mother, a hopeless optimist who ended every discussion with "Things will get better. Give it time."

"Time," Megan would remind her. "We've nearly reached our tenth anniversary, Clare."

"Some men take longer," Clare would insist.

Maybe Clare had inherited more of their father's happy nature, too, Megan thought in frustration. Sometimes, when she'd watched their father play the piano, she saw a man who was in a state of bliss. At least he had something. His piano was the antidote to any unhappiness. She should have taken lessons, she thought.

Megan had had Jennifer's birthday cake shaped like a piano, with the nine candles set on the keys.

What brilliance in Jennifer's face when that cake had been presented. Megan saw in her so much of herself as a young girl, but she saw so much of Scott as well, saw his intense look, that studied expression that told you, he—and now, she—was considering everything carefully, weighing the value of this or that. He'd surely have gotten some pleasure out of seeing her. How could he miss these precious moments, moments that would never come again? Where was the man with whom she had first fallen in love? Or was she just so blind as not to see he was never really there?

She caught the way Ernie was looking at her and at the door, wondering where Scott was. He gave her his best comforting smile, but his mere presence, his awareness of the pain in her heart from the deep disappointment, made it all even worse. Now she wished he hadn't come. His coming underlined Scott's absence that much more, but she would never say such a thing to Ernie. He was a sweet man—strong, successful, but family oriented, too. It was truly as if he knew what his priorities should be. When he kissed her on the cheek before leaving and squeezed her arm gently, she felt more like someone who was in mourning than a mother taking joy in her daughter's wonderful birthday.

Damn him, she thought, and sat staring at the doorway. The shadows darkened. She heard the garage door going up. He was finally home. He would come in through the kitchen and make his way to the family room. She heard the door to the garage open and close and then his footsteps in the hallway from the small entry into the main part of their home. Moments later, he was standing there looking in. She realized he didn't see her. She was too well cloaked in the shadows. She wondered if the realization that he had missed his daughter's birthday party had just occurred to him. After all, the streamers and the balloons were still hanging from the chandelier. The party plates with party hats beside them were on the long table she had set up, and a cutout sign with glitter borders read, HAPPY BIRTHDAY JENNIFER. There was even some of the birthday cake on the table.

"Damn it," she heard him say.

"Yes, Scott, damn it," she repeated, and he pulled his head back in surprise and then entered the room.

"Why are you sitting there in the dark, Meg?"

"I figured since you've been in the dark so long, I might just see how it is myself," she replied.

He was silent. He looked around and then raised his arms.

"Hey, look, I'm sorry. Really. I had planned to be here, but there was something of a crisis at the company. Dad was very upset. I tried to leave three times, but . . ."

"Why don't you just hit play, Scott? You've recorded that story so many times before that it surely just goes on without you."

"We're talking about a lot of money here, Megan. You don't seem to understand what it takes to keep up this place, pay for all this, including piano lessons, new cars, clothes, expensive restaurants, birthday parties, maids—"

"Stop," she said, holding up her hand. "Everything we have you wanted more than I did, and still do. I never asked for all this. I didn't marry you for all this." She paused. "Of course, I'm having a harder and harder time remembering why I married you, but . . ."

"Very funny."

"Is it? I wonder why I can't laugh."

"Meg, listen . . ."

"It's not going to change, is it, Scott? It's never going to change."

"Look. I told you. I had every intention of being here on time," he whined. "But . . ."

"You already explained that your father and the business come first." She sat back. "Never mind that he's never really been any sort of grandfather for Jennifer, and that he should have wanted to be here for his granddaughter's birthday as much as you should."

"Dad wanted to be here. He did. I told you . . ."

"He didn't even ask you about it, did he, Scott? He didn't even remember."

"Sure, he—"

"Where's her present from him?"

"He told me to give her five hundred dollars."

Megan simply stared.

"Case closed," she said, and then stood up and began to clear the table.

"If you let me hire a maid for these special occasions, you wouldn't have to do this," he said.

Megan wouldn't have a live-in maid and had agreed to have their maid three times a week, even though she'd thought two would be enough.

She turned on him sharply.

"I want to do this, Scott. I want to be a part of my daughter's life. This isn't hard, terrible work to me. This is the joy of having a child. Something you just don't get. You want to know something, Scott? I don't think you'll ever get it," she added.

She turned her back to him, but she didn't move to do anything.

She heard him sigh.

"Where is she?"

"Upstairs in her room."

"I'll go explain," he said and started out.

She turned back quickly.

"Yeah, do that, Scott. Explain. But I'm telling you this. I'm not ending up like your mother, shrinking in a closet, another discarded possession."

"Hey, that's not . . ."

"Fair? We'll see what's fair. We'll let some divorce court decide," she added.

"Megan."

She worked faster.

He shook his head and started for the stairway.

He was too far away to hear her sobs and he couldn't see her tears anyway.

"I'm not dying," she muttered to herself. "I'm not dying this way."

The shadows merged with the darkness outside. Despite the bright streetlights and the passing vehicles, the world she saw through the window looked very unfriendly and suddenly very dangerous.

For she was about to be a woman with a child, on her own, and even in Beverly Hills that was unpredictable.

CHAPTER ONE

Still in his construction-work clothes, he sat in his room and stared at the picture of his late wife. She seemed to be staring at him, too, as if she were waiting for him to answer a question. She had always had that expression on her face when she asked him something. It was an expression that told him she devalued his answer no matter what it was. She had been not unlike his fifth-grade teacher . . . all his teachers, for that matter. His answers had never been quite good enough for them. He'd stopped raising his hand to answer questions in class after a while, and if he was called upon, he'd just shaken his head, even though he knew the right responses. They had found that out later, and some had asked him why he didn't respond.

"Why should I share what I know with them?" he'd replied, meaning the others in his classes.

"How about with me?" his English teacher, Mr. Knox, had countered.

"You already know the answer."

"But share it with me," he'd insisted.

"Right, sure," he'd said, and nodded, but never had.

Ignoring people or giving them the answers

they wanted was always much easier than arguing. He'd been that way with Julia, and maybe that was why she had always worn that expression whenever she asked him a question and why that expression was indelibly printed on her face in the photo.

"What?" he blurted.

His door was closed, so his mother couldn't hear him talking to a picture on the dresser.

"You want to know why you're dead? Is that what you're asking me? Why did you agree to marry me if you didn't want to have children with me? That wasn't fair. You kept a major thing secret, and it wasn't as if I didn't run at the mouth before we were married when it came to talking about kids and raising a family.

"What's more important than family anyway? Having a bigger, more expensive house, expensive cars, lots of new clothes, your trips, jewelry . . . what? What?"

He realized he was speaking too loud even behind a closed bedroom door and stopped.

He lowered his head and clutched his hands between his thighs, swinging his wrist from right to left, pounding each knee. She'd hated that.

"What are you doing?" she would ask.

He'd stop. "Huh? Nothing."

"That's a peculiar nervous action. You really need to talk to someone about it and some of the other weird things you've been doing lately, like breaking all the pencils in two and grinding your teeth at night. You sound like you're sawing wood on a job. Why can't you just snore like most men? And why are you breaking all the pencils? It's weird!"

He looked at the photo as if she had just said this.

"Don't call what I do weird. It's weird to be a woman and not want children. That's weird. You're built to have children. What if no woman wanted to have children, huh? What would happen to the human race? You don't even want children if we hired some surrogate mother to carry the fetus. Don't you think that's weird?"

He waited for her answer, but just as it had been when she was alive, there was no response. She would simply turn away and do something or change the subject.

He'd tried getting her to see it his way, hadn't he? He'd made sure they were friends with couples that had children, but whenever they had attended a dinner at one of those couples' homes, she'd always complained about the noise the children made, or how the children demanded too much attention and didn't let them enjoy themselves.

"They're just children," he would tell her. "You were a child once and just as demanding and as noisy, I'm sure."

"Yes, I was, and that's why I don't want to go through it."

Some answer. She was a miserable kid, so their children had to be? Where's the logic in that? He could ask, but she wouldn't answer. She wouldn't give in; she wouldn't have children.

It didn't matter that he'd said he would volunteer to do everything for their children. He'd cook the meals, clean their rooms, take them for walks or to the playground, whatever. Whatever she didn't want to do for them, he would do.

"You say that now," she'd told him, "but after I

give birth, you'll be too busy working or going out with your buddies. I know how it gets. Didn't you tell me it was that way with your own father?"

"I'm better than my father," he'd cried. "I swore I would be and I wouldn't be like him. I made a sacred promise to myself on the day we were married that I'd be a better husband and father, if you gave me a chance."

"Right. Promises are like balloons. They float for a while and then lose their air and sink to earth. There's nothing as ugly or as disappointing as a balloon that's leaked all its air. It feels like . . . a glob."

"Feels like a glob." He'd shaken his head. "And you call me weird," he'd told her.

He stood up and walked to the window in his room. He was back living now with his mother in the house in which he had grown up. After Julia's death, he hadn't wanted to remain in the apartment. There was too much of her still in it and so he was back in his old room, which now felt more like a prison cell. He incarcerated himself more than he had to because he knew what his mother would be saying out there in the kitchen or the living room.

"Why don't you go out and look for another nice woman?"

"I didn't have a nice woman. Don't say 'another.'"

"Oh, she wasn't bad. I got along with her."

"She was selfish. I would have hated to be locked in a broken elevator with her. She would have breathed all the air."

"Oh, stop. Don't talk that way about the dead."

He looked out at the house that was practically attached to theirs. In this part of West LA, the developers squeezed every inch into every possible lot. There were homes so close to each other, the inhabitants could reach out of windows to shake hands. But this was the best his father could do and his mother certainly wasn't left with enough money to go find something different. Besides, the mortgage was paid. It was the least expensive living condition for her. Every time he talked about getting her out and finding a better place for them to live, she replied, "This is where I'm supposed to be until I die. Besides, you should be thinking again of a new home for yourself and a new wife and family."

Of course, he thought about it, but he wanted to be extra cautious this time, extra sure. God forbid that he would make another mistake similar to the one he had made with Julia. It was highly likely these days, too. Women these days were so into themselves that they made Julia's self-centeredness look absolutely altruistic. Most of them weren't interested in getting married early anyway. All the women he met were thinking about career first and a family second. They wanted to realize their potential, whatever that meant. They were competitive with men and didn't see why they had to be the ones to stay at home and raise the family. Remember *Mr. Mom*? Or look at a woman running for president . . . or what about all the women who run big companies? Marriage and an immediate trip to the maternity ward were seen as a personal defeat.

Go romance one of them? he thought. Maybe he

should take his mother out with him so she could see for herself. That possibility amused him. He could just see her sitting there beside him, sipping her famous whiskey sour, practically the only hard drink she would ever drink, and listening to the conversations he was having with possible candidates for romance. He would turn to her after a while and she would shake her head.

"Next," she would say.

"Next? Next is the same, Mom, but I'll call up another one for you to see and hear."

Maybe then she would stop her nagging.

He watched the shadows spread and slowly thicken until it was dark. She was calling him to come to dinner. He had almost gone out to eat tonight. She was still a good cook and all, but the conversation would inevitably return to his starting anew, finding another wife.

"Julia's dead now two years," she had reminded him. She'd paused and shaken her head and said, "I still don't understand what happened that day on your boat. I can't get it through my head."

"That's because you never would go on my boat, so you don't understand what's involved. You can't be careless on a boat in bad weather," he'd repeated—chanted, he should say. That was what it had become, a chant. "Navigating in the ocean is serious business. You can't be doing your fingernails at the same time or sitting there with earphones on, listening to some stupid music while I'm telling you what to do."

"But didn't you hear the weather before you went out? You told me you always check on the weather before you go out to sea."

"Weather can change quickly over the ocean," he'd told her. "Let's stop talking about this already. It won't bring her back and it doesn't make me feel very good."

"I can't help feeling sorry for her," his mother had said. "I think about her a lot lately. You think a shark ate her body, or what?"

"Whatever did eat her soon after surely had a bad case of heartburn."

"Stop that talk. I did get along well with her. She was like a daughter to me."

That was true, he thought, although he didn't know why there had been any affection between them. Why hadn't his mother resented Julia for not giving her grandchildren as much as he had resented her for not giving him a son or a daughter, or both? It was at her insistence that he had put up a tombstone in the cemetery just so she could have a place to go to pay her respects. How stupid was that?

"I would have had a daughter, you know," his mother told him. "They told me it was a female. You would have had a younger sister. I had that miscarriage and then your father wouldn't try again."

He never understood that.

Why wouldn't he try again?

Did that mean they didn't have sex again?

All she would tell him was his father had said, "I don't want to go through that again."

"What did he go through? He wasn't the one who was pregnant. You were," he'd replied.

"A pregnant woman is not an easy woman to live with sometimes," she'd said. "Both husband

and wife share the ordeal. I was also very depressed after the miscarriage and he lost patience with me. It wasn't his fault."

"Of course it was. He was a self-centered bastard."

"Don't speak of your father that way, and never talk that way about the dead."

"Ma, please," he'd moaned, and rushed away before he said anything worse. He always fled from these conversations. And she always sat there looking stunned by her own words and thoughts as if she didn't know she was capable of saying them or thinking them.

"Dinner is ready," she said, knocking on his door.

"Coming."

He rubbed his cheeks and stretched.

On the way out he paused at Julia's portrait.

"I'll tell you why you're dead," he said. "You're dead because no one really cares about your being dead. My mother moans about you once in a while, but she didn't go to your tombstone this year. She doesn't lose sleep over you, and your parents are both gone. We had no children, Julia. There's no one to go visit your grave, not that you really have one. There's no one even to think about you under the water, your bones rotting under the sea. How's it feel, being all alone down there with fish making homes in your skull?

"Family, that's what gives us immortality and a reason to live. Maybe your cosmetics advisor or your clothes saleslady talks about you once in a while, huh? Don't bet on it, Julia. I doubt they even remember who you were.

"I might as well go to the cemetery and scrape your name off that stupid tombstone. What good's a name to a woman without any children, dead or otherwise?"

"It's getting cold!" his mother screamed.

He glared at the picture and then he turned it down on its face. He still couldn't make himself get rid of it. If he did that, his mother would never stop asking him why he had done so. He hated the image of her suspicious eyes, but at least he didn't have to have her staring at him and asking him questions all night, even when he was sleeping.

And dreaming about that day on the boat and the look on her face when she was struggling to stay afloat in those rough waves, screaming for him and reaching up for his hand while he knelt there looking down at her. He'd watched her swallowing water and spitting and gasping. She'd extended her fingers and he had almost touched them, but then he'd quickly pulled his hand back and shaken his head.

He was confident that someday he would forget that look of surprise on her face, the way she had simply accepted his refusal. Was she smiling? Did she dare smile? He was confident that when the right time came, that image would sink to the sea as well, and in its place much-welcomed darkness would come.

Good night and good-bye, he thought, and went to eat his mother's dinner.

It didn't surprise Megan that Scott didn't believe her. He lived in a world where 90 percent of what people said was either exaggeration or outright untruth. She also had the sense that Scott believed she simply wasn't capable of striking out on her own. She needed him too much, was far too dependent upon him for nearly everything. Why, she didn't write a check without his approval and got her spending money weekly like some child getting an allowance. Her girlfriends teased her about it and she pretended it didn't bother her. Her comeback was always, "I hate bothering with money." All this surely contributed to his lack of respect for her.

Actually, she couldn't blame him for this opinion of her. Because she had come so much later in her parents' marriage, nearly eight years after Clare, she had been coddled by them. They had been nowhere near as wealthy as Scott's parents of course, but that hadn't stopped her father from lavishing gifts upon her, buying her anything she wanted or even simply gazed at with interest. No matter what childhood illness she had, her mother had treated it as if it were nearly fatal. This overprotective childhood had continued into her teen years and even into her first year at college. Clare had teased her about it. She was already married and had her three children, so there hadn't been the usual sibling rivalry for their parents' attention. For Clare it had been more a subject of amusement.

She'd had the foresight to kid her after she married Scott and say she thought Megan had leaped at Scott Lester's marriage proposal to get away from her overwhelming parents.

Of course, now she was prone to look for every excuse to explain how or why she had gotten into this marriage. The truth was, she really did love Scott, and all through their dating, he was one of the most sensitive, loving young men she had ever met—not that she was any expert, when it came to that. She would never call herself experienced when it came to boys and young men.

Throughout high school, she had been quite shy. No matter whom she liked, her mother or her father seemed to be able to find something to criticize, something to use to discourage her from getting too deeply involved. Consequently, she never had. In fact, even though she tried to hide it from her roommates at USC, she'd been a virgin.

She'd tried to imitate the other girls, to be just as carefree and wild when it came to meeting boys. The truth was, she was uncomfortable with the pursuit, and for the most part found that most of the boys who showed interest in her were quite immature. She was afraid of being thought a snob, so she'd dated even when she had little enthusiasm for the boy asking her out. Her parents were always asking her about it. After all, she was away from home and beyond their protective reach. And then there was Clare, always telling her to "start having a good time, Megan. You don't get to do it over." Maybe Clare had regretted her own quick marriage and motherhood.

Megan had met Scott quite by accident. Her roommate, Dana Morris, was meeting her cousin Alice who had flown in from Dallas to audition for a Hollywood agent. They'd met Alice in Brentwood at a coffee bar. Scott, who had already graduated Harvard Business School, was meeting a client. His client never showed. Afterward, both of them thought that proved they were meant to be. At least, she had.

He was sitting at the table beside theirs, and because he was alone, he was obviously paying attention to their conversation, which was mostly a conversation between Dana and Alice about their relatives. She caught him smiling at her, and at first—as usual—avoided eye contact. But something kept her turning his way until he leaned over and said, "Excuse me, girls, but I couldn't help hearing one of you mention Jeff Gerson. If that's the Hollywood agent, I handled a big commercial building investment for him. In this town that means I have some juice, when it comes to him."

Of course, Alice was intrigued and quickly asked him to join them.

"Thanks. I've got a client who's apparently a no-show," *he said, taking the seat next to Megan. Again, she tried to avoid his eyes, but it wasn't easy because he was so good-looking and obviously not some college boy. He was dressed in a pinstripe suit and wore a Rolex and a large diamond pinky ring in a gold setting.* "So when's your audition?" *he asked Alice.*

He was a polite listener, but his attention moved quickly to Megan, firing one question after another.

"What year are you in?"

"First," *she said.*

"You're a freshman? You looked like a senior to me."

She blushed of course, and Dana nearly giggled, but he remained serious.

"I'm a pretty good judge of character. You have to be in my business," *he told Alice and Dana,* "and when I looked at you . . . Megan, is it?"

"Yes, Megan."

"When I looked at you, I thought, there's a young woman who looks serious. Freshmen . . . no offense,

*girls ... have a flighty demeanor. They're still caught
up in the social stuff and not yet thinking seriously
about the reason they're in school. Am I right?" he asked
Dana.*

*"I suppose, but there's nothing wrong with that," she
said defensively.*

*"Absolutely not," he agreed. "In fact, these days, I
wish I was back to being a freshman."*

*That was his opening to tell them who he was and
what he was doing. When Alice asked Dana to go along
with her to the audition, Scott told Megan he'd be happy
to run her back to the dormitory. It wasn't out of his
way. None of them were more surprised than she was at
her quick decision to let him do so.*

*"You guys still have a lot of family catching up to
do," she explained.*

Dana gave her a "wow" look and agreed.

Megan often thought about that first meeting,
and not just about Scott's client not showing. Often
she reviewed her own feelings, especially her sudden power to overcome her usual shy ways. It had
to have meant something, she concluded. True
love will not be denied. What helped also was
Scott's manner. He wasn't overly aggressive. He'd
never struck her as a womanizer, despite his looks
and his wealth.

Later, of course, she discovered he was an only
child, but his parents didn't dote on him. It was
quite the opposite. His father was always challenging him, pushing him to be independent. "Nothing," Scott had once said, "makes a man feel better
about himself than having his son try to be just
like him. It reinforces his self-image and gives jus-
tification for the choices he made in his life."

So there she was, a freshman in college who had

never been far from home, whose experiences were quite limited when it came to socializing and travel, dating a man who had graduated two years earlier and who was already in the real world, a man who had traveled a great deal with his parents, was passably adequate in speaking and understanding both French and Spanish, and knew movie stars.

During every date, every moment they were together, in fact, she'd felt like his student. He seemed to know everything about anything, whether it was what food and wine to order in expensive restaurants or to how she should wear her hair or do her makeup. He had never made his suggestions in a condescending manner either, and whenever she followed them, she always felt better or looked better. Compliments began flowing her way, and for the first time, her girlfriends at school were seriously envious. Everyone had wanted to listen to her talking about her dates. She had, through Scott, suddenly risen from being the inexperienced virginal fish out of water to Miss Sophistication.

It had been that way with their sex, too. He'd been delighted she was still a virgin. He, obviously, had long since not been, and when he made love, he knew exactly how to please her. In those early days, he had never made love without being sure she had gotten as much or more out of it than he had. In a sense, he was teaching her how to be a complete woman.

But it was all this guidance, all this growing because of him, that gave Scott the impression she would never be able to get along without him. He'd kept her afloat. He'd convinced her to marry him before she completed her second year of college. Her parents were surprised at how quickly she had decided. Ironically, her father, who was a cracker-jack insurance salesman, hadn't seen how effective Scott was when it came to convincing someone to buy something or take a chance on an idea.

"You're only in liberal arts anyway," Scott had told her. "You don't seem inclined toward any particular subject or career. Why not make a career out of being Mrs. Scott Lester? You won't regret it."

You won't regret it, she thought. The words haunted her now as she opened the office door that read, EMILY LLOYD, ATTORNEY AT LAW. She couldn't help feeling numb all morning. Scott had repeated his apologies and regrets even as he rushed out before having breakfast with her, because he had a breakfast scheduled with one of his father's and his clients. She had said nothing. She had given him the silent treatment before, but he had shrugged it off. She could see it in his face: *You'll break down and talk. What else will you do?*

Here's what else I'll do, she thought, and gave her name to Emily Lloyd's secretary. She was led into her office immediately. Despite her inner rage, she couldn't keep her hand from trembling when Emily Lloyd extended hers. The five-feet-two-inch woman with a stern, no-nonsense look in her eyes picked up on it immediately.

"Relax, Mrs. Lester. Tell me your story and we'll do the right things for you and your daughter."

Megan took a deep breath and began to relate her life with Scott and especially how it had been during the last year and a half. When she was finished, Emily Lloyd shook her head, looked out the window a moment and then turned to her and said, "Sounds more like a case of desertion. Forget incompatibility."

"I should warn you before we start, Ms. Lloyd. Gordon Lester, Scott's father, is a very powerful man. There won't be an attorney sitting across from you; there'll be a battery of attorneys."

"David and Goliath."

"No, Meg and the Lesters."

Emily Lloyd laughed.

"No doubt, I wasn't the woman Scott's father wanted him to marry, but it was the one independent and firm decision Scott made. I think as punishment, Scott's father gave him more responsibility, more to do, so there would be a strain on our marriage."

"Maybe, but that's not a good argument for us. Scott's the master of his own destiny. He's old enough. Any affairs?"

Meg laughed.

"Sometimes I wish there were. It would make it easier to hate him."

"Then, you don't?"

"No. I'm just tired of it. Scott's been walking in his father's shadow so long, he can't see anything. I'm stifling. Get me out of it. Get me into fresh air."

Emily Lloyd nodded.

"I'll do my best," she said. "But let me explain how this works. First, we file a petition, which will be served on Scott. The petition asks that the marriage status of you and Scott be terminated and a judgment entered. The required period is six months."

"Six months?"

"We can't speed that up, I'm afraid. The concept is to give the two parties time to calm down and perhaps reconsider. He'll have thirty days to respond with his view of the pertinent facts. Then the case will be set for a court hearing.

"In this instance, of course, there are child-custody matters as well. I don't see him fighting your primary custody, but if he has any arguments about it and/or visitation rights, it will go to mandatory counseling at what we call conciliation court.

"If we don't get into any serious disputes over these matters, we'll move toward a marital settlement providing for equal division of community property, child support, et cetera. We'll have to have the assets valued, so this will take up time.

"Now, I always ask my clients this question. I've already asked about Scott. Are you having an affair? Can he bring up anything to challenge the custody of your daughter? It's best I know what he will tell his lawyer."

"No, absolutely not, absolutely nothing. He's going to be more shocked by this than anyone."

"Well, then, if this is truly what you want after six months, I can assure you, you will get it," Emily Lloyd said. She was silent a moment and then added, "Just be sure it's what you want."

"I'm sure," Megan said. "It took all my courage to get this far. I don't know if you understand, but . . ."

"I understand," Emily Lloyd said, leaning forward. "I got a divorce after ten years of marriage. Fifty percent of marriages these days end in divorce. Welcome to the club."

Megan said nothing.

Despite how she felt now, this was one club she wished she couldn't join.

Her hand trembled when she called Clare that afternoon and told her the news. She asked her to do her a favor and break it to their mother.

"I know she's not doing so well these days with her diabetes and all. It's good she has you nearby," she added.

"From the sound of you, you might need me nearby," Clare responded.

"I'll get through it. Thanks, Clare."

She was sure both of them were thinking about how hard Daddy would have taken the news and how quickly he would have gone to his piano.

That night when he went to sleep, he immediately dreamed of a new life for himself. He was married again and his wife was pregnant almost hours after they performed the wedding ceremony. This was a fantasy he enjoyed, but more and more it was a fantasy out of necessity.

His mother had done the usual nagging at dinner, making him feel inadequate. He didn't believe she had intended to do that, but it was the way he felt when he heard her talking incessantly about his failure to find a good woman. It was as if she believed they were out there, growing on trees, and all he had to do was get into the female orchard and pluck one for himself. It wasn't their fault; it was his.

"I can't believe all the women you meet are so bad," she told him. "You're giving up too quickly."

He hated that expression more than anything—

"giving up too quickly." He was certainly no quitter. She was parroting his father now. With him gone, she had to pick up all his miserable expressions and throw them around the house, scatter them like chicken feed. Every time he was unable to do something, no matter how daunting the task, his father had hit him with that "you're giving up too quickly" line. There were many others as well, and before he had met Julia and married her, many that mocked his still living at home.

"If you had a wife and your own home and family, your mother wouldn't be washing your clothes. *She* would."

"Your mother's got to cut that umbilical cord. I trip over it every morning."

"You're already ten years older than I was when I got married and we had you. Those were the days when men were men and women were women. Now you can't tell a man from a woman no more."

"Cut your hair or I'll have your mother braid it."

On and on, like a flood of derision. Why had his father wanted to have any children? Maybe his birth was a mistake. On more than one occasion he had heard his father tell someone that God rains children down on us as punishment for former sins. He'd say that right in his presence, too.

Some day, he thought, I'll take my wife and children to the cemetery to see his grave and I'll have my kids stand on it. I'll tell them to stamp the ground so that it will feel like a heavy rainfall. They won't understand why or why I'd be smiling, but that's fine.

He woke up from his fantasy dream and turned over to look at the moonlight cutting through the trees outside. Moonlight made him feel lonelier. So did soft music and a woman's laugh. The world was a symphony of painful noises when you were by yourself, he thought. He really didn't enjoy anything.

He hated going to the movies by himself, so he didn't go.

He hated eating in a restaurant by himself, so he didn't go.

He hated going to shows by himself. Hell, he even hated driving by himself.

The idea of a vacation seemed terrifying.

And he hated making friends with guys who were married and had children. All they did was talk about their families and when it was his turn to speak, there was a deep silence that echoed in his head.

All he did enjoy was going on his boat by himself, but he never felt he was by himself then.

He knew most men claimed to envy him. He could hear the dumb expressions. *When I was single, my pockets did jingle.*

So did your brains, he thought.

One thing he really hated was to be invited to a party and have to go alone or go to meet one of the single women who sat around waiting for someone to be thunderstruck with their beauty and personality. Women his age were all rejects, he thought. It was like eating leftovers.

No thanks.

Sorry, can't attend.

A cloud moved over the moon and the darkness that ensued was like a needle in his heart. He groaned and turned over on his back to look up at the ceiling.

Julia's face appeared on it. She was smiling down at him.

He could hear her from the bottom of the sea, her words coming up in bubbles and popping in his ears.

You think you're better off now. Look to your right. Anyone lying beside you?

You don't even have good sex anymore. Go out and make some poor girl pregnant and then volunteer to be her husband. That's the only way you'll have a family.

"Shut up!" he screamed. "Shut up!"

His mother came to the door. He could hear her standing out there waiting to hear him shout again.

Julia smiled.

He turned over on his stomach and pressed his mouth to the pillow.

He was screaming inside, screaming at himself.

"You all right in there?" he heard his mother ask.

He didn't answer.

She waited and then she went back to sleep.

He knew what she was mumbling to herself: "I wish he'd find someone and get off my back."

"I'm not just going to pick someone to make you happy," he muttered. "She has to be the right one. I'm not making that mistake again."

His firmness and determination gave him relief. This was, after all, the only reason why he was still alone. He was particular and intelligent about his choices. His friends wondered why he had to be so serious with a woman. Why couldn't he just go from one to another, one sexual encounter to another, enjoy it and move on?

He wasn't religious, but that idea was truly sinful to him. He'd wasted enough sperm with Julia.

The truth of the matter was, and he'd never tell anyone this, that he couldn't get it up unless he felt he was in a potentially serious relationship. Otherwise, it was simply an animal act. Every mature civilized adult, especially priests, ministers and rabbis would applaud that, wouldn't they?

Or would they congratulate him and then, when he turned away, shake their heads and snicker? He'd often thought they were laughing behind his back when he was in high school, and even men he met at work who had conversations about sex and love nodded at him but ridiculed him when he wasn't around.

It didn't matter.

I am who I am, he thought.

And she, wherever she is, is just waiting for me to find her.

She's out there, waiting because she's just like me, serious and responsible like me.

She might even know my name. It was given to her in dreams.

That was the only magic fairy he had ever believed in.

CHAPTER TWO

It was another one of those gray, marine-layer-overcast days for which Los Angeles is famous in the summer months. Sometimes, it didn't break until midafternoon. In the land of otherwise-glimmering sunshine and promise, a veritable garden for dreams of fame and riches, these hours of gloom were as unwelcome as a hurricane or a tornado, not to mention a too-frequent tremor. Convertible tops were still up. Auto headlights on late-model cars were still on, and joggers, especially the fanatical ones, looked unhappy and depressed. Even the rare pedestrian had his or her forehead down over soured eyes.

There always seemed to be more fender benders on days like this, too. Part of that was because people were so intolerant of each other that even if one tapped the other rather gently, the tapped driver would pop out of his or her car and dramatically study the car for the slightest damage. It wasn't surprising. Drivers were distracted by their daydreams and fantasies. Everyone was in a rush, as if getting to where he or she was going would bring on the sunshine.

Megan was no different. She nearly hit the side

of a city bus when she squeezed in a lane to pass it. The driver let her know it with a loud and long beeping that seemed to rattle her bones. She bit down on her lower lip and squeezed her eyes to keep from crying.

Yesterday, Emily Lloyd had gotten Scott and his attorney to agree to Scott's moving out during the period of separation. She was deliberately staying away from the house all morning and into the early afternoon to give him a chance to take out whatever he wanted. She knew he was still reeling from the reality of her quick and decisive moves to end the marriage. He called her, not to beg forgiveness and ask for a second chance, but to reassure himself that she was really going through with it and that this wasn't simply some overly dramatic gesture. She could hear the disbelief in his voice.

"You really want to do this?"

"It's done," she told him. "Get used to it."

"I'm trying to be patient, to understand, but . . ."

"I no longer want your understanding, Scott. I'm not the one who needs therapy here."

He was fuming. She could almost feel it through the phone.

"Just get your things," she added, and hung up.

Five minutes later she called Tricia Morgan.

"It's done," she told her.

"It's not done, Meg. It's begun, is what you mean. Don't forget, I've been through it."

"Yes, that's what I meant. I feel numb though."

"And frightened. Don't forget that. Just keep thinking about all the disappointment and pain you've felt these past years and how tolerant and forgiving you were. Stupidly, I might add. That will give you the strength."

"I know you're right. It's just . . ."

"Hard. I know. So is losing weight. Listen. I'm taking you out tomorrow night. It's what I call a 'good for you' night out. Get a sitter."

"Night out? Where?"

"The Cage, on Robinson."

"The Cage?"

"Might as well get right back into the scene, Meg. Wear something sexy as hell. You've got the figure. Most of us don't. And start thinking about this as the beginning of your life and not the end."

"But tomorrow night? That seems fast."

"It's like falling off a bike, right? If you don't get back on, you never will."

"I guess you're right. I guess I have to try."

"Try hard," Tricia said. "Call me in the morning. I'm seeing that cable-television executive Brook introduced me to at her husband's office party last week. He called. I didn't think he meant it. It did take him a week, but maybe he's shy. Wouldn't that be a change? A man who was insecure and not bleeding testosterone all over you?"

Megan laughed. It felt good.

"That's the sound I like to hear," Tricia said. "Contrary to what they tell us, smiling and laughter does not bring on wrinkles."

"What time do we meet at the Cage?"

"We don't meet. I'll pick you up at seven so you don't come up with some phony excuse. Prepare to get soused, too. If I'm not sober, I'll find someone else to drive you home."

"Okay," Megan said, and made the turn into her

street. "I'll call you in the morning to get the blow-by-blow."

"Watch it. I never said anything about blow," Tricia quipped. "These phones are tapped."

Megan laughed again and shut off the Blue-tooth. She was actually feeling better until she approached the house and saw that Scott's Mercedes was still in the driveway. She almost drove past, but he came out of the house carrying a suitcase and saw her approaching. He stopped to wait. She drove into the open garage and got out quickly to head for the door.

"Meg, wait."

She paused and turned to him.

"You were supposed to be finished much earlier, Scott, but I'm not surprised you're late. The stock market is still open."

"Actually, I had to see my attorney. This is crazy. Can't we have a sensible, reasonable and quiet discussion about all this?"

"Don't you ever get tired of talk, Scott? Don't you ever just want to do what you say?"

"I'm not saying I'll do anything."

"Well, I am."

"I don't see what we'll be accomplishing here. If we just keep trying . . ."

"We?"

She laughed and took a step toward him.

"Why is it you're smart enough to make thousands of dollars in an hour, but not smart enough to see your own failings? Maybe you just don't want to see. I have to keep reminding myself that Lesters have no failings, right?"

She turned around and headed for the door again, her heart thumping like a flat tire.

"Meg!"

She didn't turn.

"What about Jennifer?" he shouted.

She paused, took a breath and turned back to him.

"What about her?"

"You see what the kids from broken homes are like around here. We've talked about that."

"Jennifer is and has been in a broken home for some time now, Scott. To her it will seem like just another day in the Scott Lester homestead."

His expression hardened.

"I'm not going to let you do this to us."

"Really? Is that another one of your soon-to-be-broken promises, Scott, or will you actually do something?"

She held her glare for a moment and then turned and went into the house.

Scott stood there looking after her for a moment and then turned and put the suitcase into his car trunk. He was torn between his anger and his sorrow. The Lester in him wanted him to beat her down, make her submissive, hear her regrets and apologies, but the softer side of him tried to get him to see her point of view.

He got into the car and drove away, arguing with himself. Anyone seeing him would assume he was talking on a Bluetooth speaker phone and would think nothing of a man waving one of his hands in the air and apparently screaming behind closed car-door windows.

It had actually become a common scene on these streets.

* * *

On his days off from whatever construction work was out there for him, Steve went to this boat. At first his mother thought that Julia's death would turn him off the boat and deep-sea fishing, cause him to suddenly see it all as dark and unhappy. She thought he might even sell it. He never said it aloud, but he did have an entirely different feeling about his boat now. He didn't see it as the setting of an ugly fatality. On the contrary, the boat—his boat—came through for him. It took action where he couldn't, action for his benefit.

He had no trouble thinking about a boat the way someone might think of a good friend. The truth was, he didn't have anyone he would call a best friend, or even a good friend. He had acquaintances, coworkers with whom he might go out for a beer or something, but there was no confidant, no one in whom he could trust with his deepest feelings and thoughts.

He wasn't much different growing up. Other guys had palled around together, developed at least one close friend, but he never did. He hadn't been totally unpopular, but he wasn't someone others thought of first when it came to parties or just hanging out. If he was there, fine. If he wasn't, they never thought about him or he about them for that matter. Maybe it was simply the indifference that kept him an outsider.

It was really the same thing when it came to girls in high school, too. He'd gone on dates occasionally, but he traveled through his high-school years without once stopping to pick up that one special girl whom he could say he was going steady with or even seeing frequently. He saw most of the girls around him as too flighty, bimbos, girls he could never picture becoming serious mothers and wives.

Perhaps he'd turned them off by having serious conversations, especially about family. Most of them saw marrying and having a family as something so far off, they didn't want to think about it, much less talk about it. Who talks about that in high school? It was weird. Didn't he have any real ambitions? In that sense he was actually a bit frightening to them.

It got so his father began to suspect that he was gay. He'd come right out one night and asked him. It was a Friday night, a night he should have been out with friends or with a girl. He was a senior and had his driving license, but there he was, sitting in the living room with his mother, watching an *I Love Lucy* rerun.

He caught his father staring at him and shaking his head.

"What?" *he finally asked him.*

"Are you gay? Is that what it is?"

His face got hot. It got even hotter when his mother turned to see what his answer would be. Did she think it could be anything else but no?

"No."

"You don't have any pictures hanging up. When I was your age, I had dozens of Playboy pictures on my walls, and I wasn't reading only Motor Trend and Boating Life magazines."

"I'm not gay. Don't worry about it."

"I'm not worried about it. You should be worried about it. The day I find out for sure, you're outta here."

He turned away from his father. He didn't want to

keep denying it because he could see from his mother's face that the more he did, the more she thought it was possible. A good comeback came to mind.

"Why you asking me that? You have gay tendencies when you were my age or something? Worried I might have inherited some gay gene of yours?"

"No, wise guy, that's not why I'm asking. In fact, it's just the damn opposite. When I was your age, I was out getting laid, not sitting with my mommy watching television on weekend nights. Tell me. You get laid yet?"

"Boris, stop it," his mother said.

His father shook his head.

"Always depend on Mommy to come to your defense," he muttered, and went back to his newspaper.

Whenever he recalled that scene, he felt his insides twist. After a few more minutes that night, he rose and left the living room with his father's laughter trailing behind him. He'd gone out even though he had no idea or plans to go anywhere and drove off, cursing and spitting. He'd almost got a speeding ticket but caught sight of the motorcycle cop on the side street just in time to slow down.

Most of the other guys in his class had had pretty good relationships with their fathers. Many did things with them constantly. He couldn't remember doing anything special with his father. No, he had to become his own father or invent an imaginary one to talk to.

Maybe that's why he loved his boat so much, loved being out to sea. He felt he escaped the turmoil and the tension. Out there he could talk to his boat and say things that would bring laughter or weird looks if he said them on shore. Out there he was truly himself. His boat never disappointed him. His boat was his hero. His boat was his real companion.

No, Mom, he thought, there's no way Julia's death would turn me away from my boat.

It wasn't a large boat when it was compared to some of the yachts in San Diego, where he had it moored, but it was impressive enough. It was a twin-diesel eighty-six-foot Cantiere di Lavagna Admiral 26 he had bought used. It had a salon and three staterooms, all with en-suite bathrooms, and a large galley with up-to-date equipment. He lucked out when and the owner, an Italian man who lived in San Diego and had brought the yacht over, was near bankruptcy and sold it in desperation. Over the years, Steve had improved its electronics. It had a large deck for sunning and relaxing and a Bimini top on the flying bridge. He knew that Julia had fallen in love with the boat before she'd fallen in love with him, but that was all right. In his mind he and his boat were inseparable. Nothing broke down that he didn't fix with love and affection.

A man and a woman with one or two children could really enjoy this boat, he'd thought the day he bought it, and when he took his trips alone, he would spend time imagining his family on the boat with him, teaching his young son or daughter how to fish, teaching his wife how to navigate. Imagine the dinners they'd have out on the water and the fun they would have visiting Mexican ports.

He had put all his money into the boat. He had a relatively inexpensive pickup truck and nothing expensive in his wardrobe. He wore a cheap watch and modestly priced shoes. Because he spent so little on entertainment and lived with his mother now, he had no trouble keeping up the maintenance of his boat and investing constantly in some improvement here or there. Few apartments in Los Angeles were as nice and had kitchens as well equipped as his boat.

No, when the time came, he would court his new woman on this boat. She would surely be impressed. She'd see what a good husband and father he would make. She and the children she would give birth to would complete him.

He thought these things as he sped up and bounced over the water. He wasn't heading anywhere special, just out there. Amazingly, he knew almost exactly where Julia had fallen off the boat during the storm. He was fascinated with it and had to go to the exact longitude and latitude. Sometimes, when he went past it, he would look off to the side and swear that he saw her just under the water, floating, her hair looking as though it were growing so it could break clear of the water, her eyes and her mouth open, and coming out of her mouth, small fish, which out of curiosity visited her insides and discovered she was barren.

They couldn't get out fast enough.

Instinctively, Scott knew he shouldn't return to work, even though his father was holding a very important meeting with their staff and attorneys. He was certainly in no mood to listen and contribute, but he also knew what his father was going to be like. Gordon Lester never avoided anything unpleasant or disappointing. In fact, he enjoyed looking at potential failure and daring it to take one step forward. He was that strong.

Scott himself was an athletic-looking six-feet-one-inch man who never doubted that he had inherited his broad shoulders from his father. All of his relatives on his mother's side were slight, physically inconsequential people, but his father was a burly former college-football halfback who even in his sixties looked as if he could put on a uniform and get on the field.

When Scott was younger, his father—whenever he was around enough—was always challenging Scott to one form of physical activity or another and warning him to stay fit.

"A man who takes care of his body usually takes care of his life and his business. He exudes confidence and gives those who deal with him a sense of security. A wimp might inherit his father's business, but he won't command loyalty and respect. Don't forget that."

Like he could forget anything his father told him. He suspected one day he might test him on these sound bites and grade him on how well he did.

Almost anything his father advised him to do he did anyway. There was no denying his father had made a success of himself and was highly respected, not only by his peers and associates, but more important perhaps by his enemies. Why shouldn't he listen to him and try to be like him? It was just difficult to be like him and still maintain some independence, some qualities that were his and his alone.

Megan wasn't the only one who accused Scott of walking in his father's shadow. His mother had actually accused him of it herself, but this was in her later years, when she was in her physical decline from too much closet drinking and drugs. She hadn't died as much as she'd faded away, drifted into a ghost. Either his father truly hadn't noticed what was happening or had but no longer cared. One thing was for sure, he hadn't wanted to admit to having a wife who was an alcoholic and drug dependent. It reflected too much weakness onto him. It was better to bury it.

Other fathers would tell their sons, "You'll do better next time" or "Wait until next time," if they failed at anything, but not his father. Failure, defeat of any kind, no matter how small or insignificant it might appear, was intolerable. "You failed because you didn't try hard enough," he would say, or "You underestimated the competition or the task." In his father's mind he wouldn't succeed the next time if he took his defeat too lightly the first time.

Scott knew from the start that his father expected him to bring the same philosophy into his marriage to Megan. His father saw her as a burden, a task, an obstacle. "You have a lot of groundwork to do there," he'd told him, nodding at Megan at their engagement party. "Our world's like going to another planet for her."

"She'll do just fine," Scott had told him.

His father had shaken his head.

"You thought with your pecker," he'd replied, "and not with your head."

"She'll be fine, Dad," Scott had insisted.

"Don't convince me first. Convince yourself," his father had told him.

Gordon Lester was relentless when he came to a conclusion. Changing his mind was like trying to shake a fully grown old hickory tree. Not only would you fail, but you would feel stupid making the attempt.

Nevertheless, Scott did try. Every time he had an opportunity to show off something Meg had done, he did so, whether it was simply the way she rearranged furniture to make it all look better and fit in a room or some household expenditure she had made intelligently. His father would simply smile and shake his head as if Scott were delusional.

Now Megan's taking the first steps toward obtaining a divorce certainly gave his father the gleeful "I told you so" look. He didn't go into any long lecture. In fact, all he said was, "Do I have to say anything?" He added, "Let's see how you handle this."

Scott's hands actually trembled as he turned into their parking lot and took his reserved space. He looked back at the gates closing. Despite how successful he was working under his father, he couldn't help having the feeling he was being put under lock and key every time he drove in and watched those gates close. After all, he was giving up a great deal of his freedom. So many choices were already made for him, including his secretary, Arlene Potter, who he knew was so loyal to his father that she doubled as his spy. Arlene probably knew as much about his personal life as his father did. She surely eavesdropped, read anything and hacked into his personal computer. Maybe it was just his paranoia, but this was what he sincerely believed. He would never confront her about it, and never even entertain the thought of replacing her—not while his father was alive.

She was practically waiting at the door when he stepped off the elevator and walked toward his office.

"Everyone's waiting for you in the conference room, Mr. Lester," she told him.

Arlene has her hair pulled back more severely than usual today, he thought. It seemed to lift her sagging fifty-year-old face, but instead of smoothing out emerging wrinkles, made it look more as if she were wearing a mask. He never liked the way she wore her makeup either. It was never understated, as Megan's and most of her girlfriends' makeup was; it was more old-fashioned, more like the way his mother had worn her makeup.

"Thank you, Mrs. Potter," he said. Even though he was her boss, he never called her Arlene. She was still older than he was and too prissy to be called by her first name. He even envisioned her husband, Lewis, calling her Mrs. Potter at home. The few times Scott had seen them together, Lewis had cowered in her presence, always fearful of saying or doing the wrong thing in front of a Lester.

He hurried into his office, picked up the folder Mrs. Potter had prepared for the meeting and shot out again to walk down the corridor to the conference room. The Lester Building, as it was now known, had fifteen floors. They rented out offices on every floor but the top two, which they used for their business. His father's office had the best view because on that side of the building, the west side, there were no taller buildings. On very clear days he could see Santa Monica and the Pacific. Scott's office looked out toward South Los Angeles, and usually there was a view of settling smog hugging the buildings and creeping into the windows to distribute its cache of allergies, asthma and lung cancer.

There were five other executive employees waiting in the conference room. Three were their attorneys, Elliot Green, James Carrus and Ward Young. One was Scott's competition, his father's other prodigy, Nick Haber, the company's second vice president. Last was his father's accountant, Earl Hanson, a rather thin, balding man who had the long fingers ideal for working adding machines and computers. They all looked up when Scott entered.

"Sorry, I'm late," he said, avoiding his father's eyes and moving quickly to the seat on his right.

"Punctuality has never been much of a value to most of the people in Scott's generation," his father remarked.

"It couldn't be helped," he muttered. "I had to see Mike Benton first this morning and then . . ."

"Scott, as some of you might have heard from that ever-present mysterious grapevine, is having a small marital problem, also characteristic of his and younger generations."

He saw the wry smile on Nick Haber's face.

"Since my father chose to bring it up, it's not exactly a small marital problem, gentlemen. My wife has hired an attorney and is filing for a divorce."

Nick lost his smile. No one spoke. Then his father leaned forward.

"You don't intend to let that happen, do you?"

"She's determined this time. What can I do?"

Gordon Lester sat back, but instead of looking upset, formed a deep and wide smile.

"What can he do? Does that capture the problems this country's experiencing today or doesn't it? The younger generations either throw up their hands and say, 'What can I do,' or go to a therapist."

Everyone smiled. Nick chuckled and nodded.

"What can you do?" Gordon snapped, raising his voice and freezing everyone in their seats. "You can take action, seize the moment, be the captain of your soul. Divorce court is messy, especially in these community-property states. Right, Elliot?"

"Yes, but not only because of the asset allocations," Elliot said, coming in as if the entire conversation had been rehearsed. "There are also social workers cross-examining your child and digging out the most intimate details of your private life."

He looked at the others.

"There are some women who marry just to get divorced and independently wealthy."

"No? Really?" Scott's father said with great exaggeration. Everyone but Scott laughed.

"Meg is not like that," he said softly. It stopped the laughter but didn't wipe away the smiles.

Gordon Lester nodded.

"Well, one way or another, Scott, we can't let this happen to us."

"It's happening to me, Dad."

"And you're my son. What happens to you, happens to me," he replied sharply. He held his glare a moment and then sat back again and softened his lips. "Don't worry. We'll figure out a solution. We always do, don't we, gentlemen?"

Everyone but Scott nodded.

Nick stared at him, waiting for a reaction. Scott opened his folder.

"Yes," his father said. "Let's get off this nonsense and down to serious business."

Later, when Scott was alone with his father in his father's office, he turned an uncharacteristic antagonistic tone on him.

"That was an unfortunate and unnecessary display of family problems in there, Dad. You made me feel this big," he said, holding his hand a few feet off the floor.

"That's how big you make me feel, putting up with this nonsense, rushing off to your attorney."

"What do you expect me to do? Really?"

"You don't just jump when she tells you to, Scott. Forgodsakes. Counter. Hire a private detective today to shadow her so you can come up with something. She's probably having an affair."

"Megan? No way."

"I don't know how you can be my son and continue to be so naïve. Why couldn't she be having an affair? What is she, Mother Teresa? Get all your telephone bills together. I have some friends in the telephone company who will track some of the calls for us."

"This is crazy. Forget about it. I'll take care of my own situation."

"Right, but when you come crying to me because you found out I was right, be sure you apologize first."

Scott glared at him a moment and then left the office to show his defiance.

But when he closed his own office door and stood there thinking, the accusation his father had made suddenly seemed possible. Look at how fast and how determined Megan was now to end the marriage. She couldn't do this on her own. She couldn't have gotten the courage. Surely she was being encouraged by one or more of her girlfriends, or maybe even Ernie Cornbleau. He was in criminal law, but a lawyer was a lawyer. He could have recommended an attorney to her.

Megan did seem changed these past weeks. Her voice was harder, what he thought of as her delicious vulnerability gone. That takes a surge of self-confidence. Should he hire a detective? It seemed to be a plausible idea, but he hated taking his father's orders on this.

Maybe when she got right into it, saw the actual paperwork, went to court, she'd have a change of heart. If he was just the opposite of what his father wanted him to be, he might win her back. Once he threw down the gauntlet, went aggressively at her, it would be permanently over, and despite how he had behaved and where his priorities had gone, he still loved her very much.

No, he thought, I'll wait to see. To put it out of mind, he buried himself in his work.

Megan looked at herself in her bathroom mirror and thought, I look like I've aged years in weeks. I'm in no shape to go out with Tricia tonight.

Scott always hated it when she went out with her girlfriends. "Especially these girlfriends," he'd say, "and especially Tricia Morgan." Tricia was a divorcee, but without any children. Her marriage hadn't lasted a full year. Sometimes, she thought it was more Tricia's fault than that of her ex-husband,

Phil Myer, a radiologist working at Cedars-Sinai. She hated socializing with his medical associates and complained about their wives being "too Stepford." The more frustrated she became, the more carefree and irresponsible. It was as if she wanted Phil to be the one to ask for the divorce first. Scott loved to say, "Phil should have turned the CAT scan on her and seen how flighty a woman he married."

Megan had to admit that Tricia was flighty, but she couldn't help liking her. Tricia was never depressed, even when she was in the middle of her divorce. Her carefree attitude about men and marriage was refreshing at times. Everyone else Megan knew was so serious, so sensitive to every little hiccup. Also, one thing Tricia didn't do that most divorcees were prone to do is flirt with other women's husbands. She never came to any event without some man she was seeing at the moment—and "the moment" was a good way to put it. Since her divorce, she had yet to find anyone she thought was worth more than a couple of weeks of her time. Maybe the men thought the same of her, Megan thought. That was Scott's take on it.

But one thing was certain: Tricia was up on the dating game for women of their age. Megan's other girlfriends were married with families, and when most of them learned what was happening between her and Scott, they would treat her as if someone in her family had died. She didn't want that. She knew she would lose quite a few of them as friends and probably not be invited to any of their family functions. Jennifer would be hurt the most by that, she thought regretfully. Before these women had even shown their reactions, she was angry at them.

"Some friends," she muttered at her image in the mirror. No, there wasn't any question about it. There wasn't a better guide to help her navigate through these new rough waters than Tricia Morgan. Tricia knew the places to go and how to handle the men who frequented them. Despite her laissez-faire attitude about love and romance, Tricia never went for any extremes. She never dated much younger men. She was no Mrs. Robinson.

What's more, Tricia wasn't in any rush. She didn't buy into that old idea that her biological clock was running down. Whenever she was serious about it, she would shake her head and say, "I'm not rushing into anything. I didn't have enough fun out there to start with, and paid for that inexperience."

Was that true for me as well? Megan would often think. She was thinking about it tonight.

Is that why I'm in this place I'm in, this situation? Maybe Clare was right. I jumped too quickly into my marriage, and now I'm paying the price for that impulsiveness.

She had no idea what to expect out there. She might fall on her face and look foolish. Or she just might regain some desperately needed self-confidence. What woman wouldn't want to be thought of as pretty and sexy? It was just important not to lose her head over any compliment and to be careful about whose compliments she welcomed. Surely, Tricia would be a good advisor when it came to that.

Maybe there wouldn't be any compliments.

Maybe she was fantasizing. She knew that no matter what, however, she wasn't going to go running back to Scott.

I might as well find out sooner than later, she concluded, and went about fixing her face and her hair and then choosing the sexiest outfit she had. That was easy to find.

It was the one Scott hated the most.

CHAPTER THREE

Maybe his mother wasn't all wrong, he thought. The possibility occurred to him on his way to a swimming-pool construction job in the valley. He had picked up the job when one of the company's regulars had to go into the hospital for a double bypass. Matt Lowenstein, for whom he worked regularly, was friends with Paul Stanley, the CEO of the company, and he had just completed working for Matt on a pool in Brentwood. Matt appreciated his work ethic and how, unlike the others, he didn't look for every possible opportunity to slack off.

Maybe his mother was also right about the women he sort of pursued. Perhaps he just wasn't looking in the right places because he relegated himself to a certain . . . how should he say . . . level, category, of watering holes? Perhaps he should be setting his sights on better prey. The truth was, he did himself a disservice by settling for this class of woman. True, he hadn't attended college and he was nowhere near rich, even with owning his boat, but he had always been a good reader, kept up with news and had done some traveling. He'd always felt head and shoulders above his fellow construction workers. He was confident that he could hold his own anywhere, if he so chose. He would just have to dress better and watch the way he spoke. Can't sound like a redneck.

Of course, he really didn't know where to go. He didn't hang out with lawyers and businessmen. He didn't take three-hour lunches and work in a tie and jacket. What was he going to do, turn to the Yellow Pages and look up "High-class Watering Holes"? The problem discouraged him, but maybe, maybe, he could do some reconnaissance—say, in Beverly Hills.

The whole idea seemed more and more far-fetched and stupid as the day rolled out. He couldn't help thinking about it, however, and being in such deep thought as he worked alienated him from the others who liked small talk, coffee and cigarette breaks or just general bullshitting. Maybe it kept them from thinking about who they were and what they were doing. He could see the way they were looking at him as the day drew closer to an end. A man as silent as he was couldn't be trusted.

Matt's friend Paul Stanley, however, was very pleased with him. He didn't know he was being watched so closely, but before the day ended, Paul came over to him.

"Nice work," Paul said, standing beside him and looking at the Pebble Tec they had been pouring. Paul was about his height, with blue eyes and curly blond hair that belied his age. In fact, it was his youthful appearance that kept his employees from holding him in great respect. The truth was that even though he looked like he was in his early thirties, he was well into his forties.

"It's a nice property," he told Paul. "The pool's

well placed, too. I like the natural privacy those trees provide, and I can see you didn't have to do much grading here to prepare."

"Yeah. The jerk who owns this just got divorced and bought the place to show up his ex-wife. That's what he told me," Paul said.

"Any kids?"

"That's why he's building the pool. He's got three—nine, twelve and thirteen, all boys."

"Why did he get divorced?"

"Says he caught his wife with another woman."

"What? But they had three children?"

"You ever hear of AC/DC? She liked it both ways. That's what he says. 'Course, he admits to screwing around himself. He's some business exec at an independent film studio. Claims the temptations are just too great for any man to withstand."

"That's bullshit," he said.

Paul laughed. "Hey, live and let live. I got this job out of it and you got some work."

"You married?" he asked.

He didn't think Paul Stanley was going to answer and he figured the man thought he was being too personal now, but after another moment, Paul nodded.

"Was," he said. "My wife was killed in a horrendous car accident on Cold Water Canyon. Some teenagers after a wild party slammed into her. As usual, they weren't harmed seriously and later, through legal manipulations, were slapped on the wrist and sent off to do it again."

"Sorry," he said.

"What about you?" Paul asked.

"My wife was killed in a boating accident a little over a year ago. No kids," he added quickly.

"No kidding? Two widowers?" Paul shook his head. "What are the chances of that?"

He shrugged.

"You start dating again?" Paul asked him.

"Not really," he said. "You?"

"A little. It's not easy. Some friends of mine are always on me, getting me to go out with them. Two of them are bachelors, so that's easier."

"Where do you go?" Steve asked.

"Usual kind of places. I mean I go to some charity events, but it's not easy meeting someone there."

"I don't know where to go these days," he admitted.

"Well," Paul said, "I can give you a few where the choices are usually pretty good pickin's."

"Anything in or around Beverly Hills?"

"Beverly Hills? That's trouble. There is one place my friend Sandy takes me to occasionally. It's on Robinson. The Cage. Ever hear of it?"

"No."

"You ever hang out in Beverly Hills?"

"Not really."

"Don't blame you. It ain't cheap," Paul said. "You'll pay three to five dollars more for a drink than I bet you pay at the places you go to. If you go, put on all the jewelry you own," he added with a laugh. "And bone up on your clothes designers, Hollywood gossip, and the latest world hot spots." He laughed. "If you're anything like me, you won't last ten minutes in the place. Anyway, thanks for filling in and giving me a good day's work. I'll see you on Monday."

"Right," he said.

He caught the way the others were looking at him as they wrapped up. Not one looked pleased.

All looked as if they resented him for making them look bad.

This isn't a job I'll have long, he thought.

He wrapped up and headed for home. Paul's description of the Cage both interested and frightened him. He would hate to make a fool of himself or be the object of some mockery, especially by arrogant and snobby women. It probably made little or no sense to go there, given his motives.

But on the other hand, he was tired of the places he did frequent. Three to five dollars more a drink wasn't one of the things that frightened him. He didn't drink that much anyway, but what if he had nothing to say to any of the women there or anything he did say was uninteresting to them? He could fall on his face. What would that do to his self-confidence?

He drove on, realizing he had picked up the train of thought he had followed going to the job. It was as if it had been kept on hold, just waiting for him to return. I can't do it, he concluded.

I can't be someone I'm not. That's what Julia tried to do to me.

When he arrived home, however, and saw the way his mother looked at him when he entered the house, he reconsidered. Staying home with her would be veritable torture tonight, he decided.

He went directly to his room and searched his wardrobe, choosing what he thought were his nicest clothes. Even those shirts and pants looked inadequate, however. He berated himself for taking so little interest in himself, this past year especially. He hadn't bought a single new item of clothing, not even a new pair of shoes. His dress shoes looked old-fashioned and needed a good polishing, and as for jewelry, what did he have? A emerald pinky ring that had been his father's, a sort of dress watch, even though most men would wear it as an ordinary daily watch, and a stupid name bracelet Julia had given him on his birthday.

I know nothing of Hollywood gossip, he thought. He looked at himself in the mirror.

Who are you kidding? You couldn't be successful in a place like the Cage. Go off with your tail between your legs and hang out at Mahoney's or something.

"No," he told his image in the mirror as if he really were two different people. "I'm going to try it. Maybe, just maybe, there's someone there waiting for a real man like me. You can go hide in the closet and wait here for all I care."

He liked that burst of outrage. It gave him encouragement. Moments later, he was in the shower shampooing his hair with the sweet smelly stuff Julia had used.

How ironic, he thought. I'm using her stuff to find another woman.

Ain't that poetic justice?

He started singing and when his mother saw him all dolled up, she broke into a wide smile.

"Got a date?" she asked.

"Not yet, but maybe I will by the end of the evening."

She pulled her head back.

"What's that mean?"

"I'll tell you in the morning, Ma. I don't know myself," he said, and left her shaking her head.

Jennifer Lester looked up from the puzzle she was working on with her teenage babysitter, Margaret Sanders, when Megan walked into the family room. Megan could see the confusion in her face. Jennifer was more like she was, Megan thought. She had no deception, no connivance, at least not yet. She revealed everything going on inside her honestly, openly.

On the other hand, Megan hadn't been entirely honest with Scott. Jennifer wouldn't treat his absence from their lives as just another day. Despite how poorly Scott had invested himself in their daughter's daily life, she still loved and missed him. His presence was something she not only relied upon, but cherished. She didn't understand why he was as aloof as he was when it came to her and Megan, but she didn't love him any less for it. He would always be her father, absentee or not.

"How do I look, honey?" Megan asked, hoping to get her mind off the impending divorce. She spun around in her designer leather slacks, high heels and a black leather vest over a frilly blouse. The slacks clung like another layer of skin. She added long, silver earrings and had her hair brushed down.

Jennifer stared in semishock. She was quite precocious, as are most nine- and ten-year-olds these days.

"You look . . . different," she offered first. "But very pretty," she quickly added. She'd almost said "sexy."

"You do, Mrs. Lester," Margaret seconded with so much enthusiasm, Meg couldn't help but laugh. "If I didn't know you, I'd think you were still in college or something."

"Really? Well, thank you, Margaret."

"I wish my mother would dress like that sometimes."

Jennifer looked at her, considering, wondering why her mother was going out dressed like this.

"You going to see Daddy tonight?"

"No, Jen. I told you. Your daddy and I won't be seeing each other socially anymore."

"He'd be sorry if he saw you now, Mrs. Lester," Margaret blurted.

For a moment Megan didn't know what to do. She finally smiled and shook her head.

"Why is it young people can see clearer than adults most of the time?" she asked hypothetically.

"We're just not as cluttered, Mrs. Lester," Margaret said. Margaret was an honor student, very responsible but, Megan thought, as unsophisticated when it came to socializing as she had been when she was her age. Sometimes, she wished she could take her aside and tell her not to be so choosy. Have some fun and be less judgmental.

Megan nodded.

"I think you're right, Margaret. I'm about as cluttered right now as anyone can be. Okay, give me a kiss good night, Jen, and please make it easy for Margaret when she tells you it's time to go to bed, okay?"

Jennifer rose and went to her. She gave her a quick peck on the cheek and returned to her puzzle.

Scott's warning in the driveway about children from broken marriages returned to her. She saw how Jennifer was trying to organize and digest all this and how difficult it was and would be when things were made final.

It's still going to be better for us, Megan thought. We won't have to suffer so many disappointments.

Megan heard the doorbell and started for the front door.

"I'll call if I'm going to be any later than twelve, Margaret."

"No problem, Mrs. Lester. I've got lots to read and do."

Tricia Morgan burst into a smile the moment she saw Megan.

"Wow. You're really a hot chick tonight. Where have you been keeping these clothes, and why?"

"Scott hates them," Megan said.

"Hated. He's gone, baby, gone. I feel like a schoolmarm or something dressed in this," Tricia said, turning.

"It's a pretty nice dress, Tricia. It's complementary too."

"Which is another way to say it hides my flaws. Ready?"

"Ready, but I'm not sure about the able."

"You will be."

"Bye, kids," Megan shouted back and walked out.

"I love those shoes," Tricia said. "I didn't realize you had such a firm rear."

"All those hours of exercise waiting for Scott to come home," Megan said.

"Now I'm beginning to regret asking you out. I'll be the wallflower."

"Stop it, Tricia. I'm nervous enough as it is."

"Good," Tricia said and they got into her BMW 335i convertible.

"Want the top down? It'll give you that bedroom look."

"No thanks. My hair's wild enough."

Tricia laughed and backed out of the driveway.

"Here we go," she said, and shot off so fast, Megan fell back against the seat.

They both laughed.

It was as if they had become teenagers again.

Less than fifteen minutes later, they pulled up to the valet at the Cage. Megan hesitated on the sidewalk. The music spilled out of the front double doors, which had bars embossed on them from top to bottom.

"Why did they want to call this the Cage?" Megan asked.

"It's all about bondage," Tricia said, winking, and started for the door.

"What?"

"C'mon, you idiot. You'll see. It's fun."

Megan joined her and they entered the dance club and bar that was indeed designed to look like a great cage. There were bars from floor to ceiling inches from the walls and bars comprised the ceiling above them. The floor of the club, except for the dance floor, was built out of wide raw-looking planks with dark knots. Off to the left, a DJ spun the music and looked down at the crowd of dancers, which Megan thought was already drummed into a frenzy. To the right and also up a level was the L-shaped bar with a glass top that pulsated neon colors in sync with the beat of the music. It was heavily populated, but not yet too crowded.

In the bar area and to the right side below were black-topped tables and chairs. Most were already taken. Waitresses wearing skimpy outfits decorated with chains made of nothing more than tinfoil navigated through the partygoers to deliver drinks in tall glasses and bottles of beer. Megan panned the room and shook her head.

"Everyone here looks ten years younger than us, Tricia."

"Not if you look closely," she replied, and steered them to an opening at the bar. "I'll bet thirty percent of the women and men here are either in a divorce, separation or recently broken-up relationship. You get so you know what places they favor," she said. "Let's get a drink. You want that Cosmopolitan Scott always orders for you in fancy restaurants? They make good ones here."

Just the mention of Scott and her Cosmopolitans deflated some of her excitement. He had introduced her to the drink.

"What are you having?"

"Simple. Vodka and soda with a twist of lime."

"Me too," Megan said.

A couple moved off the stools nearest them and they quickly took them. Tricia ordered their drinks.

"I really feel like a fish out of water," Megan said.

"Just give yourself a chance to get wet again."

"Ladies?" the bartender asked.

"Two vodkas and soda with a lime twist, please."

"Coming up."

"Hope so," Tricia said, and he laughed.

"Hey, you were here last weekend, weren't you?" he asked.

"I can't remember," Tricia replied. "It's too far back."

He laughed again and started to make their drinks.

Suddenly, a tall stout man with short graying

brown hair stepped up behind Tricia and tapped her on the shoulder.

"Hey, hi again," he said when she turned around.

"Oh, yeah, hi."

"I thought you were coming back on Wednesday night."

"Something unexpected is always coming up to interfere with your plans. Don't you find that to be true?" she asked, and looked to Megan for confirmation and support. Megan nodded.

"Absolutely," he said, and looked at Megan too.

"Oh, this is my best friend, Megan. I'm sorry. I forgot your name," Tricia told him.

He laughed. "Someone said we'd be better off wearing name tags in here. I guess she was right. I'm Harry, Harry Kaufman," he said, holding his hand out to Megan. She shook it quickly.

The bartender served their drinks.

"I thought we had a pretty good time together last week," Harry told Tricia.

She sipped her drink and nodded.

"And I remembered your name, so I know it was a memorable night."

"I'm convinced," Tricia said. She took another long sip of her drink and put it down hard on the bar. "So let's dance." She got off the stool and then leaned toward Megan to whisper. "You have a better chance alone."

Before Megan could respond, Tricia grabbed Harry's hand and tugged him toward the stairway and down to the dance floor. She watched them go and then turned around to drink her vodka and soda.

* * *

He would always believe she and he were meant to
be. It was the way he was immediately drawn to
her when he entered the Cage. She was sitting
alone at the bar. For a few moments, he just stood
there watching her to be sure she was not with
anyone. It was certainly a wild enough place. He
hadn't expected it. He was thinking it would be
more sedate, young men and women having conversations over cocktails with soft music in the
background, everyone dressed like window man-
nequins. Instead, the place looked like it could
break out in a veritable orgy at any moment.

Something about her, about the way she looked
meekly around and hovered over her drink, gave
him the impression she was just as uncomfortable
in here as he was beginning to feel. That gave him
more encouragement. He started for the bar.

Two stools down from Megan, a chubby man
with thinning brown hair downed an Irish whiskey and pulled his shoulders back. He was obviously building his courage to ask her to dance. He
had been eyeing her ever since she had come in
with Tricia, and when Tricia went off to dance with
someone and left her alone, he was elated. She had
no date.

He slipped off the stool and took a few steps toward her to lean on the bar and look at her. For a
moment Megan didn't realize he was there.

" 'Scuse me," he said.

"Oh. Yes?"

"I'm Tyler Barton."

"Yes?" Was she supposed to know him?

"I just wanted to introduce myself before I asked
you if you wanted to dance."

"Oh. Thank you, but no. I'm not in the mood for that right now."

"Not in the mood? Why would you come to a dance club then?" he asked.

"It's complicated," she replied, hoping he would take that as a final answer and go away. He didn't look much older than twenty-five at the most, but with a face and body most Santa Claus impersonators would covet, he was anything but attractive. Even though it was a nonsmoking club, he reeked of cigarette smoke, and a quick glimpse of his teeth revealed a layer of nicotine yellow–stained enamel.

"Hey, there's nothing complicated about dancing. C'mon," he pleaded. "It'll make you feel better."

"No thank you. Thanks," she said, turning away and hoping that would end it.

"C'mon," he whined.

"Didn't you hear her say no twice?" Megan heard. She turned to see a strapping six-feet-three-inch man with chiseled, perfect facial features and emerald green eyes standing between her and Tyler Barton.

Tyler didn't move. He looked at him and at her and smirked.

"What are you, the complication?" he asked, the last syllables dripping out of the sides of his thick lips.

For a few moments, Megan didn't realize the man had punched Tyler Barton in his rubber-tire stomach. He was that fast. Tyler gasped and bent over, falling back against another stool.

"Jesus!" he screamed loud enough to get the attention of most everyone at the bar. "He hit me!" he shouted, straightening up with great effort and pointing at the man beside Megan.

No one spoke; no one looked as though he or she much cared. Everyone went back to their conversations. The man stepped closer to Megan and faced Tyler, who turned—more like spun—over the stool, and rushed down the stairs toward the dance floor.

"You all right?" the man asked Megan.

"Yes. You hit him?"

"You can't reason with guys like that. It's like trying to talk a mosquito out of biting you. Best to just swat them and move on."

Megan laughed.

"Well, that's a folksy way of putting it."

He shrugged.

"I tell it like it is. Always have."

"I guess I'm out of practice. I haven't had to drive them off for a long time. Thanks."

He shrugged again.

"Couldn't help myself from coming to your assistance."

Megan smiled.

"Why, are you a guardian angel or something?"

"Something," he said.

Before he could order a drink and sit beside her, Tyler Barton returned with two friends, both of whom looked younger, one of whom looked like he could be his brother. He wasn't quite as heavy, but he had similar facial features and the same color hair.

"This the guy?" he asked.

"That's him," Tyler said.

"You hit my brother," he said, stepping forward.

Again, Megan never saw the punch coming. Most of the arguments and fights she had seen between boys while she was growing up were usually much slower in developing. It was always as if one or the other boy was trying to find a way to extricate himself from the situation without losing face. Rarely did she see one boy swing unexpectedly at another, and she had never witnessed a violent confrontation since high school, except in a movie, of course.

One thing was sure, she had never seen anyone hit so hard in the mouth that one of his teeth flew out and his head snapped back with such force that it actually broke the skin around the middle of his neck. A thin red line instantly formed. His companion and his brother moved quickly to keep him from sinking to the floor.

"Call the cops!" Tyler screamed at the bartender.

Megan's guardian angel looked at her sorrowfully.

"More mosquitoes," he muttered. "I better go. Don't want to make any trouble for you," he added, and started away, forcefully separating two other men standing with the gathering crowd. No one tried to stop him.

"Call the cops!" Tyler screamed again. "And an ambulance for my brother."

They had lowered him to the floor. He was obviously dazed.

Tricia came running up the steps with Harry.

"What's going on?" she asked Megan. They both looked at Tyler and his brother.

Megan shook her head.

"Mosquitoes," she said, and laughed to relieve

the boiling tension that threatened to blow off the top of her head.

The club manager and two waiters helped get Tyler's injured brother off to the side. Megan started to explain to Tricia and Harry what had happened, but before she finished, two Beverly Hills patrolmen entered the club and the bartender sent them over to Tyler first, and then they came over to her. She quickly described the events as she remembered them. Tyler stood off to the side listening.

"I wasn't begging her to dance," he moaned.

"Just a moment," one of the officers said, and turned to Megan. "Do you know the man who hit his brother?"

"No, I don't, Officer."

"He sure acted like he knew her," Tyler said.

"He's wrong," Megan said. "He never even told me his name. This man and two others came up from the dance floor before he could say much to me, and threatened him."

"Threatened him? He hit me!" Tyler cried.

"All right. Just go see to your brother. There's an ambulance on its way. Paramedics will be here any moment," the police officer told him. Reluctantly, Tyler Barton retreated.

"What's your name, miss, and your address?" the officer asked Megan.

She looked at Tricia.

"Why do you need that? She didn't do anything. She was just sitting here," Tricia said sharply.

"I need her name and address. Whether she did anything or not, she was involved in this violent incident. We don't know how serious the injuries are yet," he replied just as sharply.

"She doesn't need this."

"It's all right, Tricia. My name's Megan Lester," Megan said, and gave him her address and phone number.

"And you're absolutely positive you don't know the man?"

"I am, Officer."

"Let's get a description then," his partner said.

"I didn't get all that much time with him," Megan began.

"What did he look like?"

"He was about your height, well built, light brown hair with green eyes. He was wearing a black button-collar short-sleeve shirt and a pair of black dress pants with cuffs. He was cleanly shaven with high cheekbones."

"Not bad for not much time," the patrolman quipped. He looked at Tricia. "You should hear the descriptions we get from people who spend hours with perpetrators."

"He didn't say anything about himself?" the second patrolman asked.

"He just said sometimes when you're dealing with mosquitoes, you can't talk them out of biting you. You have to swat them," she said.

The two policemen stared at her a moment. One of them finally smiled.

"Let's get their description of the guy," the other patrolman said, just as the paramedics arrived.

"Can we go?" Tricia asked them.

"Yes, but let us know if you see this guy again. Here," the patrolman added, giving Megan a card.

She took it, but didn't put it in her purse. She just held it.

"Tricia, get me out of here," she said in a low but firm voice.

"Will do," Tricia said. "See you later, Harry," she told him, and they walked out of the Cage. Tricia gave the valet her ticket and turned to Megan.

"Holy mackerel, as my grandfather used to say. None of the girls are going to believe this."

"I don't," Megan said. "Take me somewhere where I can get a calming cup of tea."

"I will," Tricia said, and then knocked Megan's shoulder with hers. "That cop was right. You did a pretty good description of him for someone who barely saw him."

"He had the sort of face you don't easily forget. Actually, he was . . . in and out like . . . Batman," Megan said. She looked back at the entrance to the Cage as if she wanted to be sure there was no one close enough to hear her and then she leaned to-ward Tricia to add, "And probably just as exciting."

CHAPTER FOUR

He sat in his truck well in the shadows across the street and watched Tricia and Megan come out of the Cage. He was prepared to wait all night if he had to and was happy to see them come out so soon after the police had arrived. He had a strong feeling she would come out as soon as she could. She didn't belong there. The fact that he was so instinctively right about this woman continued to build his confidence.

When they drove off, he followed slowly, and when they pulled up in front of a small café, he drove past so they wouldn't see him. Then he turned around and parked across the street again to wait. From where he was, he could see through the front window. They had taken a table up front, so she was quite visible.

Every gesture she made, the way she held her head and sipped from her cup when she was served, amused and pleased him. He was glad to see that before they paid their bill and got up to leave, she was laughing.

Again, he waited for them to emerge and then started his truck and followed the car. When he saw it pull into the driveway of an enormous two-story Beverly Hills house, his heart sank with his hopes. She couldn't be single and live in a house like this, he thought. Sadly, he watched her emerge from the BMW, say something to her girlfriend and head for the front door. He sat there staring at the house after the girlfriend left. A few minutes later a teenage girl appeared and got into her car in the driveway. He watched her drive away as well.

A babysitter, he thought. She has children or a child, but where is the husband? If she was out with her girlfriend, why wouldn't her husband watch their children or child? Unless he had something to do, too and they got a babysitter. Families in Beverly hills can afford babysitters. That's for sure, he thought.

He saw the lights go off downstairs and then some turned on upstairs. He wasn't going to go home this early. His mother would drive him up a wall. He thought about going to one of the hangouts, but that was even more unattractive to him now. Instead, he just sat in his truck watching the house, seeing the light go out upstairs. Hours passed, but no one else came. The husband must be away on business, he concluded. He checked the time and then started his truck. As he turned around to head home, he thought there were another couple of possibilities, of course. The husband could be dead, or maybe she was divorced. Divorce was practically a national pastime, especially in this city. It was worth looking into, he concluded, and went home far less depressed than he had anticipated.

His mother was asleep, so he didn't face the usual inquisition when he returned from a night out. He slipped as quietly as he could into his bed-room and closed the door softly. He knew he was going to have trouble falling asleep. He was still quite excited. The look on her face when he'd punched that guy in the stomach and then his brother in the mouth was adorable. She'd been shocked, but he would swear there'd been a pleas-ant kind of surprise in her eyes. She really appreci-ated him. He stopped pacing and conjured her face. She wasn't just cute or pleasant to look at; she was beautiful. She was the kind of woman who re-ally got under your skin and crawled right into your heart.

Got to get up a plan, he thought. He knew how to find out who owned a property, so he would get her name. Then he would do some investigating to see why she needed a babysitter. Did he dare have hope? Let's put it this way, he told himself: if it turns out she's available, I'll devote every free sec-ond of time to winning her. His determination filled him with hope, but then he suddenly stopped again and thought, Why would a woman who lives like that want to have anything to do with me?

The question sent a chill down his spine. He sat on his bed and stared down at the floor.

Look at the impression I just made. She must think I'm a crackpot. This whole idea is stupid.

He thought he could hear laughter and looked at Julia's framed photograph. When his mother came in and cleaned his room today, she'd put it right side up again.

"What's so funny?" he asked. "You think the idea of anyone with class liking me is funny? What were you before I found you, huh? A waitress at

Denny's. Where were you going with your life? Like all the others, you came running out here expecting to be discovered. Well, I discovered you. Instead of being grateful, you had me regretting it."

He turned away and thought again. There was something more than beauty in her face. There was a vulnerability. She was . . . looking for help.

She called me her guardian angel, probably because she needs one.

His hope began to build again. He would pursue her. He would find out her name and what was going on in her life. She was basically alone, wasn't she? He could feel it, sense it in her eyes. She was just like him, searching, hoping, needing.

And the best thing was, he was sure she wanted children, wanted a family. She already had one or two. Of course, she might think that was enough, even though she was surely young enough to have more. If she were with him, she would see how good a husband and father he was and she would want to have a child with him. He was confident of that.

"Tomorrow," he declared. "Tomorrow my life will start again."

He started out to the bathroom, and on the way he put Julia's picture facedown.

Maybe if he did it enough times, his mother would stop putting it back up.

Somehow, for some reason he had yet to understand, he couldn't put it in a drawer or throw it out. He would have to admit that for now, at least, she was company.

* * *

Despite how the evening had gone, Megan couldn't help being pleased. Men were fighting over her. It was difficult for men to understand, perhaps, but women, especially women who had been married or were in the process of getting a divorce, were for the most part insecure about themselves. It was only natural for any woman to ask herself, Am I still pretty? Would anyone else want me? Can I compete out there against women who were in the minds of men fresh and exciting?

She never understood why Benjamin Braddock in *The Graduate* was attracted to Mrs. Robinson. Why didn't he look for a girl his own age, or just a little younger? Why would girls his age be more intimidating than a woman Mrs. Robinson's age? Was it just her coming on to him? Are men that simple, that easy to figure out?

Maybe it was unfair to judge poor Benjamin. He had other problems. She wouldn't want anyone looking at her life and doing the same. She had her own particular problems. Who would have ever thought her marriage would come to this? She remembered vividly how amazed she was with Scott's determination to make her his wife. Yes, she'd liked him and then she had fallen in love with him, but why was he so determined it be she?

Surely the question on the surface looked like a question someone who didn't think much of herself might ask. *Why not me? I was just as pretty if not prettier than the next girl, and I was just as intelligent. I had a nice personality. I wasn't as aggressive as most girls, perhaps, but that was probably just the sort of woman Scott wanted for his wife. He was around*

*enough barracudas at work and in the business world. I
had a lot to offer.*

Why had it all gone so sour? She was certainly
not overly demanding. In the beginning she'd put
up with his lateness and his missing important
family events. She'd put up with his 24-7 mentality
when it came to his father's and his business. She'd
tolerated him running off to do something his father needed done on weekends. She had even put
up with their having to cancel their first vacation
so he could complete a project his father wanted
completed. No, this can't be blamed on me, she
thought. No way, José.

Anyway, what good was it now to fix blame on
anyone or anything? It was over. It sickened
her still to think that, but she had to face it and
be grown up about it. She had to be more like
Tricia Morgan and some of the others. She had to
have grit. The Lesters weren't going to push her
around.

She loved her lawyer. Emily Lloyd looked as if
she was so determined to help her, she would take
on her case pro bono. She was that enraged about
it, all from a purely female point of view. She was
champing at the bit just waiting for their first court
session. She wanted to get her teeth into Scott and
his father as deeply and as soon as possible.

"You're going to come out of this all right," she'd
promised. "Both you and Jennifer."

Despite all that, despite Megan's anger and her
determination, she felt a pang of regret and still
even some sympathy for Scott. You just don't turn
on and turn off love like some water spigot. It takes
time to die, time to be buried. She was just starting
her period of mourning. She still wished it had all

turned out differently. She would just not say these things to anyone, especially Emily Lloyd.

Now that she was crawling into bed alone, she did pause to think about the man she called Batman. Tricia got a kick out of how she had reacted to him. At the café, all she'd wanted to hear about was Batman, but Megan really couldn't tell her much.

"After all, he was only there beside me for minutes."

"I should have such minutes," Tricia had said.

She had seen something in his eyes—some sincerity, some real concern. He'd looked like he genuinely cared about her feelings and how this Tyler creep was treating her. It was more than just a big-brother protection act, however. She'd seen how much he was enjoying being near her, how his eyes explored her face and how frantic and disappointed he was when he knew he had to get away.

Funny, she told herself, but I should be turned off by someone so violent, not excited by it. She tried to imagine how Scott would have reacted. He wouldn't have punched Tyler, but he would have attacked him with choice words. In that regard, he was his father's son. Gordon Lester could dissect someone with some quick phrases and cutting remarks. He was Zorro, when it came to verbal dueling.

That wouldn't have been half as stimulating as this was, however. She was too embarrassed about it to tell Tricia, but she was actually aroused. Right now, she fantasized her Batman scooping her off that bar stool, kissing her and taking her out of the club. Would she have gone if he had asked her to flee with him?

Of course not, the reasonable part of her said.

"Too bad," she muttered.

She turned over, looked at the side of the bed where Scott slept and overcame any sad feeling by telling herself, He's away again. This is nothing new, except . . . this time it will be permanent.

Jennifer was there to wake her in the morning. Megan was disappointed, because she was right in the middle of a helluva sexual fantasy with her Batman when she felt herself being shaken.

"I'm hungry. I made some oatmeal. You want some?"

"You did? That's terrific, Jen."

"It was only putting it in a bowl and into the microwave, Mom."

"Nevertheless, that's . . ."

She paused. She was going to say, *More than your father would have done,* but bit down on her lower lip instead and started to get out of bed.

"Did you have fun last night?"

"Fun? Yes, I think I did, in a strange way," she said, reaching for her robe.

"Why strange?"

"Not strange, so much as unexpected. C'mon. I'm hungry too now," she said, putting her arm around Jennifer's small shoulders. "Besides, we're going to that movie this afternoon, remember? I promised."

"Right," Jennifer said surging forward to the stairway. "You want toast, right?"

"Toast it is," Megan said and followed after her. "We're going to make it," she muttered as she descended. "We're really going to make it."

The phone rang while they were eating breakfast. Jennifer leaped up before Megan could and got to the receiver first.

"Hi, Daddy!" she cried. Megan froze. "I made

Mommy her breakfast," she added. She listened. The expression on her face grew serious. "I can't, Daddy," she said. "We're going to the movies."

"What's he want?" Megan asked.

Jennifer, mimicking what Megan and Scott did when they were on the phone and someone asked something, put her hand over the mouthpiece.

"He wanted to take me to the Getty Museum to see stuff and have lunch."

"You can go if you want to, Jen. I'll take you to the movie tomorrow."

Jennifer thought, but also studied Megan's face for signs of disappointment.

We're already in that game, Megan thought: tearing the kid apart with her loyalties. She could feel the oatmeal coming back up.

"Okay, Daddy. Mommy said she'll take me tomorrow." She listened. "I'll be ready," she said. "Bye. Oh, where do you live now?" She listened, nodding as if he were standing right in front of her, and then said, "Bye," again and hung up.

"He's living in a hotel," she whispered.

Megan looked up sharply. She'd been confident he was going to move in with his father. That house was twice the size of this one and his father was living alone with his servants.

"Hotel? He said a hotel?"

Jennifer nodded and sat.

"At least he doesn't have to make the bed," she said, which brought Megan her first really good laugh of the day.

She wondered if it would be her only laugh.

He couldn't wait for Monday to find out information about her.

He had a better idea. He was out early, even before his mother got up to make breakfast. Once again she would have no opportunity to ask him any questions about his night out, grilling him on the women he'd met or hadn't met. Sometimes, he did think she believed he had gay tendencies.

The sun was barely up, and on Saturday in Los Angeles, that made for light to no traffic. It took him no time at all to drive to Beverly Hills and he parked near her house, near enough to see her front lawn and the driveway. His hope came true. There in the driveway was a newspaper. As inconspicuously as he could, he got out of his truck and strolled down the quiet street. There weren't even any joggers out this early.

When he reached the driveway, he turned sharply and scooped up the paper. All he wanted to do was read the name on it. Unfortunately, it had only her husband's name, Scott Lester, but at least he knew that. It was as if he had some sort of an addiction to her already and had to know even the smallest possible facts, anything more than just the address of the house.

He dropped the paper where he'd found it and crossed the street to walk back up to his truck. There he sat thinking and staring at the house. So her husband was getting his newspaper. He wasn't dead, obviously, and if he was getting his newspaper, he wasn't gone. A lead ball of disappointment settled in his stomach. Everything he had felt, every instinct he had relied upon had told him she was perfect for him. It didn't make sense. There just had to be something to justify his intense interest and hope.

Like a stubborn four-year-old, he pouted in his truck cab and glared at the house. Even his hunger pangs didn't send him off. He sat and stared, as would some lovesick teenager waiting and hoping to catch sight of his dream girl. The sun grew higher in the sky and the street began to come alive. Out of one house, a husband and wife emerged to jog. Another door opened a few houses down and an elderly lady came out with a Scottish terrier on a leash. She headed in the opposite direction. Traffic began to build. At one point he had to take a bad leak, but he didn't budge. He was mesmerized by her front door.

Open, he willed. Open and let her out.

When a Beverly Hills patrol car cruised down the street toward him, his heart began to thump. What if they had somehow found out who he was and there was an APB out on him? Beverly Hills was supposed to have one of the best city police forces in the country. They surely had a description of him. Maybe she had given them great detail. Naw, he thought immediately, she wouldn't betray him like that. He could see it in her face. She wouldn't give him up.

The patrol car did slow down a bit more when it approached him. He looked at his clipboard and pretended to be checking something off as the car passed him. The patrolman gave him an interested glance, but nothing more. He looked up in his rearview mirror and watched the car turn at the corner and disappear. Relief washed over him.

Once they spoke to those creeps at the Cage, they'd probably decided the whole incident wasn't worth their time. They had more serious work to do than scour the neighborhoods for someone who fit his description. He was confident no one had seen him get into his truck. He had parked far enough away from the dance club. He wasn't going to pay any valet, not because he was cheap. He was a little embarrassed about the truck. No, I'm safe, he thought. He turned his attention back to her house and the street, waiting for some sign of movement.

Finally, a sleek black Mercedes sedan turned into the driveway and a tall man with wavy blond hair, wearing a light green sweater and jeans, stepped out. As he started toward the house, the front door opened and a young girl came bursting out to run into his waiting arms. He lifted her and kissed her cheek. Then she came to the door and he saw his dream lover.

She stood in the doorway and watched but didn't budge. He couldn't hear her, but she shouted something to the young girl, who nodded. The man looked at her and started to speak. He started toward the door, but she closed it before he finished speaking and got too close. He remained staring at it for a moment and then turned and walked back to the car to open the door for the girl, who was clearly his daughter. After she got in, he closed the door, looked back at the house, shook his head and got into the car to back out and drive off.

It was as if someone had shouted, *Happy New Year!*

This, he thought, is a broken marriage. And it was clear that she had nothing but anger and disdain for her ex-husband. His instincts were right after all. Thank goodness he had come up with the idea to drive over here early. The fact that the husband's name was still on the newspaper, however, told him this breakup was not too old. That worried him for a moment, but he recalled how she had closed that front door on him. There was no forgiveness looming in that woman, he thought happily.

He had a chance. Sure, he wasn't rich enough to keep a house like this; few men were. But he was confident she was not the sort of woman who judged people on the basis of their bank accounts. Maybe he was talking himself into it, but he was still convinced that she was his kind of woman, the kind of woman Julia could have been but wasn't.

He started his truck engine and turned on the radio. He would eat a helluva breakfast this morning, after he took one helluva leak.

Megan stood just in the entryway, half expecting Scott to keep coming and ring the doorbell. A wild thought occurred to her. Someone he knew had witnessed the scene last night at the Cage. Or, more likely, someone his father knew had been there. It could easily have been the son or daughter of some wealthy client or associate who had seen her at some social event. Maybe Tricia had been on the phone immediately after dropping her off, and the information had shot through the ears and mouths of a good dozen links in the gossip chain, dropping right in Gordon Lester's lap.

Maybe I shouldn't have been so abrupt with Scott, she thought. Maybe that made me look guilty of something.

But he had made no reference to last night, she countered, arguing with herself.

I'm being paranoid already, she thought, and chastised herself for having these crazy ideas. Was this the way it was going to be? Why should she be ashamed or afraid anyhow? She had a right to go out and meet people.

Nevertheless, the phone was ringing already. First call was naturally Tricia.

"How are you, the morning after?"

"Still in a bit of a daze. Scott called first thing this morning."

"He found out?"

"No, he wanted all of a sudden to spend a Saturday with Jennifer. He's taking her to the Getty for lunch."

"Typical. I could write the whole scenario for you. He'll be acting like he should have for weeks now and doing his best to make you feel guilty, make you feel you jumped too quickly.

"Don't laugh," Tricia warned before Megan could even think of it. "It works with most women."

"It won't with me."

"I'm here for you, if you feel yourself slipping. What are you going to do with your day now?"

"I don't know. I had promised to take Jennifer to the new Disney film, but . . ."

"Let's go on a wild shopping spree and have a fattening lunch. I'll pick you up in an hour or so. You've got to spoil yourself for now, Megan. There's too much opportunity for these dry, dark and depressing hours."

"You're probably right. Okay. In an hour or so," she said. "By the way, you haven't told anyone about last night yet, have you, Tricia?"

"Don't worry. I know exactly what you're concerned about. No one has heard anything from me."

"Good," she said, but wondered why Tricia had qualified with *from me*. "Did you see anyone who might know me or Scott there when you were dancing?"

"Harry wouldn't let my attention wander," Tricia replied.

"Who is he?"

"No one. I met him there. I never gave him my phone number and I didn't give him my name. I gave him my ex-husband's surname."

"Oh?"

"Just a little thing I do until I'm convinced the man I'm with is worth some truth. That's something you'll have to learn how to do now. But don't worry. You have a really good teacher."

"I'm beginning to think so," Megan said.

"See you soon."

She hung up and went up to shower and dress. What a roller coaster this was all turning out to be, she thought. She didn't know whether this was a symptom of a woman's being involved in a divorce or not, but she found herself spending much more time on her coiffure and her makeup. She even pondered longer on what to wear. Funny, how all that didn't matter as much a week or so ago. Oh well, she thought, it's a good change.

Tricia's right. I should be spoiling myself and nothing fits that bill like buying new clothes and new shoes.

With a spurt of welcome energy, she finished up and bounced down the stairs, when she heard the doorbell. Full of new self-confidence, she seized the doorknob and thrust the door open, prepared to go "Ta-da!" and spin around for Tricia.

Her jaw dropped.

Her heart seemed to go on hold and her breath caught in her throat.

He stood there, smiling at her, a bouquet of magnificent red roses in his hands.

Before she could utter a sound, he stepped in and handed her the roses.

"I wanted to come by and apologize for ruining your night last night."

She looked at the flowers without taking them.

"Please," he said, urging her.

She took them slowly.

"I'd like to do more to make it up to you," he continued.

"I . . . How did you find me?"

"That was easy," he said. "I stopped on a corner in Beverly Hills and asked the first person I met where the most beautiful woman in Beverly Hills lived," he replied.

She held her incredulous smile.

"You were expecting someone else, I gather?" he asked.

"Yes. My girlfriend, the one who was with me last night. We're going shopping," she said, and wondered why she had to explain anything to him.

"Well, maybe I can find another opportunity to make it up to you. Can I have your phone number?"

She shook her head.

"But . . . how do you know . . . ?"

"That you're free to call?"

"Yes?"

"Same person I asked about the most beautiful woman."

She saw Tricia's car turning into the driveway

and felt a mixture of relief and disappointment. The conflicting emotions stole her voice for a moment and then she nodded at Tricia's car.

"My girlfriend."

He turned to look.

"Oh, right. Okay. Your number is?"

Someday, she would ask herself why she gave it to him, but she did. She blurted it out and he smiled and started down the walk.

"Wait," she called, and he paused.

"Yes?"

"What's your name?"

"Steve," he said. "Steve Wallace."

"I never told you mine," she realized.

"Oh, why rush things? You will," he said, laughing, and continued walking away.

Tricia stood by her car, staring at him in shock. He waved to her as he walked by and down the street toward his truck.

She turned immediately to Megan, who was standing there holding the roses.

"I'll be right there," Megan called, and held up the roses to illustrate she had to put them in water.

For the moment, she was too stunned to say anything else.

CHAPTER FIVE

Steve Wallace didn't simply walk away; he floated. He couldn't feel the ground beneath his feet. Every part of him, down to his pinky toe, was energized. A day never looked any brighter, the sky any bluer.

She had given him her telephone number. And she did that before he had even given her his name!

He had taken a big gamble back there by suddenly appearing like that, giving her no warning. She could easily have viewed him as some kind of nutcase, panicked and shut the door in his face. Maybe she would have even run to the phone to call the Beverly Hills police to tell them he was there. Although it added to the shock, he was happy he had thought to buy the roses and give them to her. Flowers, especially to women, had a magic entirely of their own.

The look on her girlfriend's face was precious, too. Women like surprises sometimes. They like a man who can be spontaneous. Steve imagined her husband wasn't anywhere like that. He had no tangible proof of anything, but it was the report he was getting from his own instincts again. Why would a woman living in a house like that in Beverly Hills want a divorce, especially if she had a child? Maybe he cheated on her, the bastard. That type of guy is always going to cheat. Things always look greener on the other side to them. Being faithful isn't important.

Of course, these Beverly Hills women could be like that, too. Her girlfriend looked more like that type. He was good at telling the difference. He knew in every cell of his body that his dream woman was different. He could see it in her eyes. There was that vulnerability, that innocence that cried for someone to protect her, to believe in her and love her. She hungered for it now. He was going to be her cool drink of water after years of surviving in an emotional desert.

After all, really, why didn't she run to call the police? That told him she more than approved of his actions last night. She valued his protection. She obviously saw something in him that gave her comfort. How could this be any better? He didn't know if he should thank fate, God or just his own good and true instincts, but he was thankful.

He got into his truck just as she came out of her house. He sat there watching them, laughing at how emphatic their gestures were. There was no doubt that what they were talking about involved him. His surprise appearance was probably the most exciting thing to happen to them since . . . since . . . last night. He laughed to himself as they got into her girlfriend's car. He was surely going to be the topic of conversation most of, if not all of, their day.

They backed out and drove off. He started his truck and slowly followed. He wasn't sure what he was going to do. He just knew he didn't want to be

that far from her right now—maybe ever. He kept
far enough behind so they couldn't see him. He felt
confident that they hadn't seen him get into his
truck. They were both in too much shock to be ob-
servant. Even now, when he pulled around a taxi
and drew a little closer to her girlfriend's car, he
could see her hands going as they chatted. They
were still quite excited. Maybe they wouldn't calm
down all day!

He followed them all the way to the Beverly
Center, a shopping complex. He wanted to be extra
careful now. It would spook her too much if she
saw him following her this closely. He remained a
good distance behind them and was careful to find
a parking space far enough away so as not to be
noticed. After that, he put on a cap so he could pull
the brim down and shade his face, quickly changed
his shirt and left his jacket behind. Then he took
off after them.

Throughout the remainder of the morning, he
hovered at a distance that permitted him to watch
her closely but not be obvious. He studied her more
than watched her. He wanted to learn every gesture, every movement in her face. Once or twice he
nearly got too close out of a desire to hear her voice,
especially when she laughed.

At lunchtime, the two women left the shopping
area with their bags of clothes and shoes and went
down to one of the restaurants on the street. It was
impossible to observe them there. They would
surely spot him entering the restaurant, and that
would seem like far too much stalking. He was doing well. He got her phone number. Don't, he told
himself, make a stupid move now.

He remained outside, across the street, and when they emerged and went into the parking lot, he followed slowly. He wondered what they would do now. They had bought what they'd wanted to buy, he imagined. He kept himself near enough to watch them drive off, but again did not get too close. When they arrived at her house, her girlfriend got out of the car and went inside with her.

They weren't finished. He was sure they were going to keep talking about him, wondering who he was, where he came from, how he had found out where she lived. He had inserted a lot of wonderful mystery into what was currently a dark, dreary and depressing period for her.

Hours passed and still her girlfriend remained inside with her. Then her either soon-to-be or current ex-husband drove up with their daughter. He got out of his car with her and they went into the house. What I wouldn't give to be a fly on the wall in there right now, he thought. The ex-husband wasn't in there long and when he came out, he didn't look very happy. In fact, he backed his car out quickly and spun his tires, taking his rage out on his car and the street.

Steve felt his eyes narrow.

That man has a bad temper, he thought. I can't let her be abused. He glanced at the house once more and then he started his truck and took off after the ex-husband. He made some sharp turns and headed up another Beverly Hills street. About fifteen minutes later, he saw him pull up to an enormous gate and drive in when the gate opened.

From the street, he could see that the driveway for this mansion curved up and wound around.

He could barely see the top third of the house. The foliage and landscaping were so elaborate that it looked as private as a king's or high government official's private residence.

Was this where he lived now?

Who was this guy? How rich was he?

He thought about it for a while and then, more concerned than ever, drove off slowly and went home.

His mother, frustrated by his absence all day, pounced on him when he entered.

"What's going on? You working overtime?"

"No," he said.

"Well?"

"I'm seeing someone new," he said. Her face exploded with so much interest that he nearly burst out laughing. Instead, he teased her by walking away. As he'd expected, she was right on his heels.

"What someone new? Where did you meet her? Who is she?"

"I met her last night at a very expensive Beverly Hills watering hole."

"Watering hole?"

"That's what those places are, Ma, Beverly Hills or not. People go there to meet people. You just pay more for the same drink in Beverly Hills."

He took off his shirt. He was going to take a hot shower. He was hungry now, too, very hungry.

"That doesn't sound like a place you would normally go to. Why did you go there?" she pursued.

He paused as if the question were a terribly good one, one he wanted to ponder before answering. She stood waiting.

"Well?"

He turned slowly to her.

"Someone needed me," he said. "And I felt it deeply."

"Huh?"

He smiled at her.

"Got to take a shower. I'm starving. Hope you have something good going," he added, and left her standing there, shaking her head.

Maybe her husband hadn't been so crazy after all.

Maybe their son had some serious problems.

On the way out, she put Julia's picture upright again.

"I still can't believe you just blurted out your phone number," Tricia said as she prepared to leave. "I definitely underestimated you."

"Oh stop. I told you. I don't know why I did. It was just impulsive."

"No, sexual," Tricia insisted.

Megan looked at the stairway. After Scott left, she had sent Jennifer up to wash and change her clothes.

"Well, nothing will come of it."

"I wouldn't be so sure. Besides, you deserve a fling if you want one."

Megan shook her head.

"I can't imagine myself—"

"Imagine it, Meg. You're soon to be a single woman again. You don't have to run out and marry the first guy who smiles at you, but you don't have to become a nun, either."

"That was the angriest I ever saw Scott," she said, changing the subject. "He looked like he wanted to . . ."

"Slap you silly. I know. He cannot tolerate your

being so strong. If he does or says anything in any way threatening, you call Emily Lloyd."

"I don't think—"

"You don't know," Tricia corrected. "He's never been backed up to the wall like this before, especially by you, has he? You've complained and had arguments, but this is real now, and he's got to face it whether he likes it or not. That can reveal the real Scott Lester," she warned.

Megan bit down on her lower lip and nodded.

"More reason to have a good time," Tricia continued. "Get your mind off the nasty stuff. I'll call you later. Or better yet, you call me when Steve calls you."

"Maybe he won't."

"Right. He just runs around Beverly Hills with bouquets of roses. See you," Tricia sang, and walked out.

Megan stood there thinking a moment and then went up to see how Jennifer's day had gone.

She was just putting on her flip-flops.

"Did you have a good time, Jen?" she asked.

"Yes," Jennifer said, but not with much enthusiasm.

"You saw a lot of wonderful art and had a nice lunch, didn't you?"

"Uh-huh, but Daddy was on the phone a lot, too. Even at lunch," she said.

"Oh. Well, I'm sure he talked to you quite a bit, too."

She shrugged.

"He asked a lot of questions about you," she said.

"What kind of questions?"

"He wanted to know what you've been doing and especially where you went last night."

"Is that right?"

"I didn't tell him anything bad about you, Mom."

"Oh, I know you didn't, Jen. I know you wouldn't."

"He said he didn't understand why you were being so mean to him. He said he wished I could get you to change your mind."

"Dirty pool," Megan muttered. She made a mental note to call Emily Lloyd to see what could be done about his trying to pressure her through their daughter. She was angry enough to get on the phone and call him herself, but she realized that might be just what he wanted—a Lester discussion. Both he and his father were too good at knocking down their opponent's arguments. Let your lawyer handle it, she told herself.

"Well, don't you worry about it, Jen. It will all work out. C'mon. Help me make dinner and don't forget, we're going to the movies tomorrow."

Working side by side in the kitchen with Megan helped Jennifer to relax and resemble a normal nine-year-old girl again. Despite her annoyance at Scott for not devoting 100 percent of his attention to her at the museum, Jennifer obviously had enjoyed the experience. She rambled on and on about the different works of art, the statuary, even the restaurant. Megan couldn't help but shake her head and regret that it took a separation between her and Scott before he would think of taking Jennifer on such an outing. Before, if she didn't come up with the ideas for such trips and experiences, they would never come up, and too often she and Jennifer had ended up doing them without him because of another one of his last minute business crises.

They ate, cleaned up and watched television. Just before nine, the phone rang. She was expecting calls from her other girlfriends by now. Despite Tricia's promise not to get on the gossip line, she knew she would at least mention it to one or the other and that would set off a series of calls and discussions. She reviewed how each of her friends would react, picturing who would see it as a death in the family and who would be more than sympathetic, actually sound envious of her grit.

As she moved to pick up the receiver, she tried to guess who would be first.

"Sorry, if I shocked you this morning," he began.

She felt the heat come into her face. She could end it now before it even really began, she thought. It was truly as if there were a good angel on one shoulder and a bad one on the other. Both were whispering in her ears:

This guy is good-looking, but too aggressive. End it.

This guy is more than just good-looking. There's an old-fashioned kind of way about him. One thing's for sure, he's sensitive to your needs.

Hang up.

Give him a chance. Learn more about him. Don't crawl into a shell. Tricia was right.

She glanced at Jennifer, who was getting sleepy. She looked so small suddenly, so vulnerable. How could Scott not see that? How could he have neglected her even for a moment today, neglected her enough to have her complain about his being on the phone? She pictured Jennifer standing there in front of some hard-to-understand work of art, feeling alone while other parents and children moved about with excitement.

Almost out of spite alone, she decided to continue the phone conversation. But there were real concerns.

"No," she said. "That was all right. I would just like to know how you knew where I lived."

"I was supposed to meet a friend at that place last night, the Cage? I didn't see him because he was on the dance floor, but I saw what was going on with you and forgot about him. Afterward, he heard the commotion and was in the crowd when the police arrived. He overheard some things, including your name and address."

Did she say her address aloud or just write it? She couldn't recall.

"Oh, I see."

"You'd think a woman would be safe from those kind of creeps in a place like that."

"I don't know as we're safe anywhere, when it comes to that sort of thing," she said. "But . . . didn't you think I was married? I mean . . ."

"You weren't wearing a wedding ring. I took a shot," he said.

She looked at her hand. She had forgotten that she had taken off her wedding ring.

"Are you divorced?"

"In the process," she replied.

"Oh. Well, I felt you were a little down when I first saw you. Sorry."

"I'll be all right."

"You surely will. Anyway, you don't know me, except as someone who wouldn't tolerate you being abused, but I was hoping I could talk you into letting me make up for your ruined evening. I'd like to take you to dinner. Anywhere you'd like," he said. "Maybe tomorrow night, if that's possible."

"I don't know. It's a little soon, and . . ."

"You were out Friday night," he reminded her. "My mother says I'm a helluva nice guy," he added.

She laughed.

"You can choose wherever . . . Don't worry about the cost."

"You really don't owe me anything."

"Okay. Then let's pretend you owe me. Because of you, I'm a wanted man. Maybe they'll put my picture up on post-office walls or telephone poles."

She laughed again. He wasn't just good-looking; he was clever. Dare she think, charming?

"Where would you like to go to dinner?" she asked him.

"Me? Oh . . . um . . . There's this little Italian place in West Hollywood, kind of off the beaten path, if you know what I mean. Kind of a mom-and-pop operation. Nothing as fancy as Beverly Hills, but . . ."

"That's exactly where I'd like to go," she replied quickly, maybe too quickly.

"Well, that's great. How about I come by around seven? We don't even need a reservation at this place, but I'll make sure we're seated by seven thirty."

"I can't stay out late," she said. "I have a babysitter I trust, but she's still in high school."

"Perfect. I have to go to work early. How about I get you home by ten?"

Was she really going to say yes?

Jennifer's eyes were completely closed. She had to get her to bed.

"Okay."

"Great. See you at seven."

"Wait," she cried before he could hang up.

"What?"

"You better give me your phone number in case something unexpected comes up. I have a nine-year-old daughter."

"Sure . . . 555-434-5044. That's my cell. I'm usually out and about during the day. My mother has me doing errands on weekends."

"You live with your mother?"

"I'll tell you all about it. You look like someone I can trust with my story," he added.

He couldn't have said anything that would have heightened her curiosity more. Anyway, it was about time she was with someone real. All of Scott's friends or acquaintances were as artificial as sweeteners. This might be that fresh air she was craving.

"Now you do have me hooked," she said.

"Maybe it's the other way around," he told her, and then said good-bye.

Like some mime, he was yelling silently. If anyone, especially his mother, saw him, she would think he was a raving lunatic. There he was swinging his arms, stomping the floor and spinning around. After a few more moments of elation, he calmed himself. He had some real planning to do. You don't get more than one opportunity to make a good impression in this situation, he thought. Of course, he didn't count the incident at the Cage and his giving her the roses as full-blown opportunities. They just set it up for the real thing.

Tomorrow, he had to get out and do some shopping. He wanted to wear something special and get himself some new shoes too. He wondered if he needed a haircut. He could trim it up here and there himself, but he'd be too afraid of messing up. Of course, he didn't want to look like any of those Beverly Hills guys anyway. Maybe the haircut wasn't that important. She was looking for something fresh and different, someone natural. He heard it in her voice.

"Just be yourself, Stevie boy," he told his image in the mirror. "Just be yourself. It was enough to win Julia, wasn't it?"

That thought gave him serious pause. Julia wasn't up to this woman's knees. I can't measure anything using Julia, he decided. Julia was unsophisticated.

Maybe he wasn't up to this new task. What if he couldn't carry on a serious conversation? What if she started talking about art or theater? What were her interests? She didn't look like she hung out in a bowling alley, like Julia had.

What about his etiquette? He'd rarely pulled out the chair for Julia, and when he did, she'd looked at him as if he was trying to be someone he wasn't. He had to be careful about the way he used his silverware, too. He knew the difference between a salad fork and a main-dish fork, but sometimes he mixed them up. Julia had never noticed. She'd mixed them up herself often.

And make sure you put your napkin on your lap. Don't tuck it in your collar like some peasant.

What am I getting so worked up about? She didn't seem at all like that sort of snob, even though she lived in a big house in Beverly Hills. There was something downright honest and true about her. He sensed it, and once again he would rely on his instincts. It'd be just fine.

But he would spruce up a bit. That's simply a show of respect. He went to his bottom dresser drawer and dug out his father's dress watch. It had been his father's father's watch. His father hadn't actually given it to him. After his father had died, his mother brought it to him.

"Be very careful with it, Steve. It's an heirloom. It was made in Switzerland."

He'd taken it, but he wasn't excited about it then, and he certainly couldn't wear it to work. Julia was never impressed with it either, but it did have character and it was a wonderful conversation piece. He decided he would not talk about his rough relationship with his father anyway. That might not go over too well. This woman was a woman who valued family. He was positive, despite her divorce action.

I bet she gave him every possible second and third chance, he thought. *I bet going for a divorce was the very last thing she did. She'd probably put up with a great deal of misery.* He felt as sorry for her right now as he often felt for himself. *We were both in bad marriages,* he concluded.

I won't tell her that right off, but eventually I will. It will make her feel better about her own situation.

For a guy who didn't have all that many relationships with women, he prided himself on how well he could handle one. He was a natural psychotherapist.

As he stood there looking into the mirror, he conjured up scenes he hoped would soon take place between him and her. He couldn't wait to take her to see the boat. That would surely impress her, and . . .

Wait, he thought, how am I going to take her—in a truck? The fact that he didn't think of this before threw him into another panic. He couldn't use his mother's beat-up Ford. It was twelve years old. True, he kept it in working condition, but everything was worn. No way.

He hurried to find the phone book and located rental cars. Minutes later he had reserved an SUV. The gas guzzlers were popular with the wealthy. He knew that from his work. Besides, if she complained about it, even hinted at disapproval, he'd have a different vehicle the next time. Once again, he relaxed. It would all be okay, more than okay. It would be wonderful.

When he stepped back into the living room, his mother looked up and immediately saw the change in his face.

"What?" she asked.

He widened his soft smile.

"I have a dinner date tomorrow night, so don't make anything for me."

"That girl who needs you so much?"

"Exactly," he said.

He sat on the sofa but he really didn't pay much attention to what his mother was watching. He never liked her choices anyway and sat there just to keep her company or maybe just to not feel alone.

"I see you're finally wearing your father's watch."

He looked at it as if he had forgotten he had put it on.

"Might as well get some use out of it."

"Must be a fancy date. Well, what's this woman like? How old is she? Does she work? What kind of job does she have? Where does she live?"

His mother fired her questions as if she expected he would write them down. It was like being in a classroom.

"She's in the middle of a divorce," he said.

"A divorce?"

"And she has a little girl."

His mother leaned forward and stared at him. Then she shook her head.

"Leftovers," she muttered, and sat back.

She could just as well have slapped him across the face. His face became that crimson. He glared at her with so much heat in his eyes, she had to look away.

"What did you say?"

"No wonder you said she needed you. You're so naïve, Steve. A woman like that always jumps to the first man who shows some interest. She'll use you for a while, peel you like an orange and then dump you when someone else comes along."

She didn't look at him, but she nodded her head.

"You listen to me," she continued. "You stay away from her."

He shot up as if she had lit a fire under his rear

end. He frightened her, but she didn't cower. She pointed her right forefinger at him.

"Don't you look at me like that. You look just like your father right now."

"I'd never say anything good about him," he said, "but at least I understand why he looked this way so much . . . especially at you."

He turned and left the living room, slamming his door closed.

She turned back to her television show.

For a few moments, he stood inside his room, fuming. Suddenly his eyes were drawn to Julia's framed photograph. She was laughing at him again.

"Bitch!" he screamed and drove his left fist into the picture, sending shards of glass everywhere and thrusting it into the wall.

"What's that? What did you do?" his mother cried.

He looked down at the knuckles on his left hand. All but one were bleeding.

"Steve!"

"Nothing. Shut up!" he screamed. He pressed his palms against his temples.

"I'm going to start a new life," he vowed. "I'm going to get out of here and have a family. I am!"

CHAPTER SIX

"It's just a dinner and an early evening," Megan told Tricia when she called in the morning.

"I hope not," Tricia said. "What you need right now is a good roll in the hay."

"Stop it. I'm not going to bed with someone new that quickly."

"What did I tell you about falling off a bike?"

"Sex is not riding a bike."

"Sure it is. You're peddling your ass with both, aren't you?"

Megan laughed. She had woken up with a feeling of dread and regret. What had she agreed to do? What made her so impulsive, especially now? She would not be so dishonest as to say she had never looked at another handsome man with some desire, played some fantasy, while she was married to Scott, but never once did she believe she could carry out an affair. Of course, this wasn't exactly an extramarital affair anymore, but still, what had come over her? Where did she get all this new courage? Was it simply born out of anger and spite or had it always been there inside her, stifled and suffocated?

While she got up, showered and dressed to start

the day, she debated with herself, and by the time she went down to the kitchen to start her and Jennifer's breakfast, she had decided to call Steve and cancel. But before she could do that, Scott called.

"You didn't give me much of a chance to talk yesterday," he began. "And I didn't want to discuss our affairs in front of Tricia Morgan. If I were going to do that, I might as well just go directly to ABC News with it."

"What do you want, Scott?"

"On the advice of my attorney and after discussion with yours, I froze all our brokerage accounts and two money-market accounts. Your household account has lots of money in it anyway."

"Why? Did you think I would empty all those accounts and run off?"

"You wanted this," he said. "We're in it now, so we have to do what our lawyers tell us."

"How convenient. Fine. But I suspect your father was the one recommending it."

"That's not true. Look, Megan, I don't—"

"I'm busy right now. I don't have time for this," she said, and hung up on him.

Jennifer came in at almost the same moment. If she hadn't, Megan was sure she would have started to cry. Instead, she put on her best mommy face and had her help make their pancakes. All thoughts of canceling her impulsive dinner date evaporated seconds afterward.

Megan tried to get her mind off everything by taking Jennifer for some new shoes before they went to the movie matinee. It was a very entertaining film, and at least for two hours she was able to get the tension out of her body. It didn't return until she looked at the clock at home and realized she had to get ready to go out.

Jennifer was all questions.

"Where are you going?"

"I'm going to dinner with someone new, someone you haven't met yet."

"Why?"

"He seems very nice and he asked me. I'm just as sad as you are about everything and I need to have some distraction."

"What's that?"

"Something to get your mind off thinking about sad things," she said. "Like us going to the movie today."

Jennifer nodded, but her eyelids narrowed like Scott's did when he was in deep thought. It occurred to Megan that despite Jennifer's precociousness, she was still a little girl at heart and hadn't accepted, or wouldn't accept, the idea of her parents not being together. Even though she understood that lawyers and courts were soon to be in their lives, she still had that child's optimism. Hope was out there just waiting to be readmitted.

"And this new person can do that?" Jennifer finally asked.

"I'll see. If not, I won't see him again," she said. That seemed to relieve Jennifer.

She had invited Margaret to have dinner with Jennifer, and she arrived at six.

"You can just leave everything in the sink, Margaret. Lourdes comes tomorrow to clean."

She had the maid three times a week only because the house was so big, but sometimes she thought Scott wanted the maid more as a status symbol than as an actual necessity. He insisted Megan leave clothes to be washed and ironed.

"Go out with your friends. Take advantage of what we have," he urged, but she always had the feeling he wanted her to do these things mainly because all the wives of all the men he knew did them. Maybe that was unfair of her, but he didn't dissuade her when he took little interest in what she did do whenever she went out with the other women. It was only when she had gone somewhere with Tricia that he put her through the third degree.

She was as twisted as a ball of rubber bands when the clock approached seven. Right on the first gong of the grandfather clock in the hallway, the door buzzer rang. She took a deep breath and went to open the door. Once again, he had some flowers, this time a bouquet of mixed-color tulips. She thought he looked quite attractive in an embroidered black shirt and slacks with a rich leather belt.

"You'll turn my house into a nursery," she said, laughing, and took the flowers. "Thank you."

"This world has so much gray going. It's nice to brighten up the scenery—not that you need any brightening."

She smiled.

"Well, now you'll have to give me a moment to put these flowers in another vase. Come in," she said, and he stepped into the entryway.

Jennifer had come to the living room doorway and was gaping at him.

"Hi there," he said. "My name's Steve. What's yours?"

"Jennifer."

"Great name. I'm very interested in names," he continued, walking closer. "Jennifer is a Welsh name and it means 'fair one.' Fair doesn't mean the opposite of unfair here. It means very pretty, so the name really fits you."

Jennifer stared in astonishment. Megan had heard it all and was smiling in the kitchen doorway.

"How come you know so much about names?" she asked.

He shrugged. "I'll tell you later." He glanced at his watch.

"Margaret," Megan called, and the babysitter came to the living-room doorway. "We'll be back at ten. Call me if there's any problem."

"There won't be, Mrs. Lester."

Megan blanched at the name but thought, Of course, what else would she call me?

"You can start calling me Megan now, Margaret. We've been friends long enough and you're old enough."

Margaret nodded. Megan kissed Jennifer.

"Go to sleep early, honey. Tomorrow's school."

"Okay," she said, but her eyes were fixed on Steve Wallace. He winked at her and then opened the door for Megan. She looked back at Jennifer and walked out.

"That's one cute little girl," Steve said as they walked to his newly rented black SUV.

"Thank you. She's my whole life."

"I understand."

He rushed ahead to open the door for her.

"This looks new."

"Relatively new," he said. "Is it okay?"

She smiled. Okay? What was he going to do, buy a different car if it wasn't?

"It's fine," she said, and got in. He hurried around and got in.

"I think you'll like this place," he said as he started the SUV and began to back out. "I haven't had a bad meal there."

"I enjoy going to different places."

"Oh, I do, too. It's just that when I find something good, I try to support it, keep it in business."

"I didn't mean . . . That's very nice. Look—," she began the same time he said, "Listen—"

They laughed.

"Sorry, go on," he said.

"I just wanted to say that I'm a bit rusty at this."

"Rusty?"

"I'm out of practice. I've been incarcerated for ten years."

"You have?"

"Bad marriage."

"Oh, yeah. Well, don't you worry, Megan, it won't take long to get back into it. I should know."

"Divorced?"

He didn't answer right away. He made a turn and sped up.

"No. My wife died while she was pregnant. Lost the baby, too," he said.

"Oh, my God. What happened?"

"Hemorrhaged. I wasn't with her at the time."

"I'm sorry."

"Yeah. We knew we were going to have a girl. That's how I know so much about names."

"Oh."

"I always wanted a family. Bit old-fashioned, I suppose, but I go for all the corny stuff."

"Not corny to me," she said.

I know, he thought. I knew it the moment I saw you.

He smiled at her and drove on.

Scott looked out the window of his hotel room. What the hell am I doing here? he asked himself. His father wanted him to come home, but he clung to the belief that Megan would come to her senses. Moving back into the family house was truly accepting the breakup of this marriage. He knew it wasn't something his father would pine over. In fact, there would be that constant "I told you so" look on his face, and Scott couldn't imagine himself waking up and seeing that first thing in the morning, much less at dinner every night.

What frightened him about it all was Megan's heartfelt outrage. Was he really that bad of a husband and father? Was he really that oblivious to what was happening at home? Megan had once told him he didn't see his home life as half as exciting as his work life.

"For you, Scott," she'd said, "your work is an end in itself. It doesn't matter what you say you do with your financial success. It's the pursuit—the game, as you call it—that you live for and not the cars and the house and all the expensive things we have. You'd think more about Jennifer and me if we were a commodity."

At the time, he thought her words, her accusations, were so off-the-wall, he didn't pay any attention to them, but try as he might, he couldn't shake them off now. Maybe that was because deep down inside he knew she wasn't completely wrong. But rather than getting him to see things from her point of view, it only frustrated him more.

How do men of great power and responsibility balance their family needs with their work? How do they compartmentalize so well, and what did it say about him that he couldn't do it? His father couldn't do it either, only it never seemed to bother him anywhere near as much as it was now bothering Scott. He should have been more rebellious. He should have defied his father more and become more of his own man.

Shoulda, coulda, woulda—the slogan of a failed person.

Am I a failure?

He looked at the portfolio of work he had taken from the office. He didn't want to open it and begin, but it was like an addiction. His father needed some numbers crunched, and whether he was doing it to make himself feel better or just to keep him from caring about Megan, he didn't know, but he had told his father this investment was going to be totally his decision. And it was a considerable amount of money, too.

He went to the desk and opened the portfolio, but before he reached the end of the first page, there was a terrific tremor, one that shook the very foundation of the hotel. A glass he had too close to the edge of the night table fell and smashed, and the bed itself seemed to rise and fall. It lasted a good forty to fifty seconds. All the windows rattled. He anticipated glass breaking. He actually clung to the sides of the chair. His heart was pounding when the tremor stopped.

Outside, car alarms were screaming. Doors slammed in the hallway. People were comforting each other. One woman was close to hysterical. Scott rose and opened the door to see the other hotel guests milling about.

"Did you see that?" a man asked him.

"See?"

"The earthquake, forcrissakes."

"Yes," Scott said, and closed the door.

What does he think? I slept through it?

The first thing that came to his mind was Jennifer and Megan. He went to the phone and dialed, but the line was busy. He imagined Megan was calling around or friends and neighbors were calling her. He waited and dialed again and again, it was busy.

Maybe something's wrong, he thought. He tried one more time and then went for his jacket and shot out of the room.

Most of the hotel residents had gone down to the lobby and were still there. Many were out-of-towners who had never experienced an earthquake. The hotel management had the waiters from the restaurant serving drinks to help calm people. He made his way to the front and ordered the valet to bring up his car.

He had been through many tremors, being a native Californian, but it still amazed him how quickly things returned to normal. The damage was relatively light in this area. He'd listen later to see where the epicenter was and where, if anywhere, there was serious damage. Right now, the traffic looked light and there was no sign of any panic.

He got into his car quickly when it arrived and

took off toward his house. He still thought of it as his house, of course. Maybe he'd push to have them sell it and split the proceeds. It wouldn't break Megan's heart. She was never ecstatic over it. In fact, he always felt she was embarrassed by its size and opulence. That embarrassment did annoy him. He hated the way she had of making him feel guilty for being so well-off.

"What are you, a socialist?" he asked, half kidding.

"No, but sometimes I do feel like I'm living in some kind of bubble."

"Viva la bubble," was his response. "We do our charitable contributions, don't we? We do more than a lot of others who are just as well-off, if not more. I won't be ashamed of my success."

"I'm not asking you to be ashamed," she said.

"So what are you asking me to be?"

She thought a moment. He was confident that she would cave and just apologize for her attitude. But no, not Megan.

"More modest, less loud, but most of all, more concerned with what we like and want and not what your father expects us to like and want."

He was speechless for a moment, and that made him angry. He walked away and pouted, making himself feel better by berating her for not appreciating what she had. He ranted in his thoughts so long and hard, he had to take a sleeping pill that night.

Because neither of them brought up the topic for a long while afterward, he'd put it aside, but it was always there, festering beneath the surface of their marriage, part of the unspoken, unheard and unseen tension that he now had to admit he had felt as much as she must have felt. There was no pressure release. He saw that now, but now, it was probably too late.

All the lights were on in their house when he pulled into the driveway. He got out quickly and ran up to the front door. This was no time to follow any protocol. He dug out his house keys instead of ringing the buzzer, and entered.

"Megan!" he called.

Margaret Sanders came out of the living room quickly.

"Oh, Mr. Lester."

"Where's my wife? Where's Jennifer?" he asked, rushing toward her.

Margaret stepped back and he looked into the living room and saw Jennifer curled up on the sofa.

"She fell asleep there right after the earthquake, and Mrs. Lester said to just let her sleep until she returned. She's on her way."

"Where is she?"

Margaret hesitated. He could see the abject fear in her face.

"She went out with someone?"

She shook her head anticipating his next question. "I don't know who he is," she said.

He stepped back as if he had gotten too close to a hot stove.

"He?" He looked at Jennifer. She seemed quite at peace. Waking her up wasn't an option. "Anything break, fall off?"

"I don't think so, but I didn't go through the whole house. I had to stay with Jen."

"Right," he said, and started through the house. Fear had turned to rage. He? What were they, weeks into this at the most? She must have been seeing this guy before the petition for divorce.

He checked the kitchen. Nothing was broken, but a cabinet had opened and some packages had fallen to the counter. He left it and went to the den. A small trophy he and Megan had won in a dance contest on a cruise ship a year after they were married had fallen off the shelf. Ironically, nothing else had fallen. He picked it up and read the inscription. Memories of that cruise returned. It had been a Mediterranean cruise with romantic and interesting ports like Santorini, Sorrento, Nice and Monte Carlo. They had made love almost every night and sat on the deck chairs holding hands until one or both of them began to doze off. It had seemed like the whole world was opening up to them back then. How could it go so badly and end up like this?

He put the trophy back and went upstairs to check the bedrooms. When he went into the master bedroom, he saw how Megan had rifled through various outfits to wear. He could see her agonizing over the choices just the way she usually did whenever they had a place to go. Rejected garments still lay over chairs or on the bed. She wouldn't put it all away until they came home, usually, and he'd always complained about it. Right now, it almost brought a smile to his face, but then the thought of her being out there with some other man came sweeping back into his mind and he turned and charged out of the room and down the stairs.

Jennifer was still asleep. Margaret sat across from her.

"Are you all right?" he asked her.

She nodded. "My parents called. Nothing happened at our house."

"Good. Okay. You can tell Mrs. Lester I was here, checking. I'll call tomorrow."

Margaret nodded. He could see how terribly uncomfortable she was in the middle of all this. He almost felt sorrier for her than he did for himself.

"I'm sure she'll be back soon," he muttered, and left.

For a few moments, he sat in his car, tempted to remain there and confront her when she came back, but he also didn't want that sort of confrontation at this point. Instead, he backed out and then went up the block, turned around and parked across the street, far enough away not to be noticed, but close enough to observe.

There he waited, feeling as if he had just been punched hard in the stomach.

The restaurant was just as Steve Wallace had described, a mom-and-pop operation with no more than ten tables, decorated with Italian memorabilia that ranged from movie posters to pictures of little Italian villages and seaside resorts to hanging garlic. The tables were red with red-cushioned chairs. There was no bar as such, just a small area mainly for the waiters to get the wine and drinks customers ordered. When they arrived, the place was full, but their table was reserved. It was, she thought, the best-placed one because it was in a little alcove near the front window. She heard the Three Tenors singing just loudly enough to clear the cacophony of a half-dozen conversations all going at once.

The waiters seemed to know Steve well. Unlike the maître d's of the high-end restaurants she and Scott would frequent, the wife of the owner, a woman in her sixties with straight gray hair and silver and black earrings that captured the sparkle of her ebony eyes, seemed far more natural and relaxed. It was truly like being invited to someone's home for dinner.

"I love this place," she told him when they were seated. "I feel like I'm really in Italy. Have you ever been?"

"No. I haven't done anywhere near as much traveling as I would like," he said. "Different reasons."

The waiter brought them a basket of homemade garlic rolls and handed them menus and him the wine list.

"I usually go for their house Chianti, but if you have something else you like . . . ," he said, offering the wine menu to her.

"No, just order what you usually do. I'm sure it's perfect."

He did and the waiter left.

"Everything sounds so good on this menu. I'm really hungry now."

"It all is."

"What do you usually have?"

"The eggplant pasta dish, but the meatballs are to die for."

"I'll go with what you order," she said, and put the menu down.

While he ordered for them, she looked around and kept that soft smile on her face, a smile he thought would literally melt his heart.

"I feel like I'm coming back to earth," she said.

He laughed. "I'm glad I could be of some help."

"Thank you. So, how do you know so much about names? You knew what Jennifer meant."

"Oh, I was doing a lot of thinking about baby names when my wife became pregnant," he said, looking down and toying with the fork.

"I'm sorry. I guess sadness has hooked itself onto me right now."

"No, no, that's fine." He smiled. "So what does this soon-to-be ex-husband of yours do?"

"He and his father run Lester Enterprises—commercial real estate, investments. I don't understand half of it or care to."

"Lester Enterprises. I've heard of them. Might have even worked on one of their projects."

"What do you do? I guess it was rude of me not to have asked earlier."

"No, you can't be rude," he said.

She laughed. "There are two men who will vehemently disagree with that."

He nodded. "I'm in construction, self-contracting. I guess I'm pretty good at it. Never lack for work."

"Is that what you've always done?"

"I went to a trade school after high school, did a stint in the navy, which is why I fell in love with boats. I have a twin-diesel eighty-six-foot Cantiere di Lavagna Admiral 26 I keep in San Diego. I got it on a great deal and have fixed it up considerably. You like boats?"

"Scott—that's my husband, to be ex—invested in a yacht with two other investors, but we have yet to use it. It was more of a business deal than a pleasure activity for him, which is true for most everything he does."

The waiter brought their wine and poured it. She tasted it and smiled.

"Smooth. I like it."

"It's not expensive," he said as if to apologize.

"I like it more then," she said, and he laughed.

"I never understood these suits," he said. The waiter brought their salads.

"Suits?"

"Guys with these nine-to-five office jobs."

"I wish Scott's were just a nine-to-five. We might have had a chance then."

"To me, going to the same place to do the same work every day would drive me bonkers. I like going to new sites, having new challenges. Besides, you meet different people all the time."

"You do make your work sound romantic."

"I can tell you this," he said, leaning toward her. "My customers are usually overjoyed to see me and the others show up."

She laughed. "I bet."

After their main dish came, he talked more about his boat, his trips to Mexico, the joy of being free on the open sea, fishing. She sat mesmerized, and the more he saw he was capturing her attention, the happier and more talkative he became.

When the waiter cleared the dishes, he ordered cappuccinos and some homemade biscotti for them.

"I hope this is sorta making up for the night I ruined for you."

"First, you didn't ruin it. You might very well have saved it. And second, this is the first night in weeks that I've relaxed and enjoyed myself. Thank you."

"Divorce is hard, huh?"

"Yes, and especially for me. My husband and his father can get up an army of lawyers, not that I care about all his assets. They'll just find ways to make it extra difficult, I'm sure."

"I don't understand how a man can be so in love with a woman one day and the next see her as the enemy."

"Well, it might not be that exactly, but the effect is—"

The tremor struck and the tables actually began sliding around the tiled floor. Megan screamed. Steve leaped to his feet and went to her, embracing her as bottles fell off shelves and one picture hanging loosely came crashing down, the glass in its frame shattering. Other customers cried out. Alarms went off outside. The lights flickered and then finally it stopped.

Megan had her face buried in Steve's shoulder. He held her tightly, holding her protectively. She raised her head slowly.

"Nice-size one," he said calmly. Everyone was rushing around to straighten and clean up. One of the customers had a plate of food in his lap.

"Jennifer!" Megan cried. "I've got to call the babysitter."

Steve flicked out his cell phone before she could dig for hers in her purse and she made the call. She could hear the hysteria in Margaret's voice. Jennifer was crying, but got on the phone.

"I'm coming right home, sweetheart. Just stay in the living room with Margaret, okay?"

"Okay, Mommy," she said, suddenly becoming half her age.

Steve went to pay the bill and they rushed out to the SUV. When he started it up, it stalled. He started it again and it stalled again. After that, the engine wouldn't turn over.

"What the hell?"

"What's wrong?"

"This thing's acting like it has a dead battery. Has to be the alternator."

"I've go to get home to Jennifer."

"Right. I'll need to boost the battery, but I'll go in and have them call a taxi for you."

"Hurry," she said.

He leaped out, cursing under his breath. He was probably driving on the battery the whole time he had the damn thing. Why didn't they go over the vehicles more thoroughly? He had the restaurant call for a taxi, but with the street just coming back to normalcy, it took the taxi a while to arrive. He actually had found someone with jumper cables just as the taxi did arrive, but Megan didn't want to wait.

"Let me pay for it," he said.

"Don't worry about it. Thank you. I'm sorry," she said, getting into the taxi.

He stood there watching it go off. The owner of the cables was getting impatient.

"Maybe you oughta just call Triple A," he said, turned and got into his own car.

As he started away, Steve kicked the side of his car and cursed him. He hit the brakes and opened his door, but when he got out and saw Steve hovering, his hands balled into fists, he got back into his car and drove away.

He didn't look back, but if he had, he would have seen Steve still standing there, glaring after him as if he would follow him to the ends of the earth. It would have frightened him more than the earthquake had, and given him far worse nightmares.

CHAPTER SEVEN

Scott saw the taxi pull in and Megan get out and rush into the house.

What sort of a man was she with? Why hadn't he driven her home?

Exactly where had she gone with this guy?

He lowered his head slowly as if he were lowering a flag of defeat. His father was right again. He should have hired a private detective. He didn't have the time to follow her all around, but never before this had he believed it was something he had to do.

I guess I have been oblivious when it comes to home life, he thought.

He started the engine. Surely, this had something to do with that Tricia Morgan. He knew she was a bad influence on Meg. Tricia was an alley cat. Hell, there were many times when she flirted with him—and right in front of Meg, too, although Meg wouldn't believe it. She actually told him he was just like other men, always flattering himself. Hell, she was the one who had her head in the sand, not him. Tricia was out there on the make all the time, and she had surely pressured Megan and introduced her to that lifestyle. There's nothing a woman like that wants more than a companion. It reinforces her belief in herself. She's like a pot smoker who can't stand anyone in the room who doesn't smoke pot, too. He was sure she was whispering in Meg's ear all the time.

So now what? Meg petitions for divorce and gets me out of the house so she can run around with this guy or maybe other guys, he thought as he drove away.

What a fool I've been. What a naïve fool to believe her issue was not having me around enough. It was all an excuse to justify her own illicit behavior.

The more he thought about it, the more riled he became. He was a man of action, wasn't he? This was time for some action.

He decided he would move out of the hotel immediately. He hated the thought of spending one more night there, especially now, after seeing this. He felt more like a fool than ever. He was too compliant, too considerate. What did it get him?

He speed-dialed through his Bluetooth built-in phone. His father answered the phone as if he had been hovering over it, expecting his call.

"I'm coming home tonight," Scott told him. "To stay. I'm out of the hotel."

"The earthquake damaged it."

"No. It's not that."

"Anything happen to the house in the earthquake?" his father asked.

That's Dad, he thought. First concern is always property. What about Megan and Jennifer?

"No, it's fine. A few things fell off shelves, but nothing serious was broken. What about up there?"

"Lots of junk banged around, but again, nothing serious. We had a little more serious damage on one of our commercial sites, however."

"Dad, did you hear what I said? I said I'm moving out of the hotel and coming to stay with you."

"Yeah, I heard it. I don't know why you put yourself in a hotel in the first place," he continued. "You're letting her push you around. You've got to—"

"Do you have a private detective we can hire?" he quickly asked to cut off one of his father's long lectures.

"Ah, so you are coming to your senses. Good. Something else happen?"

"I'll talk to you when I see you. I'll be there in less than an hour."

"Sounds good," his father said.

He hung up.

Sounds good? What sounds good? Can't he just once think about my feelings, how all this impacts on me?

He didn't know whom to be angry at more, Megan or his father. He sped up and nearly rear-ended a BMW that was similar to Tricia Morgan's car. Maybe that was what he was thinking when he waited until the last minute to hit the brakes, he thought.

I'd like to ram her back end right into her mouth.

Just as he checked out of the hotel, his cell phone rang. He saw it was Megan.

"What?" he asked, not hiding his irritation and rage. For a moment, she didn't respond. "What is it, Megan?"

"I heard you had stopped by to check on Jennifer and the house. Thanks."

"You don't have to thank me for doing what I should be doing, Megan. That's pretty damn condescending."

"I would have thought under the present circumstances, you'd be less antagonistic, Scott."

"Really."

He was going to ask where she was and start interrogating her, but he felt it was not only below him, it was showing her how much she'd hurt him and how weak it made him feel. He wasn't going to give her the satisfaction.

"It's just good you got here," she said. "She's fine now. It was her first sizeable one."

"No kidding. I think I might have known that."

"Glad you're full of sympathy," she said, and hung up.

He stood there in the hotel lobby for a moment and then closed his cell, put it away and went out to get his car. Twenty minutes later, he was driving up to his father's house. For the first time in a long time, it looked like a safe haven, a place in which he would regain his strength and confidence. It was large, yes, and muscular and full of options. It was not a place of retreat. It was what it had always been, family headquarters. From here he could, as his father could, reach out and make things happen.

Jules, his father's house manager, was at the door before he got to it.

"Let me take your suitcase and get your things put away for you, Mr. Lester," he said. "Your father is in his office and wants you to go right there."

"Thanks, Jules."

At times when he was much younger, Scott had

thought his house was as deep and as vast as the Grand Canyon. It had very high ceilings, walls peppered with expensive and beautiful art, velvet-curtained windows, expensive imported floor tiles, chandeliers from France and furnishings from Spain. The cost of any one room would be as much as or more than that of half the homes in America. The joke was that Citizen Kane had once lived here and the only way he could upgrade was to buy the Hearst Castle. In how many homes did your footsteps and your voice echo?

His father was at his desk. A cigar rested in the ashtray, its smoke spiraling up and dissipating. Despite the size of the home office with its over-sized desk and large cushioned sofas and leather chairs, its floor-to-ceiling shelves of books and grand picture windows, his father never looked small in it to Scott. Even now, long past his youth, when everything had looked larger and grander, this office appeared just the right size for a man like his father. Senators and congressmen came here for advice and for contributions to their campaigns. Movie producers, very successful developers, owners of hotel chains and successful restaurant chains had all sat in these chairs and visited to solidify deals or get good business advice.

"Relax," his father said, nodding at the sofa on the right. "What a night. The scaffolding at the Venice Beach project collapsed, but fortunately no one was hurt. It's just a matter of getting things set up again. I've already told the scaffolding company they're liable for any damage caused. They should be putting up that stuff to resist an eight on the Richter scale at least. We just had a 7.2, with the epicenter out in Landers."

Scott nodded.

"So, what's the story with you? Before you begin, I've already gotten you an appointment with Ed Marcus. He does a lot of work for Gerry Orseck. Gerry handled Marvin Basset's divorce. You remember Marvin. We outbid him on the Westwood strip mall and it nearly drove him mad. He never sees me without crying about it. I wrote down Ed's address for you," he said, holding out a slip of paper. Scott rose to take it. "Go there first thing tomorrow morning. He's expecting you. Well? What happened to stir up your Lester juices?"

His father always referred to "Lester juices" as if they had inherited some rare hormone stronger than testosterone. How many times had he sat in this office and heard him narrate legendary stories about his father and his grandfather? Seemed to him that he was never in here without hearing some reference to a wise political or business move only a Lester would have made.

"When the quake hit, I immediately called the house."

"Naturally, and . . . ?"

"I couldn't get through. Megan's babysitter was on the phone talking to keep herself calm, I guess."

"Babysitter?"

"Megan went out with some guy."

"No kidding. Son of a bitch," his father said, shaking his head. "I hate to be right."

"Sure you do, Dad."

"Whatever, Scott. Get on your problem and get to the office tomorrow. We have to prepare for the meeting with the Consignatory Group. It's time to seriously consider investing in some good European markets. In fact, I was going to suggest you fly over to London next week, but with your personal problems growing . . ."

"We'll see," Scott said.

"Yes, we'll see," his father said, and puffed on his cigar.

Scott started out and paused.

"Didn't you ever have any problems with Mom, with your being so busy and—"

"Never. She was independent, knew how to amuse herself and take care of our home without me being there all the time. You didn't turn out so bad, did you?"

"I don't know, Dad. Didn't I?"

"Don't start feeling sorry for yourself, Scott. That's what can bring you down," his father warned. "That was my grandfather's advice to my father and his advice to me. Remember it," he said, and went back to his papers.

Scott hesitated and then went up to his room. He looked at the slip of paper with the detective's name and address on it.

Why didn't I see any of this coming? It was a question that could easily haunt him for the rest of his life if he let it. Dad was right. It was bad to feel sorry for yourself, but who'd ever believe, he thought, that I would be hiring a private detective to spy on my wife?

Least of all, me.

The poor woman who happened to be behind the rental-car counter was literally too frightened to move. Steve Wallace had come in with such intensity and force, he'd looked like he would leap over the counter and be at her throat. She gazed past him and saw the tow truck and the SUV. He slammed the keys down on the counter and handed her the tow-truck bill.

"Who the hell is the manager here?"

"We got three managers, depending on the time of day and the day," she replied. "What's wrong, sir?"

"What's wrong? You gave me a vehicle with a defective alternator. Why wasn't it checked out before it was rented?"

His eyes were blazing, the veins in his neck embossed with the strain. He hovered like a buzzard waiting to pounce on a dying corpse. She had to swallow before responding.

"I'm sorry, sir. I don't have to call the manager. We'll take this off your bill," she said, indicating the tow-truck bill. "Would you like a replacement?"

"Damn right, and I want a significant upgrade, too."

She nodded and started on her computer.

Twenty minutes later and quite calmed down, he drove out in a yellow Corvette. She'll get a kick out of this, he thought. He certainly had a lot of making up to do. This whole thing hadn't started out badly. Hell, he wasn't upset at the earthquake. If the damn SUV had performed, he would have brought her home and helped her reassure her daughter. He would have been funny and sweet. She would have seen him in action as a father. It was a huge missed opportunity, but there wasn't much he could do about it now.

He flicked on his phone and called her. It rang three times before she picked up.

"Hey, sorry," he said. "Don't mean to intrude, but how are things there?"

"Oh," she said, clearly indicating that she didn't know who he was at first. "We're okay. I'm sorry I didn't thank you properly for the nice dinner."

"Forget that. I should be thanking you for coming out with me. Your daughter okay?"

"She's fine now, exhausted from fear, and asleep."

"Yeah, don't blame her. Can't say I wasn't a little frightened back there," he said, laughing.

"You didn't show it," she said.

"Well, my experience has always been, it's best to hide your fear so someone who needs you doesn't get more frightened. I'm glad I was there for that much."

"That's very sweet. How's your car?"

"Forget that. I got rid of it."

"Rid of it? I don't understand."

"It was a rental."

"Oh. Your regular car out of commission or something?"

"No. I only have a pickup truck."

"I don't understand. Are you saying you rented a car just to take me out?"

"I wouldn't take you out in the pickup. It's not exactly spick-and-span and my mother's car is a jalopy. That's all right. I got a surprise for you next time I see you. They quickly gave me a significant upgrade."

"Well, how long will you keep a rental car?" This whole thing was getting quite strange, she thought.

"For a while. No big deal. I'm working on a real

deal for a new car. Every time I see you, it seems I have to make up for something, but how about I try again tomorrow night?"

"Oh, well, give me a little time to recover," she said. "Jennifer will be very nervous about my going out so soon after as well."

Her reasoning wasn't completely honest, but it was easier than no, and she wasn't sure she wanted to say no anyway. She really did enjoy being with him.

"Can I call you tomorrow then? After I come home from work, that is?"

"Sure. Call," she said. "And again, don't blame yourself. It was really a nice experience until Mother Nature decided to be heard."

He laughed and pulled to the curb. She wouldn't know it, of course, but he was just outside her house, just across the street. He looked up at the lit windows upstairs in front and imagined she was there in that room, maybe in her bathrobe or pajamas. She probably wears pajamas, he thought. She was that kind of girl. Julia liked to sleep naked, he recalled. There was nothing dainty about her.

"Okay," he said. "Tell you what. I'll have a little talk with Mother Nature tonight and make sure she behaves next time we do go out."

She laughed. "Thanks again for calling."

"Hey," he said before she could hang up.

"Yes?"

"You don't deserve a minute of unhappiness, Megan. No matter how powerful your husband and his father are, they shouldn't give you a moment of grief."

"Thanks, Steve. Good night," she said, and hung

up. He held the phone as if he needed to be sure she really had hung up. Even the dial tone made him feel closer to her. Finally, he put his phone in his pocket, but he didn't drive away. He sat there staring up at the house, at the lit windows, until the lights went out.

Then he whispered, "Good night, my love," and started his engine.

His mother happened to be just going into the house when he pulled into the driveway. She paused, curious about who it was. When he shut the engine and stepped out, she turned on him sharply.

"Why didn't you call me to see how I was?"

"Busy. I knew you would be okay. We've been through worse and this shack has stood up fine."

"Shack?" She peered at the Corvette. "Where did you get that car?"

"Rented it," he said.

"Rented? Why?"

"I need a car, Mom, when I go out with a woman. Can't use my truck and can't use that piece of crap you still drive. I should let it die a well-deserved death and stop repairing it."

She followed him into the house.

"You rented that car to impress this new woman, this woman with a child?"

He didn't answer. He went to his room, but she continued after him.

"Are you absolutely losing your mind? Aren't there any nice single women out there without children? Must you go and take on someone else's responsibility? This woman must be some snob if you need a car like that to take her out, and how are you going to keep such a woman happy with the money you make?"

He turned and looked at her in his doorway. She was leaning against the jamb with her arms folded. How many times she had taken that attitude and stance while firing a slew of questions to make him feel bad? he thought.

"First, she is far from a snob, and second, she is disgusted with the so-called rich Beverly Hills life. She wants to have her feet on the ground and be with someone real."

"Is that right?" She shook her head and laughed a dry, short laugh, the one that always irritated him because it was full of arrogance, like she knew it all. "You'll come crawling back with your tail between your legs, I'm sure."

He walked toward her, his eyelids nearly closed. She knew he was raging inside, but she held her ground and he calmed.

"I was planning on bringing her here to meet you so you would see for yourself how wrong you are, but I'm not sure I will, if you have this attitude, Ma. Not everyone has to be the same way."

She raised her eyebrows.

"Well," she said, relaxing and starting away. "I hope for your sake you're right."

"I'm right," he insisted. She shrugged.

He backed up and closed the door.

"I'm right," he muttered. "I won't let it go wrong. Not this time."

There were moments in the morning when Scott thought he wouldn't go through with it. He was feeling more embarrassed about it than anything and he wasn't sure he wanted some stranger to know so many intimate details of his personal life. But how could you employ a private detective without that happening? It was like telling your doctor your sex life. Sometimes, there was no choice.

As usual, his father was up and out of the house before Scott went down to breakfast. It had always been this way. Maybe once or twice a week if he was lucky, he and his mother would see his father at breakfast. It inevitably made him think about how often he had not been there for breakfast with Megan and Jennifer and how few times he was the one to take Jennifer to the private elementary school she attended.

It doesn't matter now, he thought. None of that was any excuse for what Megan was doing and maybe had been doing.

He ate his breakfast quickly and drove to the detective's office, which was on the second floor of an office building in Brentwood. Anyone would have thought it was a successful lawyer's office and not the office of a private detective. It was bright and well appointed, with expensive-looking floor tile and oak-paneled walls. The secretary-receptionist in the outer office looked up and smiled as would someone who was expecting him and knew exactly who he was. She looked to be a woman in her fifties and wore a gray skirt suit. She had light brown hair styled neatly about her ears.

"Good morning, Mr. Lester," she said. "My husband is waiting for you."

She rose to open the inner office door for him. "Would you like some coffee, bottled water, soda?"

"Nothing, thank you," Scott said.

Whatever happened to the Humphrey Bogart–style private detectives who had dingy offices and disorganized secretaries? He didn't even think a private eye would have or need a secretary these days. One thing was certain—he wasn't counting on another person knowing his intimate details, but that's what would surely happen here, since Ed Marcus's secretary was his wife.

The inner office was no less impressive than the outer, and like the outer, it was as immaculate as the office of a bank president. Marcus, a tall, slim man in his midfifties with licorice black hair cut and shaped like that of an actor from the forties, rose to extend his hand. He wore an expensive-looking pinstripe suit.

"Mr. Lester . . . Ed Marcus," he said.

Scott shook his hand.

"Please, sit on the sofa. It's more comfortable."

On Scott's left was a soft black leather sofa, a glass-top coffee table and a big cushioned brown and black chair across from the sofa. Scott sat on the sofa and Ed sat in the chair.

"Would you like some coffee? Anything?"

"I asked," Ed's wife said, still standing in the doorway.

"I'm fine," Scott said.

"Very good."

Marcus looked at his wife, who stepped back out and closed the door.

"I must say . . . ," Scott began. "Your offices are not what I expected."

Marcus smiled. He has rather big teeth, Scott thought. He smiled to himself thinking that was exactly what Megan would have said after they left. Everything else about Marcus's face seemed well proportioned. *If he kept his mouth closed, he wouldn't be a bad-looking man at all*, Megan would surely add.

"Your reaction isn't unexpected. People generally think of film noir when they think about private detectives—rundown offices, tough men of mystery packing revolvers in wrinkled suits and fighting with the police, who always resent them for making them look incompetent."

He crossed his legs and smiled.

"I've never had reason to hire a private detective," Scott said dryly.

"Right. Actually, most of my work is routine, checking on assets, data. For private detectives these days, half the day is spent on the Internet.

"As you can see, we don't lack for business. We are doing well. Most of it involves marital problems, divorces. We have some cases that involve parents checking on their children. One parent I have as a client has been watching her daughter at college for two years, matter of fact."

"You handle it all yourself?"

"I have a partner and we have some associates on a subcontractual basis. So. Let's get to your problem. Your father told me a little. You're in the first stages of a divorce, separated, and you suspect your wife is seeing someone and might have been even before the petition for divorce was served?"

"As usual, my father puts it all succinctly and completely."

"Did you bring a picture?"

"A picture?"

"I have to know what she looks like if I'm to tail her," Marcus said, imitating Bogart.

"Oh. Of course."

Scott opened his wallet. Ironically, he would have to thank Megan for this. Just a month and a half ago, she'd given him the picture of her, Jennifer and him to put in his wallet. He handed it to Marcus.

"Very pretty and an adorable little girl." He looked at Scott. "This is fairly recent."

"Yes."

"Okay. We'll draw up our standard contract for you and I'll get right on this. We'll stake out the house and we'll give you a daily report. I assume you'd like the phone tapped, as well."

"You can do that?"

"All I'm saying is, I assume you'd like it. I didn't commit to doing anything," Marcus said, smiling.

"Oh." Scott smirked.

"This is uncomfortable," Marcus said. "I understand." He leaned forward. "The whole idea of spying on someone is nefarious to start with, Mr. Lester. I'd be the first to admit it. War is nefarious, too, but unfortunately events make them both necessary. I always found the concept of fair play in a shooting war absurd. Armies by their very nature play as dirty as possible to win—to survive, in fact. We proved it ourselves recently in Iraq and Afghanistan, and I'm sure we will in the future."

Scott simply stared at him. He hadn't counted on such a well-to-do private detective and he certainly hadn't counted on a philosophical discussion concerning good and evil.

Marcus rose and went to his desk to get a legal pad.

"Now, why don't we begin by your telling me as much as you can about your soon-to-be ex-wife, where she likes to go, who are some of her friends, et cetera. I'd also like to know when you saw each other last, what that was like, if your daughter has said anything you think important. Sure you won't have some coffee?"

Scott thought a moment.

"Maybe I will," he said. "I guess I'll be here a while."

"I guess so," Marcus said, smiling, and called for his wife.

Forty minutes later, Scott emerged and went down to his automobile. Despite how civilized Marcus and his wife were, Scott couldn't help feeling he was in league now with the darker world. Somehow, he had kept himself above the fray all these married years. What happened to others didn't happen to him. The whole thing made him feel dirty and that made him even angrier. Megan was doing this to him. She was the cause and Jennifer was caught in the middle. One thing was for sure, he wasn't going to make any of it easier. He got right on the phone with his attorney to make sure he understood that. He also told him about the private detective.

"I'm sorry about all this, Scott," he said. "But it will support our position. I'll call you soon."

By the time he got to his office and met his father in the conference room, he felt his insides were twisted like pretzels. His father took one look at him and shook his head.

"You've got to compartmentalize, Scott. When you come here, you put all that out of your mind. Otherwise, you won't be worth a nickel to us."

"It's not easy."

"It's easy," his father replied. "You simply tell yourself you've hired experts to do the worrying for you. Now let's look at this portfolio. I'm not happy about the exchange rate they're suggesting."

Scott looked hard at his father. He wasn't sure if he should envy him for his emotional and psychological strength or despise him for it. Is this really who I am, too? he wondered. Megan surely thought so.

He sat and opened the portfolio.

His father began to analyze and Scott looked at him and pretended to listen.

He couldn't help it.

He was agonizing over the very thought that Megan would be intimate with another man.

CHAPTER EIGHT

Paul Stanley noticed early in the day that Steve was different. He kept up with the others, but on Friday he was way ahead of them and evinced more energy and enthusiasm for the job. Now he looked distracted, almost entirely uninterested. He couldn't help approaching him and asking him if everything was all right.

"All right?" Steve pondered the question as if it were earth-shattering.

"Any problems with the earthquake at your home?"

"Oh no, no. It did mess up an important date I was having with a perfect woman, however."

"Oh." Paul smiled. "Well, I'm sure you'll find a way to make up for it."

"Me too. I'm sure."

"She must be something."

"Oh, she is. Believe me. I know a jewel when I see one."

"Good for you," Paul said, laughing.

The little talk seemed to work. Steve was energetic again. In fact, now he looked as if he couldn't wait to get his work done and leave, and when it was time to leave, he was off before anyone else.

"What's with him?" one of the other workers asked Paul Stanley.

"He's in love," Paul said.

Steve had decided not to call Megan until he was off. He thought the more time he gave her, the better chance he had of getting her to agree to a second date. As soon as she answered the phone, he knew something wasn't right. He was encouraged by the fact that he could sense her moods so quickly without having spent much time at all with her. This was a natural, meant-to-be relationship. She was his soul mate. They had simply both taken convoluted paths to this point.

"What's wrong?" he asked. He could tell she wanted to make the conversation short. "I can hear it in your voice."

"Can you?" The fact that he could didn't surprise her. She was that upset. "I just got off the phone with my attorney. My husband's attorney is now sounding like they plan to challenge the custody arrangement. I should have anticipated it. The Lesters only know how to play hardball. Compromise is a sign of weakness and defeat to them," she added bitterly.

"Well, that's not right."

"In this world, Steve, what's right often has nothing to do with what happens. I'm sorry. I'm just upset. Thanks for calling."

"Well . . . can I help you somehow?"

"I don't see what you can do, Steve. Thanks."

"I can cheer you up. How about tomorrow night?"

"I'm not going to be good company for anyone for a while."

"But—"

"Maybe the end of the week," she added to cut him off.

"Okay. Sure. I'll call again."

"Thanks," she said, and hung up.

He flung his cell phone. Miraculously, although it bounced off the passenger-side window, it didn't break. When he got home, the sight of his yellow Corvette in his mother's driveway only intensified his rage. He didn't rent it to sit there. He got it to impress Megan and give her some fun. He would have been doing that too, perhaps as soon as tomorrow night, if it weren't for this soon-to-be ex-husband.

He had never had respect for wealthy businessmen anyway. To him they were mostly spoiled, weak excuses for manhood who managed either to inherit or manipulate businesses to give themselves a far greater piece of the pie than more deserving, hardworking Joes like himself. He was no socialist by any means, but he did see an injustice at work, an injustice built out of the luck of birth or the sneaky and ruthless deceptions in the business world. Megan's husband was just another good example of it. She was trying to pull away from it and he was throwing nails on the road.

He slammed his truck door so hard that it didn't close. He had to go back to close it softly and then he went into the house, mumbling to himself. The moment he walked through the front entrance, his mother called out.

"I defrosted a pork chop for you. Hope that's not too simple a meal for my Beverly Hills son."

"I'm not eating home," he shouted back and went to his room.

A few moments later she was at the door.

"What do you mean you're not eating home? Why didn't you call to tell me that earlier? What am I going to do with the pork chop? I can't freeze it again."

He opened the door. "I just got to get out, Ma," he said.

"Why? What's got you all twisted up?"

"Nothing."

"That woman? She turn out the way I said she would already?"

"No, damn it. It's not her. It's her husband making things hard for her and her little girl."

"Well, you got no business interfering, Steve. It ain't your affair. Don't stick your head in places it ain't supposed to be."

"Right," he said, and slammed the door on her.

"You better chain up that temper of yours, Steve Gavin Wallace," she shouted through the closed door. "It's gotten you into plenty of trouble, and what we don't need now is more trouble. You hear me? Steve?"

"Yeah, yeah. I hear you."

"Good," she said, and finally left him alone.

He pouted for a while and then showered and changed, but he didn't go to any restaurant. He had no appetite. Instead, he drove to Megan's house. He just wanted to be nearby in case that husband showed up to make more trouble. When he parked on her side of the street, he noticed another vehicle parked across the way with a man sitting calmly in it. The car was positioned so it wasn't in the direct illumination of the streetlight. Once in a while, the driver was on a cell phone, but it was clear to Steve that his attention was on Megan's house.

"Son of a bitch," he muttered. "The bastard's gone and hired someone to watch her." He waited a while longer and then drove away and circled the area. When he returned, the vehicle was still there.

He passed it, glancing at the man in the car, and then made a turn and found a place to park. It was safer to get out of his car and observe the man from a position in the shadows. Later, when he checked his watch, he realized that the guy had been there well over two hours. There was no doubt about it. He couldn't warn her, however, without revealing his own reconnaissance, and she might be turned off by that.

No, he had to handle this another way. He went back to the Corvette and drove home. Then he got into his pickup truck and returned to Megan's street. The vehicle was gone. Not satisfied, however, he parked up the street again. Suddenly he realized there was another vehicle with a different man parked not far from where the first had been parked. There was a rotation going on. He should have anticipated it. There was no concern for money spent.

He noticed the driver had his window open. It wasn't that hot, but it was warm enough to either have the air conditioner in the car going or keep the window open.

Perfect, he thought. He put on his work gloves, got out of his truck, went to the rear and found his small sledgehammer. Then he crossed the street and made his way slowly up to the vehicle and the driver, who was now on a cell phone. Steve looked around, waited for another vehicle to pass and then stepped up to the rear of the vehicle and softly made his way close to the driver's window. Suddenly, the driver noticed him in the side mirror and turned just as Steve swung the sledgehammer with both his hands to drive the head of it squarely into the man's temple. Blood splattered on the dashboard and windshield and even flew to the passenger-side window.

The man slumped over on his seat, dropping his cell phone. Steve returned to his truck to throw the sledgehammer into the rear again. Then he went back to the car, opened the door and shoved the man into the passenger's seat. Ignoring the blood around him, Steve started the engine, closed the door and drove away. He never looked at the man. He took Santa Monica Boulevard, driving as casually as he could, and turned onto Wilshire, going through the heart of Beverly Hills, continuing on to West Hollywood until he found what he considered to be an adequate side street and a parking space. He pulled in, shut off the engine and then finally looked at the man crumpled in the seat.

He found his wallet and read his identification. He was right. The man was a private detective.

"You shouldn't have taken this assignment," he told him and felt for his pulse, which was very slight. Probably bleeding in his brain, he thought, and then got out of the car. He decided to keep the wallet and the camera he had, so it would look like a robbery.

As casually as he had driven to this location, he

walked away and found a bus stop. Nearly forty
minutes later, a bus came by and he rode it to within
five blocks of where he had left his truck. He walked
quickly to it and got in. For a while he sat there
catching his breath and looking at Megan's house.
The lights were out in the rooms. She and Jennifer,
sweet Jennifer, were asleep in their beds safe now
from the prying eyes of this hired spy.

He started the truck and drove off.

That oughta put a dent in her rich and powerful
husband's surface, he thought.

In his experience men like her husband were
cowards whenever it came to any physical conflict.
This will surely terrify the bastard and he'll back
off, he concluded.

The only regret he had was that Megan wouldn't
ever know why she should thank him.

Lily Marcus called her husband's cell phone. It
rang and rang, but he didn't answer. She waited a
few minutes and called again with the same result.
She tried to keep herself busy with some house
chores so she wouldn't get too nervous. Ed had
generally given up the footwork and subcon-
tracted stakeouts and pursuits, but Gordon Lester
and his son Scott were too important to relegate
completely to subordinates.

"I want Gordon to understand we put a high
priority on his son's affairs, Lily," Ed had explained. "He can make or break us with his recommendations. You know the circles he moves in. Just
imagine the referrals we'll get out of this one. Can't
afford any mess-up here."

She didn't disagree. She simply felt street work

was not only potentially dangerous but beneath him now. He knew she was unhappy about it, but he went forward, promising not to do more than he could or should.

She checked the clock and called his cell phone again. It was nearly thirty-five minutes. He surely wouldn't be in a dead zone for cell phones, and if he was busy with someone, by now he could take a moment. This time she left a message.

"I want you to call me right away, Ed." She rattled off the time and her concern and hung up.

It was difficult to put it aside, but she went to watch television while she waited. Another hour passed and still Ed had not returned the call. Now her concern became more frantic. She called Bob Anderson, the man Ed had relieved. He had been with them the longest of anyone they used, and Ed had recently given him a junior partnership position. Ed expected Bob would eventually buy them out completely.

"Maybe it's just something wrong with his phone, Lily. This stakeout is in Beverly Hills, not South Central Los Angeles. What could happen? If anything, he must be bored to death."

"He knows I wanted him to check in with me, Bob. It's not like him to simply ignore me."

Anderson was quiet a moment and then volunteered to take a ride over to Beverly Hills to see what was what.

"I'll call you from the location," he said. "Or better yet, have Ed call you."

"Thank you so much, Bob."

"No problem," he said, even though he was getting ready to go to bed.

Less than an hour later, he cruised the street and looked for Ed Marcus's vehicle. When he didn't see it anywhere near the Lester home, he called Lily.

"Is he home or something?"

"No. Isn't he there?"

"No."

"Well, where is he?"

"I don't know, Lily. I know Tyler Barton was going to relieve him at midnight."

"Is Barton there earlier?"

"No."

"What is it then?"

"I wish I knew. Maybe he had to go to the bathroom or something. I'll hang out there until he comes around. Ed's too responsible a guy to neglect an assignment. He'll be here soon, I'm sure."

"Call me the moment he does."

"Will do," Bob said.

Just after midnight, the phone rang. Lily had dozed off on the sofa and the television was still going.

"It's me, Lily," Bob said. "Tyler's just arrived, but there's still no sign of Ed. Did he call?"

"No," she said. "What should I do?"

"I don't know. Maybe . . . maybe you had better call the police."

It was what she had feared hearing him say, but she knew it had to be said.

"I will. Even if he has a good excuse and he's embarrassed, it will be worth it."

"Absolutely. Call me if you need anything else tonight, or if the police want to talk with me, have them call me."

"I will. Thanks, Bob," she said, and as soon as he hung up, she phoned the police.

She could tell from the tone of voice of the dispatcher and then the officer she spoke with after she explained it all that they were not very sympathetic. The police always resented private detectives, even when they were doing work the police would never do, like staking out a divorce case. So she wasn't expecting they would do much about Ed's disappearance, but to her surprise, less than an hour later, the phone rang and a different Los Angeles police officer called. He was at a different precinct.

"Your husband appears to be the victim of an assault and robbery," he told her. "He's been rushed to Cedars-Sinai."

He didn't get the chance to explain much more. She dropped the phone and hurried to her automobile. Twenty minutes later she was in the emergency room, waiting to speak with the doctor who was working on Ed.

"He had a severe blow to the head," the doctor began. Lily was never comfortable with young doctors. In her mind and in the mind of most people her age, doctors should look and be older. With their age came experience. Young doctors were too technical minded, too obviously in it for the money. That was her opinion.

"Blow?"

"There was some skull damage and the pooling of blood has created pressure on the brain. We've called Dr. Skotas, a brain surgeon, who is on his way."

"You mean, to operate?"

"Absolutely. We'll be out to see you with the forms to sign."

"Forms?"

"Standard forms, Mrs. Marcus."

"Can I see him?"

"He's unconscious, of course."

"I've got to see him. I've got to call our son and daughter. I've . . . Please."

"Right this way," he said, and led her to the trauma room, where Ed was hooked up to an IV and heart monitor. His head was bandaged, but the blood stain was quite visible. The sight was too much. She felt her legs buckle and just managed a short "Oh" before she sank to the floor, her body seeming to fall in slow motion.

She woke up to find herself on a gurney in the hallway. A nurse stood by holding her hand. The young doctor smiled at her.

"You're okay, Mrs. Marcus," he said. "Just rest a while. I'll check on you shortly."

"I'm sorry," she said. "To see him like that. I couldn't . . ."

"I'll get you some water," the nurse said. "Just rest."

"I'm supposed to sign some forms."

"We'll get to it. Don't worry. There's a police detective in the lobby waiting to speak to you. Should I bring him in?"

"Yes, please."

He was a tall, African-American man with a well-trimmed mustache and a pair of gold-rimmed glasses. He introduced himself as Detective Murray. He described how a parking-enforcement officer had found Ed. His car had been parked in a permit-only area.

She shook her head.

"Was he visiting someone in that neighborhood?" the detective asked.

"No, no . . . He had no reason to be there. He was supposed to be in Beverly Hills. He was on an assignment. I explained that when I first called, when I realized something might be wrong."

"Maybe he had an errand to do in West Hollywood."

"He had no errand. He would have told me, and how could he leave his post? His reinforcement hadn't arrived. What errand would he have that time of night in West Hollywood?" she asked.

"We're looking for witnesses, but there is no way to tell when he went there exactly, during the period you said he was on surveillance," he said, without answering the question.

What does he think, Ed was doing something he was ashamed to tell me he was doing?

She sat up. "None of this makes any sense," she said.

"We'll see what we can find out. Here's my card," he said. "I'll call you as soon as I know something more, and if you can think of anything, don't hesitate to call me."

"Why would I hesitate?"

He nodded. "I hope he gets better," he said, and left her.

The nurse returned with the forms for her to sign. She didn't even read them.

"I've got to call my children," she said. "I'm okay."

She got on her feet, brushed back her hair and started for the lobby.

But she never got there.

The young doctor called to her, and when she turned to see what he wanted, she knew immediately there was no point in her signing any forms.

* * *

Scott was still in bed when his father came to his room. His knock woke him. For a moment he thought he had overslept considerably, but when he looked at the clock, he saw how early it was.

"What's up, Dad?"

"Really weird thing happened last night. Ed Marcus was killed."

"What?" He sat up quickly. "How?"

"Apparently, he was assaulted and robbed in West Hollywood. Whoever did it struck him on the head with something severely. They called a brain surgeon in, but Marcus didn't last long enough for him to even wash up."

"West Hollywood?"

"Yes. One of his associates just called. They're calling all their clients with active cases. I'll look into another agency for us," he added.

"I don't get it. Was he personally on our case at the time?"

"Apparently, but he left the location for some reason and got himself robbed and killed," his father said. "I'm calling Gerry Orseck first thing and tell him how good his recommendation for a private detective has been. Obviously Marcus didn't take the situation that seriously, if he left the location to do some shopping or something."

"Why would he do that?"

"Who knows? Maybe he had a girlfriend. Don't worry. I'll find someone else."

"My God, the guy seemed . . . more than competent."

"People, as you continually learn, Scott, are often not what they seem to be." He started out and stopped. "Under the circumstances, with all this madness going on in your life, I've decided to do the London trip myself. You'll mind the store—as best you can," he said, and left.

Scott fell back against his pillow. He was beginning to feel like someone slipping and sliding on ice. First, Megan hits him with a petition for divorce, and despite her expressions of unhappiness and complaints, he doesn't see it coming. Then he discovers she is seeing another man. There's a real possibility she has been for a while, which again is something he doesn't see coming. He follows his father's advice and gets a private detective, and the private detective is killed the very next day in a robbery. Apparently Dad was right—Marcus didn't take his situation seriously enough. But how would he ever have been able to see that coming?

Despite having one of the better divorce attorneys, he was feeling more and more like someone who was a victim of circumstances beyond his control. No matter which way he moved or what he did, the events would have their way.

He thought about this as he rose and dressed. Once it was all thrown into the machinery of the system, with the legal maneuvering, the courts, lawyers with their own egos and reputations at stake, as well as he and Megan with their egos, the person with the most to lose would be Jennifer. She was the one who would be used to get Megan or whom Megan would use to get him.

Maybe he should try to reason with her once more. He could call her and suggest a truce, take her to dinner and get her to see how they were both hurting Jennifer. He would do anything she wanted, write out a contract, in fact, that he would behave differently, anything, if she would reconsider and give him—give them—one more chance. He would, and he had to swallow hard to get himself to agree to this, even overlook her affair with another man. He'd even take the blame for it.

She'd have to go for this, he concluded. It was more than fair and more than reasonable. He'd never tell his father about such a meeting and offer, of course. He'd say Scott had no spine, and if for some reason it didn't work out still, he'd blame him for every new concession they would have to make. But that didn't matter. This was his life. These were his choices, and most of all, Jennifer was his daughter.

The idea seemed to restore his energy. He ate a good breakfast and headed off, with the decision when to call to propose the truce the only question left. He checked the time. She'd be bringing Jennifer to school about now, he thought. He'd give her time to get back home and if she agreed or even wanted to talk about talking about it, he would leave work and meet her. It didn't have to be a dinner. It could be lunch, or maybe just a meeting in their living room. Whatever she wanted was fine with him.

He had a renewed bounce in his step when he entered the office. Arlene Potter looked up with a smile of surprise on her face. Of course, she knew all the details about his current crisis. She expected he would be depressed. He hated the tone of pity in her voice.

"Good morning, Mrs. Potter," he practically sang.

"Morning, Mr. Lester. Oh, Mr. Lester . . . ," she called before he entered his office.

"Yes?"

"There's a message on your desk from a Bob Anderson. He was quite insistent that you call him as soon as you came in," she said.

"Anderson? Don't recall the name. What real-estate company is he with?"

"Not with any real-estate company. He said he was a partner with Ed Marcus."

Mrs. Potter knew who Ed Marcus was and that Scott had gone along with his father's suggestion to hire a private detective to spy on Megan. She was discreet enough not to say it, however. He nodded and went right to his desk, saw the message and called Anderson.

"I heard the news about Ed Marcus this morning," he began as soon as Anderson said hello. "I'm sorry."

"Yeah, it's terrible, but I'm calling you because I don't want you to think I won't be on your case."

"Well . . ."

"No, please listen, Mr. Lester. I've been with Ed for nearly ten years. I know the man. He wouldn't have left your house unattended and driven off to do some errand or something in West Hollywood. If he couldn't be there, he would have had me or one of our guys replace him or spell him. We've got excellent communication on the job."

"Well, what are you saying? I don't understand."

"Something smells about all this. I think . . . I think this isn't just about marital difficulties."

"Well, what is it about then?"

"I don't know. That's why I think you shouldn't just drop us."

Scott knew exactly what his father would say when he heard about this conversation: *The guy is just trying to hold on to a commission.*

Maybe he was. Maybe his father was right.

But he woke up this morning thinking about the one who was really the victim here, Jennifer.

Protecting her was more important than who was right and who was being a sap and falling for someone's effort to save his commission.

"Okay," Scott said. "Stay with it and keep me well informed."

"Will do, Mr. Lester. Thank you," Anderson said.

Scott hung up and sat back. Was he doing the right thing? Less than twenty minutes ago, he'd been ready to call Megan and propose a truce.

What kind of a truce is this if I'm having her followed and placed under twenty-four-hour observation?

His father would say she could tell you she's going along with the second chance, but continue with the other guy. How would you know for sure? Keep the detective.

Do what Dad says, he told himself, and rationalize it by telling yourself that you're doing it only for your daughter's sake.

CHAPTER NINE

Megan froze for a moment after she pulled into the school parking lot. He was in the far-right corner, standing next to what she assumed was his pickup truck. The moment he set eyes on her, he started in her direction.

"Come on, Jen," she told her daughter and went around to open the door for her.

"Morning, Megan," he said.

She looked up at him as she closed the car door behind Jennifer. He could see she was shaken by his surprise appearance.

"Why are you here? How did you know to come here?"

"You mentioned the school at dinner," he reminded her.

"Well, what are you doing here?"

"I didn't have to be at work until early in the afternoon. We're waiting for some equipment to arrive at the site."

"So?"

He wasn't happy about her reaction, but he calmed himself, told himself it was understandable. She was under a great deal of pressure, pressure put on her by this creep husband, which was more reason for her needing him now.

"I have some news for you, news you'll want to know immediately."

Jennifer held Megan's hand and stood silently looking up at him.

He squatted and reached out for her hand. "Hey, Jennifer. You going to have a good time at school today?"

She nodded.

"Hey, here's something for you. It's a tiny flash-light, see? It's on this key chain. You just push it here and a light goes on, see?"

Jennifer nodded.

"It's yours. Whenever you're frightened again, you just push the button and the light comes on and chases away anything that scares you, okay?"

He practically pushed it into her hand. She looked up at Megan.

"Say thank you to Mr. Wallace, Megan."

"Thank you."

"I have to take her in, Steve. What is it?"

He looked up at her and then stood and leaned to her left.

"You were right with your suspicions."

"What suspicions?"

"Last night I thought I would drop by. I didn't like the way you sounded on the phone, and I thought I would just stop in to say hello. I bought a box of candy to give you. It's in the truck," he added, gesturing back at it with his head.

"And . . . ?"

"As I was getting close to your house, I noticed a vehicle parked across from it. The man in the front seat had a camera aimed at the front door. He clicked off some pictures, so I rode by, went around the block and returned. He was still there. I parked on a parallel street and walked to your block. He was still there. I waited for nearly an hour, Megan. He never left, so I knew it had nothing to do with real estate. The house hasn't been put up for sale yet, right?"

"No, but I imagine it will be. Who was he?"

"I think it's pretty obvious that he's someone your husband's hired to spy on you, probably some private detective." He looked out at the street. "He or an associate of his might have followed you here this morning."

She looked more hurt than angry.

"It's something husbands and wives do when they are in the middle of a nasty divorce. They hire these people to try to get something they can use against the other one in court, especially if there's any question about child custody," he added, nodding at Jennifer. "It's a slimy thing to do to someone like you," he added.

She looked speechless.

"I didn't mean to spook you, but I thought you'd want to know right away."

Some other parents drove in to drop off their children. Megan smiled and waved at a few.

Keeping her smile, she said, "I can't believe it. I mean, I don't want to believe it, but it is easy to believe. Gordon Lester, Scott's father, doesn't like to lose anything. Rules, morality, ethics, even the law doesn't mean anything unless he can use it to his advantage. Sometimes, I feel like I married some Mafia don's son."

"Sorry," Steve said.

"I've got to take her in."

"Sure. You want to go for coffee?" He looked at his watch. "I've got another two hours or so. I'll follow you home afterward. You'll pull into the driveway and go into the house and I'll check the street and call you. How's that?"

She thought a moment, nodded and started for the front door of the school. He smiled.

She knows she needs me, he thought. He waited by his truck and when she came out, hurried over to her again.

"There's a Starbucks on the corner," she said. He nodded and followed her out of the parking lot. Ten minutes later, after they both had parked, he joined her at the outside patio.

"What would you like?"

"A latte. With nonfat milk," she called to him. He smiled and went in to get their coffees.

As he turned to bring them out, he saw how deep in thought she was. He was confident that deep thought would evolve into anger, and he knew that the more antagonistic this divorce became, the more she would depend on him. At least, that was what he hoped. She had yet to mention another man or even another woman she would consider a trusted confidant. As far as he could see, so far it was clear sailing if he handled her right.

"I'm really sorry I had to tell you all that this morning, Megan," he said as he gave her the latte and sat. "You'd think he would want to be civilized about it and also would give more consideration to Jennifer."

"Yes," she said, sipping the coffee. She looked around. "Someone might be watching us right now, snapping pictures of us."

"What are you supposed to do, hide in a closet until the court action begins? You're not doing anything illicit. You have a right to enjoy yourself and make new friends."

"Of course, but I know how Gordon Lester works. Even Scott has been amazed at some of the things his father has done to drive competitors away from a property investment he wanted. I'll call my lawyer as soon as I get home. She'll love hearing this."

He nodded and she smiled at him.

"Thanks for telling me, for taking the time, Steve."

"Hey, no problem. As I told you before, I saw something in your eyes that first night that convinced me you were a very nice person. Look at how beautiful your daughter is and how she behaves. A woman like you should have more children. How come you don't, if you don't mind my asking?"

"No, I don't mind now. It was a reluctant mutual agreement. When I saw how Scott was behaving with his firstborn, I decided to wait to see if he would change. He didn't and he didn't seem to want another child anyway. I know his father wanted him, and still wants him, to have a son, but I don't want to have another child just because his father wants it. I want Scott to want it."

"Wanted," he corrected.

"Yes, wanted."

"Well, don't give up on the idea for yourself," he said, and she raised her eyebrows. "In the future, when things settle down. You'll go on with your life, Megan. Divorce isn't death. It's death of something not meant to live, but it's not death for you."

"Thanks for saying that," she told him. "What's the project you're on today?"

"Just finishing up an oversized pool for some rich dude who just bounced another wife, as I understand it."

"Oversized?"

"For the property. It's part of the gaudy way the guy lives. No sense of proportion in anything he does, I bet. Why guys like that are lucky enough to have so much bugs me, but hey, I don't have to live with him."

He sipped his coffee and studied her reaction to his words. She liked what he was saying, so he felt he could add, "Just like you don't have to live with Scott."

"Yes," she said. She looked at her watch. "I guess I better get home and talk to my attorney."

"Okay. Like I said, I'll follow you and call you, so give it five minutes after you get into the house."

"It's really very nice of you to do all this for me, Steve."

"I hope to be able to express just how much pleasure it gives me," he replied. "Maybe try another dinner?"

"And give the private eye something to gloat over?"

"I can lose him in a flash. It'll be fun."

She laughed. "Maybe."

She headed for her car and he hurried to his truck. He didn't expect there would be anyone watching her house this morning. He imagined they were thrown for quite a loop and did not have time to regroup, but he would tell her there was someone anyway. He wanted her to need him more and more.

He remained far enough behind her to look inconspicuous and almost didn't bother to look around as they approached her house, but there he was, sitting in his car almost parked in the exact spot the man he knew as Ed Marcus had parked. He still had his identification, license, gun-permit registration, health insurance card and credit cards.

An ironic and funny idea occurred to him. He drove around once more and as he passed the car with the new private detective in it, he used Ed Marcus's digital camera to click a picture. He'd print it out for Megan so she would have something concrete to show her attorney.

After he went by, he pulled to the side and called her.

"He's out there. Look north about a hundred yards across the street. A blue Ford."

"Thank you, Steve."

"Hey," he said. "I forgot I had my digital camera in the truck. I took his picture. He didn't see me do it. Don't worry, but I'll print it out for you to hand to your attorney."

"Oh, that's great."

"Hey," he said. "I'm here for you. Just like some guardian angel, the guardian angel you accused me of being."

She laughed and then said she had an incoming call and it might be her attorney.

After he hung up, he started for the work site. Normally, he rode in silence, but right now, he felt like turning on the radio to a station he tolerated, one that played oldies, and singing along with every song he heard.

Anyone watching him would think he had just won the lottery.

Scott checked the clock in his office and decided it was time to make the peace-pipe call. It took four rings, so he knew she was on another call.

"Morning, Megan. How's Jennifer?" he said quickly.

"She's in school, Scott. You should know by now what time I take her."

"Yes, I knew. I just meant . . . Listen, I'm calling to ask you to consider meeting me for a quiet, nonconfrontational, no-lawyer conversation."

"Really?" she said dryly. "Nonconfrontational? Did you get your father's okay for such a conversation?"

"Listen to me, Megan. No one's coming out of this a clear winner. Everyone suffers."

"Yes, how do you like that? Up until now, only Jennifer and I were suffering."

"It's no good to talk like this over the telephone. Why can't we sit down over lunch and behave like two grown-ups?"

"Because only one of us is," she replied.

He closed his eyes and sucked in his breath.

"My father doesn't know anything about this call or this idea. Can't you calm down at least enough to listen? I'm trying to make a real effort to see things from your side of the street."

"Oh, I know you are," she said, laughing.

"You know I am?"

"Yes, I said I know. One of your—or should I say, your father's—spies is outside the house right now so you can see things on my side of the street. I wouldn't try to deny it. I'll have a picture of him to give to my attorney to give to yours."

He was quiet a moment. He thought these guys were professionals. How the hell did this Anderson fellow get spotted so quickly? What good would he be? Now, Scott thought, he'd really screwed up. His father had told him he would find another agency and here he'd gone on his own and rehired the Marcus agency. He'd blown it. Megan's tone and his own bad decision came in on a tide of new rage. No matter what he tried, this thing had a life of its own and was determined to have its own way.

"I wouldn't have needed that if you weren't screwing around out there, Megan," he retorted. "How long have you been seeing someone else, huh? Who is he? Someone your bosom buddy Tricia introduced to you? Or did you pick him up yourself?"

"This civilized conversation is over, Scott. You might as well tell your father he can save some money and fire the private detective," she said, and hung up.

He held the receiver away from his ear. It felt as if smoke were coming out of both his ears. He was that hot. He slammed down the phone and then after a moment picked it up and called Bob Anderson's cell.

"Anderson," he heard.

"She made you," he said.

"What?"

"My wife . . . She knows you're out there, knows what you're doing. I just spoke to her."

"That's impossible. I'm not right across from the

house, but I saw her drive in and go in. She didn't even look this way, and besides, I haven't taken a picture or anything. What would she base it on, a man sitting in a car? I could be waiting for someone. And I just got here twenty minutes ago. She's been in the house less than . . . less than fifteen minutes, Mr. Lester. How can she come to that conclusion so quickly? There's nothing about my car or about me to suggest . . ."

"All I know is I just got off the phone speaking with her and she told me you were out there."

"Something doesn't sound right."

"Look, just send us the bill for what you've done so far and drop it. Don't charge us for what Ed was supposed to be doing," he added.

"But . . ."

"Thanks for the effort," Scott added, and hung up. At least he was decisive about it. His father would like that. He rose and went out to his father's office to tell him what he had done and what had occurred all within the morning hours.

"Why didn't you wait for me to find someone new?" his father asked immediately.

"Anderson made it sound frightening. He said he was convinced something somehow related happened to Ed Marcus. I thought we shouldn't leave the house unobserved."

"Just a gimmick to get you to let him work up the bill. He was probably worried he lost his paycheck. Well, what's done is done. I'll speak to someone else and find us people who will disappear into the woodwork and not be discovered."

"Why don't we forget about all that, Dad?"

"She's screwing around and probably was

screwing around on you before, and you want to forget about it?"

"It could backfire on us and—"

"Go back to work, Scott. Let me handle this part of the mess, will you?"

"I—"

"You're showing some weakness here at exactly the wrong time, Scott. Get hold of yourself. This is not a Sunday picnic. It's nasty business. She'll wipe the floor with you if you're not firm. Now go. I have to speak to Orseck to see what he thinks the damage might be, if any.

"I did some research or had some research done on this attorney of hers, this Emily Lloyd. She's a ball-breaker and rarely loses, Scott. I'm sure she has her sights aimed high. I'm having Earl review what could possibly be tracked to you financially or where she could bite your ass good—and mine too, I might add. We have to consider whatever maneuvers are open to us. Your name is on a number of LLCs we've formed. This is complicated business, damn it."

"Sorry, Dad."

"Sorry doesn't work right now. As usual, you're not looking at the whole picture here, so you lose sight of what connects to what, what affects what."

There were many things Scott wanted to say in response. He wanted to talk about how his father kept him from doing more, kept him from understanding it all, but he didn't. He just nodded and left. He could almost hear Megan complaining about it, chastising him for once again permitting his father to browbeat him. He used to drown out her words or simply turn himself off to them, but they were deposited in his memory bank and eager to echo again and again.

He returned to his office and tried to concentrate on the project he was reviewing, but one thought continually interrupted.

Who was this guy she was seeing?

Was it someone he knew, someone he considered a friend, someone who had wormed his way into her life? He began to review the possibilities. Maybe she was having an affair with a married man who promised eventually to leave his wife. Some other marriage would be ruined.

This thing did have a mind and will of its own, like some crawling rot that fed on everyone's lusts and egos. The more you resisted, the stronger it grew. Despondent, he thought that maybe it had always been there. Maybe nothing he had done really gave birth to it because it was already born, dormant, lying in wait. Maybe he never really knew Megan or deliberately blinded himself to whatever was in her that would lead her to surrender her body and destiny to another man.

It was so easy now to hate her, he thought, which made him realize how easy it could have been for her to hate him as well.

Maybe the world was meant to be a garden only for men like his father after all.

Only that sort of man would grow and prosper. Everyone else would struggle for a sip of the rain and a time in the sunlight but eventually would find himself bathed in the shadows of defeat. He would wither and die, never understanding why he was born in the first place.

* * *

Before he reached the work site, Steve stopped at one of those places where he knew he could print out copies of the digital photograph he had taken. The picture he had snapped turned out to be pretty good. He had slowed down enough and caught the man, his car and enough of the surrounding street to identify the location. He made various sizes of it, blowing it up to an eight-by-ten, which revealed enough of the man's face to enable an identification. She'll love these, he thought, and put them all in a manila envelope.

Paul Stanley was waiting for him when he pulled into the work site. He charged over almost before Steve got out of his truck.

"Where the hell have you been?" he demanded. "You know how late you are, how this affects the job?"

"I had trouble with my truck this morning," he replied.

"Why didn't you call? I'd a sent someone for you."

"Then you'd have two guys off the job. I thought I could get it fixed fast enough not to make so much difference, but as usual, they didn't have a part and . . ."

Paul narrowed his eye and shook his head.

"This is bullshit, man. You know what your not showing up means."

"Are you accusing me of lying?"

"No, of being stupid," Paul replied.

Steve glared at him a moment. Paul could see he was weighing his options and one of them was definitely coming at him. He took a nervous step back when he saw Steve tighten his fists. The other workers had heard the confrontation and had stopped what they were doing. All eyes were on the two of them.

Suddenly Steve smiled and relaxed his fists. Some other thought had obviously taken over, but it wasn't apologizing and groveling. Paul Stanley could sense that in the weird smile.

"You're right," Steve said. "I am stupid to be wasting my time here when there are far more important things for me to be doing. Thanks for pointing it out, and go fuck yourself," he said, and turned and got into his truck.

"You'll be sorry," Paul shouted. "I'll make sure you don't work in this city."

Steve started his engine and then turned it off and sat there as if he were really reconsidering. All the others watched and waited. Did he realize Paul Stanley could hurt his earning power seriously? Would he beg for forgiveness?

He got out of the truck. Stanley, not a small man, but nowhere near as hard as Steve, took a few steps back. Steve approached him slowly. Paul Stanley knew all his men were watching. He couldn't just turn and run. He had to hold his ground. Steve stopped inches from him and smiled again as he leaned in to whisper.

"Make one call to turn people against me, just one, and I'll hurt you where you'll feel it the most—family," Steve said low enough for only Paul to hear.

Paul didn't respond. Steve returned to his truck and glared at him as he restarted it and backed out of the spot. He turned and pulled away. Paul Stanley watched him go and then turned, took a breath of relief and walked back to the site.

Screw him, he told himself. He ain't worth my breath.

It was the easiest way to retreat and rationalize his fear, but he would at least complain to Matt Lowenstein, who had given Wallace so high a recommendation. What he did with the complaint afterward was of no concern.

Steve didn't give any of it a second thought. He wanted to drive right over to Megan's house but he knew he couldn't. He had told her he was going to work late in the day. It was important to avoid contradictions now, to give her any reason whatsoever not to trust him. He couldn't go home either, because his mother would be on his back. He hated hanging out in the bars with losers. So he drove over to Santa Monica, parked and went down to a bench where he could sit and look out at the sea and plan.

He was confident now that he was going to inherit this family. He was happy to hear from Megan's own lips that she would have wanted more children, but was insecure about having another with Scott Lester. She was certainly young enough to have another, even perhaps two more. He wouldn't love Jennifer any less than he would his own children. Megan would understand that clearly and it would give her the comfort she needed. A woman like Megan would easily cherish him, he thought.

It was a beautiful day at the beach. Santa Monica was a favorite destination for European tourists who wanted to sample California. He heard the foreign languages as people passed by and he saw the families walking together, the children excited about the sand and the water. Off to his left, the Ferris wheel on the pier turned. He could actually hear the children squealing with delight. The wind carried their voices to him. Everywhere he looked, he saw the happiness that was born out of a good family life. What family meant to him most of all was the end of loneliness and a reaffirmation of his value as a man. These were the things Julia had denied him.

He dozed off for a while and when he woke he saw how low the sun had fallen. He looked at his watch and thought it would be fine to appear at her house now. An idea occurred to him and on the way he stopped at a good Chinese restaurant he knew. He ordered takeout and continued on to her home in Beverly Hills.

He was disappointed to see a car in her driveway, but he recognized whose it was. Her girlfriend was there. That was all right. Women needed the company and support of other women. Megan was surely rattling on and on about everything. He thought his ears should be burning for sure. He was that positive that he was the center of the conversation between them. He was glad he had bought extra food.

Grasping the bag with its delicious aromas spiraling out, he hurried to the front door and rang the buzzer. Looking behind, he saw there was no private detective in sight. Perhaps he was hiding somewhere. It didn't matter now.

Jennifer opened the door for him.

"Hey, Jennifer. How are you doing?" he cried, and handed her one of the tiny umbrellas that came with the takeout.

"Who's there?" he heard Megan call. She stepped out of the living room and saw him. "Steve."

"I have your pictures," he said, "and bought some Chinese. Hope you have no other plans for dinner."

Tricia came up beside her and the two looked at him.

"There's enough for your friend," he said.

Tricia and Megan looked at each other and then burst out laughing.

"That's exactly what we were thinking of doing—going for Chinese," Megan said. "It's comfort food."

"That's me," Steve said, stepping in. "Mr. Comfort."

Was he on a roll, or what?

Nothing would stop him now. When he got home tonight, he would tell his mother to start thinking of new baby names.

Chapter Ten

Nothing annoyed him as much, perhaps, as the idea that he couldn't simply get into his car and drive to his own house and see his own daughter whenever he wanted. Damn if he wouldn't, he thought when he got into his car after work. His father wanted him to join him for dinner at the Four Seasons later. They were entertaining some Japanese businessmen who were considering their office building in Sherman Oaks. He promised to be there, but he decided to detour through Beverly Hills. When he approached the house, however, and saw a truck in the driveway and Tricia Morgan's car, he kept going.

He turned around at the end of the street and rode by very slowly so he could look again at the truck. Megan was no good at getting things fixed in the house. The moment something broke down, she went into a small panic and always called him. Yet he felt confident this was not the truck of some repairman, especially this time of the day. The truck had no markings on it either, no company name. If he still had his private detective or if his father had reassigned one by tonight, he might know more. He was simply not making good decisions. He was flailing out everywhere and getting nowhere.

One of their neighbors, Sally Rosenfield, a seventy-five-year-old widow who had inherited fifty million dollars, came out of her driveway and stopped before turning to the right. She was in terrific health and shape for her age, a very independent sort who didn't rely on her children or servants. As far as Scott knew, she'd never had a driver. She was a major force in a number of charities and kept herself quite active. They had been to her home a number of times and Megan and he had invited her to dinner only once.

The truth was, he saw her as something of a threat. She was always encouraging Megan to be more independent, do more with her life than she was doing. She tried to convince her that exploring the world outside the home would make her appreciate her home life even more. Megan had resisted most of her suggestions, but often brought up those suggestions at dinner, and that occasionally had led to what he called little arguments. It got so he viewed Sally as a troublemaker.

"Hello, Scott," she called out her car window. "What are you doing?"

He wondered if she could see how red his face became. Here he was parked outside his own driveway.

"I'm just . . . stopping by to see Jennifer," he muttered, fumbling the words and adding to his embarrassment.

"Stopping by? Yes, I'm sorry," she said.

She obviously had heard about his and Megan's marital troubles.

"Me too."

"You're losing a wonderful wife," she said.

"Yeah, well, none of this is simply one person's fault."

"Never is," she said, but disdainfully.

"Yes, well, I wasn't looking for sympathy, Sally."

"Too bad," she said, shook her head and drove off.

His embarrassment turned to rage. Now he would become the laughingstock of this neighborhood. With Sally's connections, it would happen at warp speed. He looked at the truck again and then backed up a little and spun into the driveway right behind it. If there was a celebration going on in there at his expense, he wanted to make sure he knew Megan would be sorry. He dug out his house key when he got to the door and entered.

He didn't intend to sneak into the house looking guilty about it, but he did move softly at first so he could hear what was going on. The first thing he heard was all the laughter. Of course, he recognized Tricia's voice. She was laughing the loudest. The man, whoever he was, was telling a joke.

"And the nurse adds, 'If I had known that, doctor, I would have left the thermometer in longer.'"

Megan's laughter was louder than Tricia's. He opened the door and slammed it hard. Their laughter stopped. He started down the hallway. The man came to the kitchen doorway first, with Megan and Tricia standing behind him.

"Scott!" Megan cried.

"Having a party?" he asked.

He eyed the man like some gunslinger setting

up for a draw. The man hadn't spoken, but there was something very threatening, lethal, in his look. Scott thought he'd have to search way back through his library of images to find a face registering such unadulterated anger. It was as if they were lifetime enemies.

"We're just having some dinner. What is it? Why are you here?"

"I have the right to get my personal things whenever I need them," he said. "Where's Jennifer?"

"She's upstairs. She had her dinner earlier and is watching some television."

"Before her homework?"

"I think I know when she can watch television and when she can't, Scott. I don't know if you could."

"We haven't been introduced," he said, nodding at Steve. "One of your boyfriends, Tricia?"

Tricia didn't speak, nor did she permit one of her usual condescending smiles to form.

"He's a friend of mine, Scott," Megan said.

"Right," Scott said. "A friend."

"In need is a friend, indeed," Steve added. He took a small step forward.

The physical threat was something perhaps only another man could feel instantly. Scott hadn't been in many physical confrontations in his life and all of them had been during his younger years, one in his college days, but if he had some physical altercation with another boy, there had always been the sense that both he and the other boy had a limit, a failsafe point at which one or the other would back off. A fight to the death was never in

the mix; it was always meant solely to embarrass
or get the other to retreat.

However, he had seen boys and even men in
fights where it was clear that one or the other
would have to be pulled away. Something prime-
val and raw had come to the surface, and subduing
his opponent would not suffice. This man who
faced him in his own home hallway had that look.
Scott did all he could not to show he was intimi-
dated or afraid, especially in front of Megan and
Tricia, but he recognized he was moments away
from that sort of retreat.

"Whatever," he said, and continued down the
hallway toward his den, ostensibly to collect something he needed. Megan pulled Steve and Tricia
back into the kitchen.

When he entered the den, he stopped to catch
his breath and control the trembling in his legs
that had resulted both from his anger and fear.
Ironically, he hated himself more, for being this
way, than he did that man or Megan and Tricia.
His father wouldn't have backed away. His father
would have charged forward and brought it on,
forcing Megan to realize she had created more
than she could ever have imagined. No matter
what the outcome, she would have been the loser.

That's Dad, he thought sadly. That's not me.

He heard footsteps in the hallway and went to
the file cabinet to thumb through some documents.
Megan stepped into the doorway as he pulled up a
file.

"Why didn't you call first, Scott? That was the
agreement."

"I was nearby and I needed this for a dinner

meeting. I didn't think it would be a big deal, but now that I see you're in the middle of a celebration, I guess it was a mistake."

He turned, the pain and rage in his eyes so vivid, Megan had to step back.

"Believe me, Megan. This is a premature victory party you're having."

"It's not a victory party. It's just a simple dinner. Steve happened by and brought some Chinese food and—"

"Steve? And how long have you known Steve?"

"You should know that yourself." She pulled one of the photographs out of the envelope and held it up. "One of your private detectives parked outside this house."

He stepped toward her.

"How did you get that?"

"What difference does it make?"

"Did you have someone watching this house, too? Tell me. It's very important."

"I'll bet."

"You don't know what you're talking about, what you're getting yourself and Jennifer into," he continued, approaching her.

"Right, Scott. I don't know."

"Okay, smart-ass, you're right. I hired a private detective agency and they began surveillance last night, but guess what, the head of the agency was murdered last night," he said. He left out that the murder had occurred away from Beverly Hills and that the police were under the belief that it was a robbery, but he simply wanted to knock her off her high horse.

It worked.

Her expression of confidence and justifiable anger at him evaporated.

"Murdered?"

"That's right. I pulled off the detective who was there this morning. If you have any other pictures of other men observing this house, you'd better call the police immediately and inform them.

"Unless," he added, moving past her into the hallway, "you have some reason why you're afraid to."

"What reason—?"

"Anything wrong, Megan?" they heard. He turned to see Steve in the hallway.

"No, nothing. Thanks, Steve."

Scott looked back at her. She would never forget the expression on his face. Somewhere deep inside her, and from his pleading and tone of voice during the last phone conversation, she was convinced that somewhere deep inside him as well there was the hope that they'd find a way to stop this divorce, find a way back. But the look on Scott's face now was the look of a man who had been drained of the last drop of love for her. He looked like he had lost his soul.

"You're going to be sorry for all this, Megan, believe me. In the end, you'll be sorry."

He turned away and walked past Steve and back to the entryway. Tricia stood in the kitchen doorway gazing out fearfully. He glanced at her hatefully and continued on to the front door. The moment he stepped out, he felt his lungs relax and begin to fill up with clear, clean, cool air. It was as if he had stepped out of an oven. He welcomed and at the same time hated his craving for relief. It made him feel even more cowardly.

But he stopped thinking about himself when he opened his car door and tossed the useless folder into the rear. He looked back at the house and shook his head when the realization came to him.

He had gone in and out and he hadn't even said hello to his daughter.

"My God," Tricia said when the three of them gathered around the kitchenette table again. "When he walked out just now, I thought he was going to hit me. I was frozen in fear, Meg."

Megan busied herself clearing off the table.

Tricia looked at Steve, who was shaking his head.

"He threatened her, too," he said.

A thought occurred to Tricia. "Has he ever been violent with you, Meg?"

Meg paused and grimaced.

"Scott? Never. He's not capable of that."

"He sure looked like he was just now," Tricia insisted.

"She's right," Steve said. "As you know, I have had experience with that sort of thing. I can pretty much tell when another guy is going to start swinging. I grew up in the streets. You got so you had to know when to strike first in order to survive. Most fights I've been in and I've seen are one-punch fights, the first punch. It's not like in the movies. You hit someone in the jaw or cheek and you break bones and teeth. Why—"

"Stop!" Megan cried. "I can't stand this talk of violence. Scott's not violent. What's more, he just told me a terrible thing." She fought back tears and sat.

"What, Meg?" Tricia asked immediately.

"One of the private detectives he hired was murdered last night."

"Murdered?" Tricia looked up at Steve.

"How do you know that's true?" he asked.

"He wouldn't say such a thing if it weren't true. I showed him the picture you brought me and that was when he said it. He wanted to know if I had hired someone to watch the house."

She looked up at Steve.

"You didn't hire anyone. He can't accuse you of anything," he said. He looked at Tricia. She was looking at him strangely, too. "It was purely by accident that I discovered it. I'm not saying I wasn't thinking about it. What you told me about him and his father got me thinking they might do something like that, Megan. So I kept my eyes peeled when I was around here."

"You just said it was by pure accident," Tricia reminded him.

"Well, I meant . . . that I happened by at that time. Besides," he said, reddening some now, "you shouldn't be feeling guilty about anything. You're not the one who's doing this stuff. He is. Don't let him lay this on you. He's just trying to get out of some lowdown crap he's pulled. I've seen guys like that before."

"You probably have," Tricia said. He took it as a compliment, but Megan picked up on her tone and looked at her.

"I don't know what to think anymore," she said. "It's the first time I saw that much pain in his face."

"Megan—," Tricia began.

"I'm tired," Megan said. "Thank you both for

stopping by, but it looks like I have some hard days ahead. I'd better get some rest."

"Don't get depressed about it all," Tricia advised, rising. She put her arm around her. "I'm organizing a get-together with the girls for you on the weekend."

"I don't know, Tricia."

"It'll be good. You need support now."

"I didn't mean for this to turn out bad for you," Steve said.

Megan smiled at him and reached for his hand.

"I know. Thank you, Steve. We'll just all take a few steps back for a while, okay?"

His face darkened with disappointment. Back? She should be wanting to rush into his arms even more. She should be going forward, not back. What did that mean exactly? She would reconsider the divorce? It's not a good idea to push her too hard right now, he thought. He glanced at Tricia and then nodded.

"Sure. Let's all step back and let the system work for a change."

"Some system," Tricia muttered.

Megan walked them to the door.

"I'm glad Jennifer missed it all," Tricia said. "It would give her nightmares. It's going to give them to me. That look on his face."

"We'll be fine," Megan said. She hugged her.

Steve stood there waiting for some warm expression from her. She held out her hand.

"Good night, Steve. Thanks again," she said.

It nearly turned his stomach to do so, but he shook her hand. She could have at least kissed him on the cheek.

"Night," he said, and went out to his truck.

She and Tricia watched him go.

"I'm not leaving just yet. Come on inside and sit a moment," Tricia said. "You're pretty shaken up, Meg."

Meg nodded and let Tricia guide her into the living room.

"I don't know about you, but I could use a stiff drink," Tricia said, going to the bar. "How about my making you a martini or something?"

"Just some white wine, Tricia. Thanks."

Tricia poured a straight Scotch on the rocks for herself and a glass of Chardonnay for Megan. They sat quietly sipping for a few moments.

"I know you feel bad about it all, Megan, but you can't let him make you feel guilty. Men amaze me. He drives you away and yet he resents that another man might find you interesting or that you might turn to another man. It's just their damn male arrogance."

"I know, but there was a time, though, when I was just as unhappy whenever Scott was unhappy, and believe it or not, he was the same way. We felt for each other. I think that's a major part of love, maybe the heart of it, and when that goes, it all goes. Know what I mean?"

"Sure. And I went through the exact same periods of self-pity," Tricia said.

"You know, Tricia, I didn't pity myself as much as I pitied Scott tonight."

"That's because you're so good, Megan. You're better than me, that's for sure. But that also makes you terribly vulnerable. You actually lucked out bumping into a guy like Steve."

"Did I?"

"He's really handsome. He's funny and very sensitive for a tough guy, and he really likes you. I can see it."

"I know," Megan said with some fatigue in her voice, lowering her head. "But . . ."

"But what?" Megan asked.

"Sometimes I think he's too good to be true."

"I'm sure he has his faults, but right now, he looks pretty damn good and true to me."

"Maybe. I'm too confused right now to give any of that any thought. I just want to settle back and calm things down so I can think clearly."

"And don't forget . . . Depend on your attorney," Tricia added.

Megan nodded.

"I'd better go up and check on Jennifer," she said.

"Go ahead. I'll hang out for a while."

"You don't have to."

"It's fine. Where am I going? I'll leave when I see you're tired enough to fall asleep."

Megan smiled. "Thanks, Tricia."

The wine and conversation settled her a bit, but Megan could still feel the trembling inside. Now she was grateful she had permitted Jennifer to watch television in her room. It really was fortunate Jennifer hadn't seen or heard anything, she thought as she got her ready for bed.

"Look, Mommy," Jennifer said, and showed her how she could push the button on the tiny flashlight Steve had given her. "After you put out the lights, I can make circles on the walls and drive away anything that looks bad in the dark. It's like a magic flashlight."

Megan smiled. "Maybe it is."

"It was nice of Steve to give it to me."

"Yes," she said.

"He should have given you one too," Jennifer said. "It would make you feel better in the dark."

Megan laughed. Thank goodness for her daughter, she thought. She could bring her a little relief.

"Maybe he is trying to do just that. We'll see," she said, kissed her good night and went back downstairs to sit a while longer with Tricia so she could put off going to bed to fight with her own demons.

Steve was in so deep and so consuming a rage, the traffic before him was blurred.

Take a few steps back for a while? What exactly did that mean? This was the time to take a few steps forward. You don't retreat when a creep like that comes at you. You back him down. Scott was in so much pain? Poor Scott. Why was she telling him this? Did she expect him to feel sorry for the guy? And what about Jennifer?

This guy comes barging into her home and makes her feel guilty, and her answer to it all is to take a few steps back? She's weakening—she's slipping out of my fingers, he thought.

Hell, he threw away a good job today to be there for her and she tells him to take a few steps back?

Her husband's just a conniving son of a bitch. Look at that whole business about the private detective getting murdered last night. Why didn't he tell her the whole truth? He wasn't murdered outside of her house. He deliberately made it sound that way to get her upset.

He realized, off course, that he couldn't say anything to contradict that without revealing he knew much more. It was frustrating. He hated when these smart guys could figure out ways to twist things around and get their victories without risking anything. That's exactly what her husband did tonight. Scott got what he wanted without really confronting him.

Steve was primed to break the bastard's neck if he just came at him. The coward knew it, too. He couldn't have made a beeline out of there any faster. Why hadn't she seen that yellow streak? Why hadn't she thanked him for being there, for being stronger, for being her guardian angel when she needed one?

Was he wasting his time again? Was his mother right? She'd be all over him for making such a mistake. She would see it in his face the moment he walked into that house tonight, he thought. Mothers were like that. They could practically read their child's thoughts. Why go home? At least let sufficient time pass so he could paint over the cracks in his ego and his dream. She might not notice then.

He made a quick decision and turned toward the 405 Freeway. He decided to head down to San Diego and spend a while on his boat. Nowhere else did he think as clearly as he did when he was on that boat and out on the water. First, it had a way of calming him down and he knew it was impossible to make the right decisions unless you were calm. Second, he could avoid his mother for a while, give him the time to recuperate. He'd call her when he got there and make the conversation short, so she wouldn't pick up on anything. Of course, she would want to know about his work, but he could

tell her the man he was hired to replace returned
and they let him go. She'd believe that one. She always told him the world wasn't fair; it was just the
world.

He sped up. Traffic was never light, but it was
lighter this time of night. Still, it would take him
over two hours. He didn't listen to the radio. Instead, he listened to his own thoughts. It was as if
he had a radio in his head and could hear a talk
show that was all about him and his women. The
two commentators, two parts of himself, carried
out the argument.

*You try too hard, Steve. You have to give a woman a
chance to get used to you. She has to convince herself
she's not making a mistake. It's only natural for a woman
who has made a big one to think like that. Don't be so
hard on her.*

*That's bullshit. Any woman who is worthy of you
should immediately see that you bring the love and sta-
bility to her life that she needs, especially now when
she's feeling the most vulnerable and the loneliest. She
shouldn't be hesitating at all. If she's too afraid, you have
to be stronger yet. Patience is an excuse for inaction.*

On and on it went in his head. It actually made
him so dizzy, he had to pull off the freeway to
stop for some coffee. He found a place that resem-
bled an old-time diner and sat at the counter.
One of the waitresses serving two truck drivers
caught his attention. She looked a lot like Julia—
the same figure, the same color hair tied back the
same way Julia liked to tie hers and even the
same way of tilting her head to the right when
someone spoke to her. When she turned and
looked his way, it sent a chill up his spine. The re-

semblance was mind-boggling. This had happened to him before, but never as vividly. It was as if she could haunt him through her similarities with other women.

He turned away and hovered over his steaming coffee. What were Julia's words that had thrown him into such a rage that day? It was more than the words themselves; it was the vicious, gleeful way she had said them. Never had she looked uglier to him.

"You'd be the worst kind of father any child could have. You hated your own father, but you're just like him. You have to have it your own way, have everyone think like you, be like you. You would smother a child, especially a boy, to death.

"Having a child with you should be considered a capital crime," she added.

There they were, having this argument in the midst of a weather system while out to sea. She blamed him for it, of course. Why hadn't he checked it more thoroughly before having them go out? Lately at least seven out of ten things she said to him were criticisms of one thing or another. He thought, How did I fall into this cesspool of a marriage?

He told her to look over the side to see if they were dragging anything. It had happened before, hadn't it? Reluctantly, she did what he asked and he swung the boat dramatically. She lunged forward and disappeared. She was probably criticizing him all the way into the water. He heard her shout and took his time to get over to the side. She was nowhere in sight at first and then her head bobbed up and her arm was extended. He looked at her hand grasping the air, waiting for him to take hold of it.

Calmly, he asked, "Don't you wish you were pregnant?"

Then he walked away, thinking that was a very pertinent question to ask her. No matter how he felt about her as a woman, he wouldn't have permitted a yet-to-be-born child to drown. She would have saved herself if she had permitted him to have a child.

It was damn cold that night, damn cold and windy. He knew she wouldn't last long. She was practically completely forgotten by the time he returned to the dock.

No matter how he pressed the memories down in his mind, they had a way of resurrecting from time to time, and whenever they did, it seemed like just yesterday.

He blew on his coffee and took a sip. It was starting to rain now, too. He saw the drops zigzagging down the restaurant's front window. When he was a little boy, his mother would say, "God is crying," whenever it rained. As nasty as it was that day Julia drowned, it hadn't rained. God wasn't upset then, but he was upset tonight.

What had Megan said? Take a few steps back for while? That didn't mean for a while. That was a nice way of saying, *Maybe you shouldn't be in my life right now. Maybe I'll reconcile with my husband after all.*

If he just bowed politely and retreated, he would never be in her life and she and Jennifer would never be in his. He could hear the arguments in his head starting again, the two commentators.

How could he shut it off? He slapped his hands over his ears.

"You all right?" the counterman asked him.

He shook his head.

"They won't shut up," he said.

"Pardon me?"

He stood up, dropped a few dollars on the counter and hurried out. It all grew louder in the Corvette. He pounded the dashboard a few times and then he started the engine and pulled out of the parking lot, but when he reached the freeway entrance, he didn't go south; he went north.

This wasn't the time to retreat. One voice was winning out over the other and as it did, it grew quieter in his head. He was grateful for that. It helped him understand what he must do, how he could show her what was the wrong way and what was the right way. He got off the exit that would take him home and drove in behind his truck. He got out quietly so his mother wouldn't hear him and went to the truck to grab a flathead screwdriver. He dug deeper into his toolbox until he found the knit cap, some rope and the dust mask. He put on a pair of work gloves, rolled up his sleeves and got back into the Corvette.

By the time he reached Beverly Hills again, all was relatively quiet. Without a moment's second thought or hesitation, he turned onto Megan's street.

He was happy to see that Tricia Morgan's car was still in the driveway. Megan had not gone to sleep and therefore had not turned on the house alarm. He parked his Corvette on the street and then, sticking very close to the shadows, he made his way onto the property and around to the side door of the attached garage. It was nothing to pry it open by just moving the lock's bolt back. When he closed it softly behind him, it locked in place again. Only a very good forensics man would see the tiniest of scratches on the bolt.

The door from the garage into the kitchen was still unlocked, so he slipped in quietly. He could hear them talking in the living room. He heard his name mentioned a few times and knew they were doing some drinking. He laughed to himself and went to the alarm keypad by the door to the garage. He was quite familiar with the system. He simply opened the garage door to see what number corresponded to it and then pressed "bypass" and entered the number. Now when Megan set her alarm, probably out there, she wouldn't notice that the garage door had been bypassed. It could be opened without setting off the alarm.

Once that was done, practically floating over the floor, he made his way to the pantry and slipped inside, leaving the door open slightly so he could hear Megan move about the house. Then he curled up and waited.

He was very patient.

He had all the patience in the world.

He pulled the knit cap down over his eyes to the bridge of his nose and then slipped on the dust mask.

Just a little while longer, he thought. Just a little while longer and it would all begin again.

After Tricia finally left, Megan was still so unnerved by the evening's events, she knew she wouldn't fall asleep without taking something, but she hesitated to do that. She was afraid she wouldn't be there for Jennifer. Jennifer was having nightmares more often since Megan and Scott had broken up and the divorce proceeding had begun. She was old enough to understand what divorce meant, but she was still too young to accept it. Not a day went by without her asking a question that had as its underlying motive the consideration of a reversal. Couldn't they make up, mend the split, compromise, or simply put, think more about her than themselves?

The motive for this divorce was not as clear as motives for divorce usually were. Neither Scott nor she had cheated on the other. This was more of an insidious, cumulative series of actions, or rather inactions, that eroded the foundation of love that had brought them together in the first place. It was difficult to explain all that to Jennifer because children were more forgiving.

Daddy is a busy, important man, but he still loves me. Daddy wouldn't do anything to deliberately hurt us.

How do you explain to a child that she's right, but that isn't enough? Placing value on priorities was still too abstract a concept. Reluctantly, Jennifer would accept the situation. She had no choice, but she would never fully understand it, and in the end, when she was older, she would blame them both. Megan was confident of that and that weighed on her. However, it wasn't enough to change her mind. She was battling for her own well-being, and if she wasn't well, Jennifer would suffer more. Just maybe she'd understand that much soon.

Well, I won't take a sleeping pill, she thought,

but I can make myself some warm milk. That does work on me.

She checked on Jennifer before she started down to the kitchen. She looked so much smaller and younger tonight as she lay there with her favorite stuffed toy, an old-fashioned rag doll, beside her. The fact that Scott had bought it for her was an irony not lost on Megan. Any amateur psychiatrist would interpret Jennifer's clinging so hard to it as her deep-seated need to have him back, to have things the way they were, regardless of how rocky it was. Megan stared at her for a moment, fighting back the tears that wanted to gush, and then she saw the little flashlight Steve had given her. It was a thoughtful gift. She was positive Jennifer was using it regularly now. It brought more pain to her heart. She quickly turned away and hurried down the stairs before she could sob and wake her up.

She always left some lights on downstairs—a small lamp in the living room and a light above the sink in the kitchen. The chandelier above the stairway was dimmed, but threw enough illumination to make it safe. And of course, there were the outside lights, which went on when the sensor declared it was dark enough. Windows were lit, as was the entire front.

Scott and she once had gone out to dinner with Brody Palman, a professional bodyguard. He had begun working as a security employee for a company that protected the homes of movie stars, but quickly grew bored with that and worked for a company that guarded the lives and homes of paranoid businessmen. One had actually been under a death threat, which he'd claimed was a result of his work with Homeland Security. Brody had great stories to tell, leaving out the actual names of his employers, of course.

It was Brody who had convinced Scott to get a gun for the house. She'd been against it, having had no experience whatsoever with firearms. She had been worried about Jennifer. There were too many horrible stories about children getting their hands on weapons in homes. Brody's point, which was the one that had impressed Scott the most, was that it was precisely because of Jennifer that they should have a weapon.

"Look," he'd said, "I know you feel very safe in Beverly Hills. It probably has one of the lowest crime rates in the country, but don't forget the famous bank robber Willy Sutton's answer when he was asked, Why rob banks? He said, 'Because that's where the money is.' Burglars aren't going to rob homes in poor communities. They know there's not much booty there for them. But a home in Beverly Hills . . . guaranteed to be worth the effort. I'm not talking about only drug addicts."

Scott had bobbed his head like one of those dolls or animals placed in the rear window of cars. It was as if he had springs in his neck. She'd known the argument was over before it began, especially when Brody added, "You have two major things going to discourage break-ins: your good lighting around the house and your alarm system. If someone comes through both of those, he or they can be stopped only with a bullet."

Terrifying.

But that terror was exactly why her putting up an argument would have been useless. Scott had bought the gun and put it right by his side of the bed. She realized, of course, that it was still there, but she placed her comfort and confidence in the lighting and in the alarm system. She always armed the alarm before she went upstairs and it was armed now.

So at first she thought she might be having a waking dream when the dark figure, looking as if it had formed out of the shadows in the corner by the stairway, stepped out. She had little time to react. His arm came around with whatever he was grasping in his hand and he struck her in the back of her head just above her neck. The blow sent her sprawling on the tile, sliding a few feet on her right side. She was unable to get her right arm up fast enough to keep her face from hitting the tile, but she felt no pain there.

She blacked out before it could reach her brain.

But it was there, stinging, aching, screaming, the moment she regained consciousness. She didn't get to her feet right away. For a long moment, she tried to remember what had happened. When she lifted her head, the house was spinning too much and the dizziness wouldn't subside. She battled herself into a sitting position and took deep breaths to keep herself from passing out again. The pain in her head was so intense, she thought she would definitely faint again, and fought hard to remain conscious. Then she began to dry-heave, the acid rising in her throat and causing her to gag. She had to lie down and wait for it to subside.

When it did she sat up again and then took hold of the side of a table in the hallway and pulled herself into a standing position. She kept her eyes closed and worked at keeping steady. A wave of fear washed over her as she listened. Was whoever had hit her still here? She looked around.

What had happened?

Were they being robbed? Was it over? Were they still in the house?

The next thought that came to her was What about Jennifer? She moved cautiously to the stairway, listening for sounds of anyone else in the house. It was quiet, so she climbed the stairway, clinging to the banister, pulling herself along. It seemed to take hours to get to the top, but finally she did and then lunged toward Jennifer's bedroom.

At first she thought everything was all right. Then she turned on the light and saw that what she thought was Jennifer was just her blanket, bundled. Where was she?

"Jennifer!" she screamed, and waited to see if she was in the bathroom or in another room. She heard nothing—no voice, no footsteps. "Jennifer!" she called again and turned in the hallway.

Where was she?

"Jennifer!"

She looked at the bed again.

Not only was Jennifer gone, but so was her rag doll. Only the little flashlight remained.

No alarm had gone off and she was positive she had set it. She had been attacked, and Jennifer and her doll were gone. Who could do all that? Who could enter this house so easily? There was only one name to come to her mind.

"Scott!" she screamed. "You bastard!"

She collapsed to her knees and crawled to the

telephone in Jennifer's room. She pulled it down on the floor with her and punched out 911.

"I've been attacked!" she screamed. "And my daughter's gone! He did this."

She just managed to get out her address before she fainted again.

CHAPTER ELEVEN

Scott remained at the table while his father walked the Japanese businessmen out to their cars at the Four Seasons. His father had done most of the talking, noting immediately on his entrance that Scott was in something of a sulk. Scott tried his best to show interest, but he was raging so much inside himself, he could barely contain the anger enough to eat anything. He drank too much too quickly, which was another thing that clearly annoyed his father. As he sat there waiting for him to return, he anticipated another severe chastisement, and that was one thing he didn't need right now.

His father smiled at the maître d'. They had a few words and then his father returned to the table.

"If I knew you were going to behave like a child tonight, Scott, I wouldn't have had you here. Insult added to injury, you came late."

"I stopped at the house before I came here."

"What house?"

"My house, Dad. It's still technically half my house!"

"Lower your voice. I didn't say it wasn't. So?"

"She was having some sort of celebration with

that whore friend of hers, Tricia Morgan, and this guy she's met."

His father sat back.

"And . . . ?"

"And nothing. I let her know I know what the hell she's doing. Then she came at me and showed me she had pictures of Ed Marcus's partner watching the house."

"She did?"

"Right."

"So she hired someone as well. She's playing hardball," his father said. "Probably a suggestion that attorney of hers, Emily Lloyd, made. She's a real ball-breaker. What about this man of hers? Who is he?"

"I don't know. Never saw him before. He looked like someone who had just walked out of some penitentiary. I can't imagine her with someone like that, exposing Jennifer to someone like that."

"Yes, well just be patient. You'll wipe the smug smile of celebration off her face soon enough.

Well," he added, rising, "this went well tonight, despite your sitting there and sulking. I think we have the deal."

Scott nodded, but he was unable to show even a hint of satisfaction about it. Right now, all of that was meaningless to him.

"You're losing your focus, Scott. Once a man does that, he falls in all sorts of ways. Grow up. Get hold of yourself. You're playing in the big leagues now."

Scott glared up at him. This was about as much sympathy as he would ever get, he thought, but he understood why. His father saw him as weak, and the truth was, he saw himself as weak as well. He should have done more back at the house. He shouldn't have rushed away with his tail between his legs. It simply added to his rage.

"Let's go home and get some sleep," his father said.

"I'll be home soon," he added. He wasn't ready to retreat to the Lester compound and curl up in a fetal position in bed to find relief in sleep. That was another form of escape. His mother used to sleep away half her day. He was beginning to understand why.

His father leaned over the table.

"You had better start acting like a Lester," he said, and walked out.

What the hell did that mean?

Scott ruminated a while, drank the rest of his Scotch and soda and then finally got up and left. When his car was brought around, he simply couldn't just get in and drive home. His curiosity and anger seized him, so he drove back to his Beverly Hills home to see if that yellow Corvette was still in the driveway. It wasn't, which made him feel better until he turned his head and saw it parked just a few feet up from the house. He slowed down. The man called Steve was not in it. That meant he was in the house, and parking the yellow Corvette outside was just some pathetic attempt to hide it. They were probably in bed, screwing away.

He didn't have the nerve to go back in there and catch them in the act, so he drove on and ended up at one of his old hangouts, a bar in West Hollywood. He hadn't realized it was one of those that had evolved into a gay bar, but he didn't care. A drink was a drink and he wanted to delay going to his father's house. He found a corner away from the other men. His demeanor was enough to keep anyone from approaching him. He simply sat there for well over an hour, drinking and reviewing his life with Megan, trying to pinpoint that exact moment when their love for each other dissipated like smoke and left them with only the aroma of the fire that had once burned in both their hearts.

"If anyone looks like he's drowning his sorrows, it's you," a tall, muscular man in a tight black Polo shirt said, stopping at his table. He had a military-style haircut and a diamond earring. Scott could barely see his face in the shadows. "Why don't you come join us?" he added. "We'll cheer you up."

"Not in this life," Scott replied.

The man shrugged.

"Well, when you return to earth, pay us a visit," he said, and walked away.

Scott finally had to laugh at himself. He drank some water, sobered up enough to leave and paid his bill.

"What ever happened to Sonny Martin?" he asked the bartender.

"Sonny Martin? Never heard of him," he replied.

"Too bad," Scott said. "He could make one helluva martini."

He left feeling even more despondent. Coming here hadn't done him any good. It had simply reminded him that every trace of his former existence appeared to have evaporated. I'm ready to become my father, he thought, and drove home.

No one was awake. If either his father or Jules had heard him, they didn't care to get out of bed to see how he was or if he needed anything. He navigated the stairway and plopped on his bed facedown without taking off his shoes. He was that way early in the morning when Jules shook him to wake him.

"Mr. Lester. Mr. Lester," he said.

Scott groaned and turned over. For a moment or two, he forgot where he was. Then he sat up and scrubbed his cheeks with his dry palms and realized he was still in his clothes and shoes from the night before.

"Oh, Jules. Sorry. What's up?"

"There's are two police detectives downstairs with your father. They need you right away," he replied.

"What? What's up?"

Jules shook his head.

"Better you hear it from them," he said.

Scott's face grew hot with fear immediately. He shot off the bed and hurried out, passing Jules in the hallway and nearly tripping on his way down the stairway.

The police and his father were in the living room. The police were standing, but his father was seated and still in his robe. He looked up and stopped Scott in his tracks.

Never had he ever seen his father with a look of abject fear on his face.

"What's wrong?" he asked.

"These men are detectives from the Beverly Hills Police Department," his father said. "Come in and sit down, Scott."

"Beverly Hills police? What is it?"

"Your wife was attacked last night, Mr. Lester, and your daughter is missing," one of the detectives said.

"What?"

"Where were you after you left your father?" the other detective asked.

"How is Megan?" he asked, instead of replying.

"She's in intensive care at Cedars, Mr. Lester. We don't have any information on her condition yet."

"And my daughter . . . is missing?"

"Yes, Mr. Lester."

"I've got to get to the hospital."

"Let's have a little talk here first," the first detective said.

"But—"

"Sit, Scott," his father told him. "I told them they could ask you one or two questions, but if we go beyond that, we'll have our attorney present."

"Attorney? For what?" Scott asked, sitting on the sofa.

"Let's stay calm," the first detective said. "Our purpose here is to get your daughter back safely first. My name is Michael Parker and this is Jackson Foto," he said, nodding at the second detective.

"Why are you questioning me?" Scott demanded.

"Whoever broke into your home and attacked your wife and kidnapped your daughter knew how to get past the alarm system. It was never triggered. Your wife is positive she armed the alarm before going up to bed, Mr. Lester. When a patrol car arrived after her 911 call, the alarm did sound.

Your wife wasn't able to get to the front door quickly.

"Your wife was struck with a small statue of an angel. We have it in forensics."

"You have a pistol permit, so your prints are on record," Foto added.

"My prints. I remember when we bought that statue. Of course my prints are on it. Why would that be important? Who told you I had a pistol permit?"

"Megan told them," his father said dryly.

"Why?"

"She thinks you did it."

"What?"

"She told us that earlier in the evening you busted into the house and threatened her," Parker said.

"Threatened her? I did not."

"There were witnesses—a girlfriend named Tricia Morgan and a man named Steve Wallace. We're on our way next to speak with Ms. Morgan. And we'll be questioning Steve Wallace as well, so you might as well tell us what you said."

"Did you tell her she would be sorry? In the end she would be sorry?" Foto followed.

"Yes, but—"

"So you admit that?" Parker asked. "Thanks, saves us two trips. Can you tell us where you were at about eleven, eleven thirty? Your father says the dinner you had ended at nine thirty, but you didn't come directly home and he can't give us the exact time you did get home."

Scott looked at his father.

"You don't think . . ."

"Of course not, but the best way to convince them of that is for you and I to be truthful, Scott."

"I drove around for a while and went to a bar I used to frequent in my younger days, before I was married. It's in West Hollywood. The Underground."

"And how long were you there?"

"An hour or so."

"And after that?"

"I came right home. Look, I did return to the house after I left—actually, after I left the dinner with my father."

"Oh?" Foto stepped closer.

"I wanted to see if Megan's friend Tricia Morgan was still there, or that guy she's met. I saw his car on the street."

"What time would this be?"

"Close to ten."

"Your wife says they were both gone by nine thirty."

"I saw his car. The lights were out. Figure it out!" Scott exclaimed.

"Okay, we'll check all that," Parker said.

"Can I get to the hospital now?"

"Aren't you more concerned about your daughter's whereabouts?" Foto asked.

"Of course he is. The man is flustered. That's why people need attorneys when you guys go fishing. Conversation is over. We'll contact our attorney for any further discussions," his father said, rising.

"Okay. We'll let you know when. Since this is a kidnapping, we'll be talking to the FBI today," Parker said.

"Good," Scott's father said. He looked at Scott. "I'll get dressed and go with you to the hospital. I'll call the office and put off—"

"I'm not waiting, Dad. Meet me there," Scott said sharply, and rushed out.

Returning late in the morning from the grocery store, Steve's mother looked through the open door of his bedroom and saw him asleep on his back, clothes still on, boots off. His television set was on. He had been watching the news. She glanced at it when the anchor returned to the lead local story about a little girl being kidnapped and the mother being attacked in her Beverly Hills home. There was an AMBER Alert. She shook her head. What a world. No one was safe anywhere.

"Steve," she said. He didn't budge. She struggled with the bags a moment and then brought them to the kitchen table. She didn't go right out for the other four bags. Instead, she returned to his bedroom and this time knocked hard on the opened door.

His eyes popped open.

"Where were you? Why aren't you at work? I could use some help with the groceries," she added before he could even think of any answers. "Well?"

"I had things to do. The job's done," he said, and reluctantly swung his legs over the bed to find his boots.

"You look like a drowned rat," she muttered, and went out for the remaining groceries.

He ran his fingers through his hair and stood up. This wasn't the first time he had been up all night, but he sure was feeling it. I guess age is creeping in, he thought. But that only reinforced the urgency of everything he had to do. Don't want to be past my prime when I raise a family, he concluded.

He looked at the television. The news was over and some woman's talk show was starting. He shut it off. He had all the information he needed. Then he followed his mother out. She shook her head and gave him a look of disgust as he passed her to pick up the remaining bags.

"So?" she asked as he placed the bags on the kitchen table. "What exactly were these things you had to do?"

"I'm setting up a new home," he said casually. He opened a package of chocolate-chip cookies and started to gobble a few.

"Setting up a new home? What the hell are you talking about now, Steve?"

"Just what I said. Setting up a new life for myself and my new family."

"What new family? That divorced woman and her kid?"

"Exactly," he replied, and opened a container of milk. "I'm convincing her to start over with me."

His mother scowled.

"You hardly know her, unless you've been seeing her for a long time without telling me about it."

"It doesn't take long for a woman with some intelligence and quality to recognize the man she's meant to be with, the man who would provide and protect her. A good husband should be his wife's guardian angel, always. That should be his first priority, Ma. Trouble with Dad was, his first priority was himself."

"I don't like you talking that way about him. He's not here to defend himself."

"He's probably busy defending himself somewhere else . . . someplace pretty hot."

"Shut that," she snapped, and started to remove the groceries.

He poured himself some milk and gulped it.

"When's all this supposed to happen exactly?" she asked as she worked.

"Soon," he said.

"I haven't even met this new princess."

"Oh, you will. When the time's right," he told her.

He pulled off his shirt and started away.

"Now what are you doing?"

"Got to clean up and visit someone in the hospital," he said.

"Who?"

He didn't answer. He went into the bathroom and started his shower. His mother finished putting away the groceries and then sat at the kitchen table waiting for her coffee to perk. Something gnawed away at the bottom of her stomach. She could recall other times Steve was this cryptic about something he was about to do, and every time, it had been something bad, something either she or her husband had to fix.

This woman, she thought, must be taking awful advantage of him.

She wanted to know more about her. While he was in the bathroom, she rose and went into his room searching for some clue, something. She saw nothing unusual and was about to leave when she saw his jacket hanging on the back of a chair. She listened to be sure he was still busy in the bathroom and then looked through the jacket pockets.

At first she thought it was his wallet, but there was something different about it, so she opened it and looked at the California driver's license for someone named Ed Marcus. Another card told her he was a private detective. What the hell was this? She heard him opening the bathroom door, so she hurriedly returned the wallet to his jacket pocket and stepped out of his room just as he came out of the bathroom with a towel around his neck, the aroma of his sweet aftershave coming at her in waves.

"What are you looking for?" he asked immediately.

"Just checking to see how much mud and grime you dragged in," she replied.

He nodded. "I know, Ma. It's not easy looking after a grown man after all these years, but soon I'll have someone else looking after me and you'll be able to become what you were always meant to become."

"And what's that, pray tell?"

"A grandmother. What else?" he said, smiling, and walked past her into his room, closing the door behind him.

After he dressed, he called a florist and ordered a dozen mixed roses to be sent to Megan at the hospital.

"Please write, 'Sorry I wasn't there for you when you needed me the most, but I'll be there now. Steve,'" he told the store clerk. "Can you put a rush on it? She needs cheering up desperately."

"I'll get it out within the hour," the clerk promised.

Steve checked the time. He had the day planned perfectly, but he knew the groundwork was more important than anything. Despite his lack of sleep, he was energized. Finally, he had restored his purpose in life.

"Are you coming home for dinner tonight?" his mother asked the instant he emerged from his room.

"No, Ma, not tonight, not tomorrow night, not the night after. Maybe not ever again."

"What? What kind of talk is that?"

"I might as well break the news to you now, Ma. I'm moving out very soon."

She stood staring at him as if he had said the dumbest thing.

"What?" he demanded. "You've been after me since Julia's death to get a life, haven't you?"

"Yes, a sensible life," she retorted.

"That's what I'm doing. Get that through your thick head. Believe it," he said, and turned and walked out.

Twenty minutes later, the phone rang. He's probably calling to apologize, she thought. She decided she wasn't going to be so forgiving. He wasn't too old to be taught a lesson.

"Yes?" she said sharply after she picked up the receiver.

"Mrs. Wallace?"

"Yes."

"This is Matt Lowenstein. Steve there?"

"He just left. You can get him on his cell phone, maybe."

"No need. Just give him a message for me. That's

the last time I'll recommend him for any job in the state of California, or anywhere for that matter," he said, and hung up.

She held the receiver for a moment and then looked toward the front door.

What was he doing? Why was that stranger's wallet in his pants?

She raised her eyes toward the ceiling and mumbled a short prayer.

"Lord, please spare me," she said, and cradled the receiver.

On his way to the hospital, Steve stopped to buy a box of fancy candy. He perused some get-well cards until he found one he thought appropriate. Although it didn't specifically say it was coming from a husband or boyfriend, the sentiment in it couldn't be mistaken for much else. It was perfect. He paid for everything and casually drove to the hospital.

As luck would have it—and Steve did believe in luck and fate and the power of coincidence—Scott Lester got out of his car just a few spaces down and headed for the hospital entrance. Steve watched him walk quickly, practically jogging. Then Steve got out of his car, went to the trunk and took out what he needed to, as he would call it, seal the deal. Yep, he thought, everything happens for a reason. Whenever something helped him and his cause, it reconfirmed in his mind that all this was meant to be.

He was as familiar with car alarms and locks as he was with house alarms and locks. In only minutes, he did what he had to do. Then, after he felt a sufficient amount of time had passed, he too headed for the hospital entrance, only he didn't walk as fast; he didn't jog.

Time was on his side, as was everything else.

Patience was indeed a virtue.

Scott practically tiptoed into Megan's hospital room. Her head was bandaged and there was an IV hooked up, but she looked fully awake. How her sister Clare had gotten here so quickly, he didn't know, but there she was, sitting at Megan's bedside and holding her hand. They both looked at him with an angry, accusatory expression. Normally, there wasn't all that much resemblance between them, Clare being nearly eight years older, but at the moment, they looked like twins.

"I didn't do this," he said before either of them could speak. "I don't know how I could even be a suspect."

Megan's lips began to tremble. In fact, her whole body began to shake. Clare felt the tremors in her hand and stood up instantly. She waved at Scott.

"Outside," she ordered. "Outside!"

He backed up and waited.

"Clare, this is crazy," he said the moment she stepped out, closing the door behind her.

She leaned against the door and folded her arms, looking like some sort of palace guard. Clare was a good three inches taller than Megan and bigger-boned. She looked more like their father and didn't have Megan's dainty features.

"Didn't you threaten her last night?"

"It was only . . . I was angry, yes. She's been seeing another man. He was there. We just began this damn divorce action. How could another man be so close to her already?"

"You're accusing my sister of adultery? Megan?"

"All I know . . ." He paused. He didn't want to bring up his returning to the house and seeing the lights out but the man's car parked across the street. It was no time to make accusations.

"Look, this is way off the topic right now, Clare. Our daughter is missing and Megan's going to delay any real search and investigation with these accusations."

She didn't relent, but she relaxed her posture.

"She has a severe concussion. They don't want her falling asleep at the moment, so she's just on some Tylenol. What she doesn't need is any more tension and aggravation. She's terrified for Jennifer."

"So am I."

"Then go look for her. You're not going to help the situation by getting her into an argument now."

"You can't believe I'm capable of this, Clare."

"What I believe isn't important, Scott. It's what the police will come to believe."

He lowered his head. Maybe he would talk about the other guy.

"I wouldn't bring him around right now either," she added, nodding past him.

He turned to see his father coming up the corridor.

"Just go, Scott. I'll call you and tell you how she's doing."

"What's going on?" his father demanded.

"Relax, Dad. I'm handling it."

"Yes, Mr. Lester. Scott's handling it," Clare said, and went back into Megan's room, closing the door behind her.

"What the hell . . . ? That's her sister, right?"

"Yes, Dad. You've seen her enough times to know that."

"Well, what's going on?"

"She's suffered a severe concussion. Right now, she's still too upset to speak with me." He thought a moment. "I want to get that private-detective agency back. The police don't believe me because Megan doesn't. I need to do my own investigating."

"Oh, I do have another reference and . . ."

"No. I want this guy," Scott said, and started to walk away. His father caught up and started to pour out his advice. They should call Taylor Stewart, a very well-known criminal attorney, right away. There was someone his father knew who worked for the FBI and he would contact him to make sure the case wasn't left to these clowns in Beverly Hills. Scott should return to work to keep himself from thinking too much about Jennifer. On that one, Scott stopped and turned.

"Thinking too much about Jennifer? That's been my problem all along—not thinking enough about her. How can a father think too much about his daughter at a time like this?"

"Don't get hysterical on me."

Scott glared at him and then turned and walked faster. When he reached the lobby, he paused, but not to wait for his father to catch up.

Coming through the door was the man who had

been in his house last night, the man Steve, whom Megan was seeing. He braced himself for another confrontation. This time he would not only stand his ground, he would go at him as well, the devil be damned.

But the guy didn't pause.

He simply smiled at Scott and, carrying a box of chocolates, went immediately to the elevator. Scott started to go after him when his cell phone went off.

"Scott Lester," he answered, watching the man get on the elevator. Steve turned to smile again as the doors closed. Scott listened as his father caught up. "We'll be there," he said sharply, and shut the phone.

"What?"

"Call Taylor Stewart. They want us at the police station at two o'clock. I guess they're trying to spook me, all right. They said the only prints on the statue belonged to Megan, our maid and me. They have more questions to ask and claim they need them answered to go forward with the search for Jennifer."

His father's eyes narrowed.

"Why did you return to the house after you left the dinner? Maybe someone on the street saw you. Did you park, go in?"

"No. I did exactly what I told them I did and nothing more."

"So you came right home after you went to that dump in West Hollywood? You didn't work yourself into some kind of rage because you had seen that guy's car still near the house?"

"Thanks, Dad. That's exactly what I need right now—suspicion from my own father."

He hurried out, his compassion and sympathy in a state of confusion. Jennifer had to be the priority, but he did feel sorry for Megan, and now he was beginning to feel even sorrier for himself.

And he hated it.

CHAPTER TWELVE

Clare came to the hospital-room door.

"Can I help you?"

"How is Megan?" Steve asked.

"She's resting, but not comfortably."

He nodded.

"And you are?"

"I'm Steve Wallace," he said, trying to look past her into the room.

"Oh, you're the one who sent the beautiful flowers."

"Yes."

"I'm Clare Tremont, Megan's sister."

She offered her hand and he shook gently.

"Who is it?" Megan called.

"It's Steve Wallace."

"Let him in, Clare."

He smiled and she stepped back.

"You poor kid," he said as he walked in. "I don't know if they'll let you have any of this, but . . ."

Clare took the box of candy.

"But her sister certainly can. Thank you." She looked at Megan. "You know what? I think I'll go offer some to the nurses. That's always a good idea."

"Yes," Megan said.

Steve watched Clare leave and then turned to Megan.

"How did you find out so quickly?" she asked.

"First thing on the local news this morning. My mother heard it first and I rushed out to listen and watch when I heard your name. How long after I left did it happen?"

"Hours. Tricia remained behind until I couldn't keep my eyes open."

"What did the doctor say?"

"Concussion."

"Are you in a lot of pain?"

"It just throbs right now."

"Sorry," he said.

"I don't care about myself. My Jennifer . . . ," she said, her lips quivering. "She must be so frightened. I know if Scott had anything to do with this, she's not in any physical danger, but no matter what, I can't imagine the terror she must have gone through and is still going through."

Steve nodded.

"I saw him leaving just now."

"Scott? He tried to come in here, but I don't want to see him."

"Don't blame you. This is just the sort of situation that cries out for a guardian angel," he said. "A man's first priority should always be the protection of his family. There is no excuse, no reason to ever justify doing anything that in any way harms any of them."

Megan smiled through her tears.

"How come you're so family oriented, Steve? You haven't told me all that much about your own.

You don't have any brothers or sisters. What about close relatives?"

"My mother's only sister died last year and my father was like me, an only child. I have cousins on my mother's side, but they live on the East Coast.

"Sometimes, when I have spare time, especially on weekends, I go to the parks and watch parents and their children and try to imagine what that would have been like for me if my wife, Julia, had lived and had given us children."

"Hopefully your life would not have been like this," Megan said.

They heard a knock on the door and Tricia walked in with another woman, shorter, stouter. Steve thought the woman had her hair cut way too short for her plump face and wore too much makeup. Occasionally, Julia had put on too much makeup and he'd forced her to wash it off.

"Megan, how are you, sweetie? I didn't know anything until the Beverly Hills police called to question me about last night," Tricia said, rushing to her side. "Pat here heard it from a friend whose sister is friends with your neighbor, Sally Rosenfield."

She kissed her cheek and then looked at Steve. "Hello, Steve. How did you find out so quickly and beat me up here?"

"I was just telling Megan that it was on the morning news," he said, eyeing the other woman, named Pat.

Pat moved to Megan's side, cutting right in front of him.

"I'm so sorry for your trouble, Megan. The phone's ringing off the hook. All the girls are planning on visiting and doing whatever they can."

"Thanks, Pat. This is a friend of mine, Steve Wallace," Megan said.

Pat nodded at him and Steve worked a tiny smile around his lips. He had been hoping to spend all his time alone with Megan. He had much to say, proposals to make. Time was important here.

"Is there any news about Jennifer?" Tricia asked.

"Nothing yet."

"Well, what does Scott have to say about it all?"

"I don't know. He tried to come in, but I didn't want to see him."

"You really think he had something to do with this?" Pat asked incredulously.

"I don't know," Megan said. She turned to Tricia. "You saw how he was last night."

"Yes." She looked at Steve. "We all did, and that was what I told the police, too. They'll probably call you, Steve."

"I'll just tell them what I saw and heard," he said.

"Now don't you wish you never got yourself involved?" Megan asked him.

"No. Now I see what's happening, I'm glad I did," he replied.

The three women smiled at Megan.

"Well, what do they have on Jennifer's abduction?" Pat asked.

Clare returned.

"You remember my sister?" Megan said. Pat and Tricia greeted her.

"Clare spoke with a police detective this morning. She still hasn't told me all of it," Megan said sharply.

"Megan . . ."

"I'd like to know what you know, Clare. I have a right to know."

They all looked at her.

"They have the weapon," she said. "A statue of an angel. They're checking it for fingerprints."

"Both Scott's and my fingerprints would be on it, and our maid Lourdes', I imagine."

"They're going over the house carefully for any evidence at all," Clare added. "Megan reported that whoever took Jennifer made sure to take her favorite rag doll as well."

"But left the flashlight you gave her behind," Megan added. "She was using it to do just what you said, drive away the moments of fear in the darkness."

"How sweet," Pat said smiling. "Have there been burglaries in the neighborhood lately?" she asked.

"Not that I know of," Megan said.

"Someone is always first," Clare said.

"But didn't you have an alarm on?" Pat asked Megan.

"I did. I was very nervous, so I know I didn't forget to do that. Whoever entered to attack me must have disarmed it."

"How can anyone do that?"

"Strangers can't," Steve said. "Why would any ordinary burglar attack Megan and take Jennifer anyway?"

"Yes, that's right. Anything else missing?" Tricia asked, and looked at Clare.

"Well, Megan can't confirm anything right now, but as far as we know, no. She told me where she had some money, and that money is still in the drawer, not hard to find. In fact, the police tell me not much else was disturbed. No doors or windows broken."

"You didn't forget to lock up, did you?" Pat asked.

Megan shook her head.

"I know I set the alarm. Only one other person knows the code."

They were all quiet. Megan closed her eyes. Her body started to tremble. Clare started for her, but Steve seized her hand first and she looked at him.

"Hold yourself together," he said. "I'm sure this will work out all right. You and Jennifer will be together again real soon."

Clare froze next to the bed. Megan smiled again and took a deep breath just as the doctor and a nurse entered.

"We'll need you all to leave for a while," the nurse said.

Clare leaned over to kiss Megan. Tricia and Pat did as well. Steve lifted her hand to his lips and with his eyes opened, kissed it. Then he followed the women out.

"I must have had a half-dozen conversations before I left the house," Pat said in the hallway after the door was closed. "No one can believe this. I mean, no one can believe Scott would do such a thing."

"You didn't see him last night," Tricia said. She looked at Steve for confirmation. He nodded.

"He was pretty damn angry. I thought he was going to slug me or you."

"Really?" Pat asked her.

"Steve's right," she said.

"I've got to go. I have some things to take care of immediately," Steve said. "You girls give her comfort," he told them as if he were in charge of everything.

They watched him walk away.

"Who is that guy?" Pat asked.

"He sent her those roses and brought candy this morning," Clare said. She looked at Tricia. "Megan never mentioned him to me. When did she meet him? Is he some old friend or something?"

Tricia smiled. "No, no, nothing like that. Megan and I had gone out after the divorce petition was filed. I took her to the Cage in Beverly Hills. It's a hot dance club," she told Clare. "She was pretty down about it all. I was trying to cheer her up. She has such an unjustified low view of herself. I left her alone at the bar for a few minutes so I could dance with someone. She was being annoyed by some creep at the bar when Steve came to her aid and like Batman or something took out him and his friends.

"It was quite a wild scene for her first night out. I never really got to see much of him because he left before the police arrived. Megan said she told him he was her guardian angel. Anyway, he came around afterward and took her to dinner the night of the earthquake. He's been looking after her ever since and was the one who discovered Scott and his father had hired private detectives to spy on Megan."

"Private detectives? Scott did that?" Clare asked. "I can't believe it."

"Believe it. Steve actually took pictures of one

watching the house and last night arrived unexpectedly and gave the pictures to Megan to give to her attorney. You know she has Emily Lloyd. She's really tough in court when it comes to defending wives," Tricia said. "She was my divorce attorney. Steve brought Chinese food and we were having a fairly good time of it when Scott just burst in on us."

"I can't believe we're talking about the same Scott Lester," Clare said, shaking her head.

"Believe it," Tricia told her. "I was there. I saw it. He did scare the hell out of me."

They all looked down the hall as the elevator door opened for Steve.

"I was glad Steve was there. He is like Batman," Tricia said, smiling. She looked at the other two. "I wish he was around to come to my aid after my divorce. At least one good thing happened for Megan in this mess."

"I have something very important for you to do for me," Steve said the moment he entered the house.

His mother was sitting at the kitchen table sipping from what was now a cold cup of coffee, but too deep in her own thoughts to realize it. She looked up with an expression of surprise. It was as though she hadn't realized he had left this morning and didn't expect him to come in the front door.

"A policeman called here for you," she said. "You told me never to give anyone your cell number, so I said I didn't know it. What's he want?"

"I saw a traffic accident yesterday and told one of the drivers I'd be a witness. That's not what I mean. I have something more important for you to do for me now. Forget about all that.

"You hear me?" he followed when she didn't respond.

"What do you want, Steve?"

"I want you to read something over the phone. I'm going to make a call, see, and you'll read this to the person who answers. I'm sure it will be a woman."

He handed her a slip of paper. She read it and looked up sharply.

"What is this?"

"Just do what I say. It's important."

"I don't understand it," she said, looking at the paper.

"It's important. We need it done."

"Who's we? What is this?" She put the slip of paper down on the table. "And why did you lie to me about your job being done? Mr. Lowenstein called and said to tell you that he would make it impossible for you to get a job anywhere in California. What did you do? Why is he so angry? Why did you lie?"

"I'll tell you why. He gave me a chicken-shit job for lousy money where I had to do the work of two men. It was backbreaking and I told them to shove it."

She stared at him a moment. She could read his face better than she could read her own sometimes.

"Why wouldn't you just tell me that? Why would you lie?"

"Because I know how you can get on my back for nothing and nag and nag. Forget about Lowenstein. I don't need him and he can't stop me from getting work when I want work. I'll be just fine. Now back to what I need you to do for us."

"Who's us?"

"My future family," he said, straightening up.

"What?" She looked at the note. "It makes no sense."

"Just do it. Later, you'll understand why and you'll be happy you helped."

He started for the phone.

"I just read this and that's it?"

"Exactly."

"You going to explain it more?"

"I will. Afterward," he said, and lifted the receiver. He looked at another slip of paper and then he began to poke the numbers.

"I don't know," she said. "This sounds crazy. Maybe you should call the policeman back first. I wrote his number down there by the phone."

He stopped and looked at her.

"I told you that's not as important. Are you going to help or not? It's not a big deal, but I need a woman's voice. Well?"

"I don't like it."

He turned and slammed his fist on the counter so hard that the dishes and silverware lying there jumped. She winced. She knew how he could fall into an uncontrollable rage. When he was a child and didn't get what he wanted, he would scream and cry until he turned blue and even then continue. Her husband would let him go on and on, but she'd known if she didn't do something, he would literally suffocate, so she'd usually given in. That would trigger another fight with her husband and make him even more angry at Steve as well.

"Take him to see a head doctor," he would tell her after he calmed down. "He ain't normal."

"He's just a little boy," she would say. It wouldn't be until years later that she would regret not following her husband's advice. Steve's temper had grown even worse as he became older.

"I don't understand why I'm saying this on the phone," she protested.

"I told you. Later, I will explain it." His face lost some of its fury and redness. "You don't know it now, but you'll be helping to save a woman and a little girl. Okay? Okay?" he hammered.

She looked at the note again and then nodded.

"I hope you're not getting us into some terrible mess."

He returned to the phone and made the call. As soon as he heard the secretary say, "Scott Lester's office," he handed his mother the receiver.

She looked at it and at the note, and he jerked the receiver harder at her, almost smacking her in the jaw with the mouthpiece.

He held it as she read.

"Would you please tell Mr. Lester that she wants her rag doll. He left it in his car and she's getting sick over it. Please."

He pulled the receiver away and hung up. Then he took a deep breath and smiled.

"That's was good, Mom. You did that real good."

"What did I do?"

"I told you. You helped save a young woman, a wonderful young woman and her beautiful little daughter. Thanks."

"That don't tell me anything, Steve. What's going on here?"

"I have no time to talk now," he said.

He turned and started for the front door.

"Wait a minute," she called to him, and stood up. "I'm not going to sit in here thinking about all this. You stop what you're doing and explain everything—and I mean everything, Steve Wallace."

He looked at her and then smiled.

"It's okay. I told you. I met someone wonderful and I am getting a new wife and a new family. So, if you'll just relax and let me do what has to be done, it will all work out great." He started to turn away again.

"Just wait one minute."

"What now?"

She hesitated and then she walked past him and into his bedroom.

"What the hell are you doing?" he called.

She stepped back out with Ed Marcus's wallet in her hand.

"Explain this," she said.

He looked at it, and then with renewed rage in his face, he looked at her.

"You went searching through my room? Through my things, my pockets?"

"You've been acting pretty peculiar. I wanted to see if there was anything to tell me what's going on, especially since you don't. Now what about this? Is this the real reason that policeman called for you?"

He started to reach for it, but she pulled her hand back.

"Well?"

"I found it," he said. "I forgot all about it," he

added. He actually had forgotten, but he never thought she would go through his pockets. "You have no right to search through my stuff like that. I'm not some stranger, some little kid."

"You found it? Where?"

"Where I worked," he said. "I wasn't going to turn it over to that project boss. He was ripping me off, so I knew he would keep all the money and throw it away."

"You're lying again," she said.

"Don't tell me I'm lying!" He stepped toward her. "Give that to me now."

She shook her head and went to the kitchen table.

"It's why the policeman called. I know it is."

"Ma!"

She lifted the newspaper and opened it to point to a story.

"This man, the man whose wallet this is, was murdered in West Hollywood. They say he was struck so hard, his skull was smashed. You weren't working in West Hollywood, Steve."

He said nothing. He walked toward her slowly, his eyes narrowed into slits. She held her breath. This was a face she hadn't seen on him, a face she couldn't quite read.

"Give me the wallet," he said in a hoarse whisper.

"Did you steal this man's wallet? Did you hit him?"

He jerked his hand at the wallet and seized it, but to his surprise, she didn't let go. For a few moments, they were in what anyone would call a silly tug-of-war over it. He was amazed at her strength and determination and, frustrated, pushed her under her chin to get her off balance. She released the wallet, but she fell backward and struck her head on the edge of the kitchen table. The blow was so sharp and hard, it spun her around so that she fell face forward to the floor. For a long moment, he just stood there looking down at her, waiting for her to start to get up.

The sight before him seemed to throw him back years. He was like a little boy again, terrified at what punishment something he had done would bring. The strength and tightness went out of his shoulders and arms. He felt himself wither. His eyes began to tear basically out of fear and not out of sympathy or concern for his mother. His lips trembled as he struggled to form the words.

"Mom . . . are . . . you all right? Huh?"

She didn't move. As he started to kneel, he saw the tiny streams of blood beginning to jerk and crawl over the tile floor. Gingerly, he reached out and turned her over. Her eyes were wide open, as was her mouth, but she looked unconscious. How could she be unconscious with her eyes open? He pinched her chin gently and turned her head. The gash in her right temple looked like a bullet hole. The blood was gurgling.

"Ma!" he screamed, and shook her.

Her eyes didn't change, but her mouth closed a little. He checked for a pulse and then the shock of what he realized hit him in the solar plexus. He gasped for breath and fell back on his rear, staring at her in disbelief.

Slowly, he regained his composure and got to his feet. He stood there looking down at her. There was no sense in calling for paramedics, no sense at all. He looked at his watch. He had to go. He would deal with this later, he thought. There just wasn't any time to go through all the rigmarole, the paperwork, the interrogation, all of it. It would easily take the rest of the day and who knew if it would end there?

No, he had to go.

He started out again and then paused at the doorway to look back at her.

"What a shame," he said. "You could have finally been a grandmother."

Scott's attorney, Taylor Stewart, was waiting at the police station. He was on the cell phone and didn't see Scott and his father enter. Ironically, Scott, who was at first annoyed that his attorney was probably on another case at the same time, realized his lawyer wasn't behaving much differently from the way he himself behaved. How many times had he been about to begin a business meeting and on his cell phone talking about another project? It's the nature of who and what we've all become, he thought, suddenly turning philosophical.

It's part of what about me annoyed Megan so much.

As if his entire past few years were on replay, he heard her say countless times, "You're not listening to me, Scott. You're mind's somewhere else. Isn't any of this important, or at least as important as some deal your father's hatching?"

"Taylor," Scott's father said loudly enough to serve as a whack on the back of his head.

The attorney quickly ended his call and shoved his cell phone into his pocket.

"Sorry, Gordon," Taylor Stewart said, and shook his head at Scott. "This is a helluva mess. Before we go in there, is there anything you want to tell me? The worst thing is for your attorney to get caught by surprise."

"Everything is what I told you," Scott's father said, speaking for him.

"All right. Let's see what they want and what they have," Taylor said, and led them to the examination room where Detectives Parker and Foto waited with a tall, slightly gray-haired man.

"This is Agent Bindle from the FBI," Detective Foto said. "He's observing today, but the FBI will be the lead agency on the matter."

"Very good," Taylor Stewart said, and introduced himself to Bindle.

Scott didn't wait for any introductions or small talk.

"Is there any news about my daughter?" he asked.

"We're working on it, Mr. Lester," Parker said.

"Just a few questions here to help us structure the situation," Foto added, opening his notepad.

"That's a new way to put it," Taylor Stewart said. "What, you guys go to some new class in interrogations?"

Neither detective so much as smiled and Bindle looked like he had a face made of stone. Everyone sat.

"Let's review what you told us, Mr. Lester," Parker began. "You admit you went to the house and expressed anger, even uttered a threat, the night of the attack on your wife and the abduction of your daughter."

"It wasn't exactly a threat."

" 'You'll be sorry. In the end you'll be sorry,'" Parker recited.

"Depends on the tone," Taylor Stewart said, shrugging. "It could very well be simply a prediction the speaker doesn't necessarily wish to see occur. Instead of a threat, it might be a concerned person's warning."

"One of the witnesses, Tricia Morgan, who heard him say it, verifies the tone," Foto said. "We're chasing down the second witness."

"We have verified your being at this bar in West Hollywood and the time is approximately what you described," Parker continued, totally ignoring Taylor Stewart. "But is there any way you can confirm where you were after you left?"

"I told you. I went to my father's house where I'm staying. Everyone was already asleep."

"I thought you said you returned to the house first and saw your wife still had a visitor," Foto reminded him.

"Yes, that's true."

"Did you wait for him to leave and then enter the house?"

"No. Absolutely not. I went to my father's house."

"Mr. Lester, you hired a private detective, Ed Marcus, to keep your wife under surveillance," Parker continued, reading from his notepad.

"Who was murdered a few nights ago," Gordon Lester interjected, directing himself at Agent Bindle.

"You can remain here, Mr. Lester, but please don't offer any comments or answers," Foto said sharply.

"What about his hiring a private-detective agency?" Taylor Stewart asked. "It's not uncommon in divorce cases."

"After Mr. Marcus's death, you kept the agency on the job. You hired one of his assistants, Bob Anderson?"

"Yes," Scott said.

"But the night you arrived at the house and either threatened or warned your wife, you had already discharged this private detective?" Foto asked.

The way he asked the follow-up clearly illustrated they had planned their roles in the interrogation.

"My wife had discovered she was being watched. I was unhappy with Anderson," Scott said.

"You had no other reason to keep someone from watching the house and your wife?" Parker asked.

"Why didn't you replace Anderson, if it was so important?" Foto followed quickly.

"What, are you two practicing to become prosecutors?" Taylor asked. "Obviously, not much time had passed and Mr. Lester was considering other agencies."

"Were any called?" Bindle asked, finally illustrating he was a living person and not some law-enforcement statue.

"If I might speak," Gordon said. "I did call a friend for some new recommendations. His name is Philip Raymond."

"But you did not?" Parker asked Scott.

"I was depending on my father," Scott said, sounding somewhat ashamed of it.

"Okay. Let's move on here," Parker said.

"Good idea," Taylor quipped.

"There were no other fingerprints on the statue besides yours, your wife's and your maid's."

"So the perpetrator wore gloves," Taylor said. "Do I have to do your work for you too now?"

"Your maid says nothing of any value—besides your daughter, of course—has been taken from the house? Money was easily found, but was untouched. Your daughter's rag doll is missing, as is her blanket."

"Assailant sounds pretty concerned for the kid," Bindle commented. "He had to know what would comfort her."

Scott said nothing.

"No one has called you to ask for a ransom, correct?" Agent Bindle followed.

"No, no one has called yet or I would have called Detective Parker or Foto and I would assume they would have called you."

"Did you drive here in your car today, Mr. Lester?" Foto asked Scott.

The questions seemed so off the point, it took Scott by surprise for a moment. He looked at Taylor Stewart.

"What of it?" Taylor asked.

"It's out there in the parking lot?"

"Yes."

"Do you have any objection to our looking in your car?"

"For what?" Taylor asked. "Forensic evidence that his daughter was in the car? Give me a break."

"Mr. Lester?" Parker asked, again ignoring Taylor Stewart.

"Of course not," Scott said, and handed him the car keys.

"Just a minute," Taylor said. "You have—"

"We have at least a good argument for a warrant, Taylor. Mrs. Lester set her alarm and it wasn't triggered. There are no signs of a break-in and nothing material was stolen. Mr. Lester is in what has become an unpleasant divorce action. He can't offer a witness to his whereabouts during the time of the attack. He threatened or warned his wife that night. He hired and discharged a private detective watching the house that night. He—"

"Let them look, forcrissakes," Scott said. "The faster I get cleared of this, the sooner they'll get serious about my daughter's kidnapping."

"I'll go with you," Taylor Stewart said, rising.

Everyone but Scott and his father left the interrogation room. The moment the door was closed, his father turned to him.

"You didn't have anything to do with this, did you, Scott? There's nothing you're not telling me, is there?"

"Are you out of your mind, Dad?"

"You've been behaving strangely since this whole thing began."

"In your eyes, maybe. I've been having second thoughts. I'm not purely innocent here."

"What's that mean?"

"I haven't been the husband and father I could be, should be. Unfortunately, I've been too much like you."

"What the . . . ? You're just like your mother, not like me. You're in this situation because you didn't stay firm with Megan. Why'd you carry on like some embarrassed cuckolded husband, and in front of witnesses? Why'd you go and hire and fire that detective when I told you I'd handle it? And why'd you have to go and cry in your booze at some joint that night? If you would have just come home with me and—"

They looked up as all four men returned.

"That was quick," Gordon Lester said, figuring the blind alley would end it all, but he didn't see glee in Taylor Stewart's face.

"Can you account for why this was in your car on the floor in the rear?" Detective Foto asked, and held up Jennifer's rag doll.

CHAPTER THIRTEEN

From the expression on Emily Lloyd's face when she entered the hospital room, Megan knew something terrible had happened. She was eating some soft food. Clare was standing by the window looking out, but turned when she heard footsteps.

"This is my attorney, Clare," Megan said. "Emily Lloyd."

"How do you do," Clare said softly.

Emily took a deep breath.

"What?"

"Scott was formally arrested an hour ago, Megan."

"Oh, my God," Clare said.

"And Jennifer?"

"No news yet about her, but it can't be far behind," Emily said, settling into the chair by the bed as if she might faint if she didn't. "I like winning, but not this way. I'm sorry."

"How? Did he confess?"

"No. As I understand it, they found Jennifer's rag doll in his car and you had told the police it was missing with Jennifer. Aside from her, the doll and her blanket in fact, nothing else was missing."

Megan lowered her head.

"There's more," Emily said. Megan looked up. "Apparently, Scott's secretary received a call from a woman who sounded terribly frantic. She had a message for her to give to Scott. That was how the police located the rag doll."

"What message?"

Emily hesitated.

"What message!"

"She said Jennifer wanted her rag doll. Scott had left it in the car and, according to the caller, Jennifer was getting sick over it."

"Oh, my God."

"I'm sorry, Megan," Emily said. "You would have heard it soon enough. It will be on the news shortly, I'm sure. I got the call on my way up here to see you."

"Was it enough for the police to locate Jennifer?" Clare asked.

"They're on it. Perhaps Scott has told them by now," Emily Lloyd said. "Thank goodness he had someone working with him who was not a professional kidnapper. Have you any idea who she could be?"

Megan shook her head. Her eyes filled with tears. She took a deep breath and sat back. Clare stroked her arm and then put an arm around her shoulders.

"How can you live with someone so long and not know him?" Megan asked.

"I wish I had a dollar for every time I heard a woman say that to me," Emily replied. "Are you married, Clare?"

"Yes. Twenty-eight years," Clare said. "Happily, I might add."

"Some women are simply lucky," Emily said. "I'll be speaking with Scott's attorney later this afternoon, Megan. I suspect most, if not every, barrier for delay or whatever will be dropped rather quickly. All of it will end soon. Now, how are you? What does the doctor say?"

"I can leave tomorrow if I promise to behave. Fortunately, no damage inside my dumb head beside the concussion. Clare is staying with me for a while," she added, smiling at her sister.

"I'd like to be here when Jennifer is returned, too," Clare said.

"I'll call the moment I hear anything more. I have good contacts with the police. Unfortunately, some of my other divorce cases have involved them.

"But nothing like this," she quickly added. "Threats, some property damages, that sort of childish nonsense."

She rose.

"Thanks, Emily."

"Don't worry. Years from now you'll look back at all this and think, What a miserable time."

Clare laughed. Megan tried to smile, but the ache in her heart wouldn't cooperate with her face. She just nodded. Emily squeezed her hand gently and then started out.

"I'll walk you out," Clare offered. "I need some air. You don't mind, do you, hon?"

"No, no, go ahead," Megan said. "I'll still be here when you return."

She watched them leave, imagining how heavy the conversation about her would be, how hard it was going to be for her later and what a shock to the system this conclusion would bring. Then, there was all that rehabilitation to be done with Jennifer. Here they were, one of the wealthiest families in Beverly Hills, ironically suffering far more than some of the poorest in Los Angeles—or anywhere, for that matter. What did money troubles have over this?

She closed her eyes. *How do I gather the strength? Where will it come from?* Clare, Tricia, her other girl-friends would all be supportive, but they couldn't be with her night and day. They wouldn't be there for the lonely hours, the dark hours. They wouldn't be reliving the happier memories, early memories of a time that had held so much promise. What was left to believe in?

The ringing of the phone jarred her, and for a moment she lost her breath. Then she reached for the receiver, imagining it would be either Tricia or one of her other girlfriends. The news was probably singeing ears like streaks of lightning. Before the day was over, it would be topic A of all conversations in Beverly Hills.

"Hello," she managed in a much smaller, weaker voice.

"I blame myself for this," he began.

"Steve?"

"I shouldn't have left you that night. I should have planted myself outside your house and kept watch, at least. It was my responsibility, especially after I saw the anger in his face and how he was treating you."

"That's silly, Steve. You had no obligation to—"

"Yes, I did. I told you I would watch over you, protect you, be your guardian angel," he said. "But

I'll make it up to you, Megan. I'm on this. If the police don't find Jennifer immediately, I will," he vowed.

"But how can you—?"

"You don't think about it. I can do a lot more than you think."

"Don't get yourself into any trouble, Steve. I seem to be bad luck for people."

"Not me," he said. "For me you are only good luck. I'll be in touch. Just hang in there and don't get depressed. You have a family that will depend on you," he added.

She didn't know what to say. Family?

"I have a daughter," she said. "I know I'll have a lot to do with her. Where will I get the strength?"

"I'll be there," he insisted. "You'll get it from me."

The conversation was giving her a little headache. She was still not over the blow resulting from the news Emily Lloyd had brought.

"I've got to rest now, Steve. Thanks for the call."

"You don't have to thank me for anything, ever," he said.

She heard him hang up and then she did. Her thoughts began whirling, making her dizzy. She felt a little nauseous again, too, and pushed the buzzer for the nurse.

"Where will I get the strength?" she muttered to herself.

She grimaced, reviewing Steve's assurance. He's just being nice, she thought.

But how weird for someone to be so nice, so dedicated, so willing to sacrifice so quickly. Education, refinement, social graces and wealth did not guarantee the quality of anyone. In any line-up, without any further information about the men standing before her, she would most likely choose Scott over Steve.

Men. I guess Emily's right. We'll never understand them.

All this had taken much longer than he had anticipated. He didn't want to risk getting a speeding ticket. He had seen and read enough detective stories to know how police could place a suspect at a scene when they had information like speeding tickets or parking tickets. He followed the line of traffic, taking great care not to attract any highway patrolmen. A yellow Corvette certainly stood out, but he was sincerely worried about Jennifer locked up in the boat. He had left her enough water and food, and she had a bathroom to use as well as a television set, but for a little girl to be in such a strange place alone was surely a frightening experience. He would make it up to her tenfold. In time she wouldn't even think about it.

When he reached La Jolla, he pulled off the freeway and searched for that quaint shop he had visited with his mother last year. It was one of those hard-to-describe stores that sold antiques, incense and candles, all sorts of old pictures, including framed needlework pictures, beautiful diaries and notepads, ribbons and, he remembered, old-fashioned dolls. He had to replace the rag doll.

Unfortunately, as a side effect, his finding the store brought his mother to mind. When he had taken her here, it had been one of the happiest days that they had spent together in years, maybe the happiest day since his father's death in fact. He'd taken her for a nice lunch and then a short ride on his boat to finish up the day. The only sour point occurred when she'd asked him where Julia had been on the boat when she fell off and drowned. He'd told her he hated thinking about it and asked her not to talk about it. That had worked, and they returned to enjoying each other and the wonderful weather.

Now she was lying dead on her own kitchen floor. It was her own fault, though, he told himself. If she hadn't poked around in his room, in his personal stuff, she would never had found that wallet. Of course, that was a blunder, one of his first. He should have tossed the wallet after he took the money, but he thought he might need the information later to prove things to Megan. Blunder, and now what? His mother was dead. Granny was gone.

He wasn't going to think about it. He would deal with it later, when everything else was accomplished. Surely he would find a way to handle it perfectly. Except for the wallet, he had done everything else perfectly, hadn't he? Deep within him, he realized his mother might not have accepted it all anyway. This was probably for the best.

He got out and went into the store to find a rag doll as close as possible to the one Jennifer had. He panicked when he saw none, but the teenage girl behind the counter said there were three and showed him where they were located. One did look close enough, so he bought it and some old-fashioned all-day suckers, too. She would be a happy little girl soon enough, he thought, and got back into his car to continue the journey to his boat.

What he had done was taken the boat out a ways and anchored it so no one passing by on the dock would hear a little girl crying or screaming. It was only natural for her to do that until she realized what a better father he would be for her. He had a dinghy on the boat, so going back and forth was easy.

The only one who knew him at all at the dock was a Mexican fisherman, Rosario Sanchez, who made his living mainly by taking gringos out to deep-sea fish. Their conversations were restricted mainly to the weather, the sea, the routes he liked into Mexican waters and equipment. Sanchez was even better than he was when it came to servicing and fixing engines.

When Steve arrived, he saw Sanchez setting up two men to go out with him. While the men settled themselves in, Sanchez walked over as Steve loaded the dinghy. He was a short, stocky man with thick black hair he kept tied in a ponytail. He had grown up in Cabo and came from a family of fishermen. He'd told Steve he had salt water in his veins instead of blood.

"Hola, Steve," he said. "I caught me two live ones this morning," he added, nodding at the tourists on his boat.

Steve looked and nodded, but kept loading his supplies into the dinghy.

"You going out for a while, *si*?"

"A while, but not right away," he replied. "Any weather coming up?"

"No, *es perfecto* right now, but maybe later.

There's a storm wants to visit from the south. So why you anchor out instead of in your slip?"

"Checking some things," Steve said.

"Things? What things?"

"Things," he replied sharply. He nodded again at Sanchez's boat. "You'd better attend to business."

"Oh. *Si.* Well, have a good day, Steve."

Steve grunted but turned his back on him.

Sanchez shrugged to himself and returned to his boat and his tourists. The man was never much of a talker, he thought, and in his heart, he did not trust men who were so penurious with their words and thoughts. Sanchez watched him, however. Before he set out with his tourists, he saw Steve leave the dock and headed for his boat.

Steve gave his Mexican neighbor little thought. His mind was solely focused on Jennifer now. He was convinced that once he was able to get her on deck and she saw how exciting it was to be out there, she would become one happy little girl. After all, this was how he wanted Megan and him to honeymoon—on his boat, touring the Mexican Riviera.

Jennifer would love it as well. Maybe they would get a place in Cabo or even farther south and spend summers there. There were all sorts of new possibilities on the horizon. If Julia had agreed to have a family, he would have looked for such a getaway for them, too. What that woman lost she would never know, he concluded as the sea spray reached his face.

It seemed to wash away all his troubles and open the sky above to wondrous sunshine and hope, but when he tied up at the boat and boarded, he was surprised not to hear a sound coming from where he had left Jennifer. He had at least expected to hear the television going. It would keep her company and he knew kids her age liked to watch television anyway. He loaded on the supplies as quickly as he could and then made his way to the master stateroom, in which he had left her.

He listened for a moment and then unlocked the door. Jennifer was sprawled on the bed face-down, hugging one of the big pillows. When he had rescued her from the troubled house in Beverly Hills, he had kept his face masked. She had not seen enough of him to know who he was. He'd wrapped her in her blanket and tied it securely with the rope. He'd pulled off the pillowcase from her pillow and tied it gently around her face. He'd grabbed the rag doll. She was crying and screaming, of course, but he hadn't tried to calm her down—there was no time for that. He had put her over his shoulder and made his way carefully down the stairs and out the door to the garage. He had been cautious and very careful about the way he carried her to the car. She'd flailed about, but he was able to secure her quickly and drive off.

During the trip, he had played the radio loudly to drown out her screams and eventually she grew hoarse and exhausted and actually fell asleep. It had been easier then to get her onto the boat and into the stateroom. With his face still masked, he had untied her.

She'd woken up and had been too frightened to cry or scream. She had just watched him move about, setting up her food and water. He'd handed her the television remote and, still without speaking, left the stateroom, locked the door and driven back to Los Angeles.

Now he saw no more reason to be covering his face. He stood there looking at her sleeping peacefully. Look at how safe and content she appears already, he thought. He cleaned up the dishes and replaced the food, including a nice chocolate cake this time. He checked the bathroom and then watched her slowly wake up. He smiled down at her and she stared, her recollection of him obviously returning.

"How are you doing, Jen?" he asked. He knew Megan called her Jen.

"Where's my mother?" she asked.

"She'll be coming along soon."

"Did you bring me here?"

"Yes, I did. Sorry if I frightened you."

"Why did you bring me here?"

"It's my boat and now it will be your boat too. We're goin to go to lots of nice places and see wonderful things and you'll learn how to fish and even steer the boat. How's that?"

"Where's my mother?"

"I told you. She's coming. Meanwhile, do me a favor and put on this sweatshirt for a while. I need your pajama top."

"Why?"

"Got to show your mother you're okay, don't we? Otherwise, she might not want to come—and you want her to come, don't you?"

"Why does she have to know I'm okay first?"

"That's what a mother always needs to know. Is my baby okay? When you're a mother, you will have to know the same things. So will you let me have the pajama top?"

Jennifer nodded.

"Great. Here," he said, offering the sweatshirt. "It's a nice one. See? It says, 'Sailor Girl.' That's who you are now—Sailor Girl. As I said, I'm going to show you how to steer this big boat and fish for huge fish. You can swim off the boat, especially when we go into nice lagoons, and we can fly kites off the deck. You'll see, we're going to do lots of great stuff."

"I don't want to be on the boat. I wanna go home," she said.

"Now don't say stupid things, Jennifer. You're too old now to say dumb things like that. You know what's been happening. You need a new home," he said. "Too many bad things happened in that old home.

"Here," he said again. "Give me your pajama top. Hurry up," he said a bit more sternly.

Reluctantly, full of suspicion and confusion, Jennifer sat up and unbuttoned her pajama top. He could see she was shy about it, so he smiled and turned his back.

"You're growing up fast. Lucky I came along now; otherwise I might have missed all the good things. It's an exciting time when a girl starts to become a young lady."

He turned back and saw her pull the sweatshirt down over her head.

"Thanks, Jen. I appreciate your help here."

He picked up the pajama top and folded it neatly.

"Sailors like us always tie things up and fold

things neatly," he said. "Got to keep shipshape. All right. We're going to be a while, so you have to continue to amuse yourself here. There's lots of goodies to eat, and guess what," he said, reaching into the bag from the store in La Jolla. He produced the rag doll. "I got some great lollipops, but most of all . . . ta daaaa! . . . a new one of these for you."

He handed it to her, but she didn't take it.

"I want my own," she said.

"Oh, you can't have that one for a while, Jen."

"Why not?"

"That's what is known as evidence now. It'll be a while before we get that back. In the meantime, you can use this one. She's a beaut, isn't she? Check her out," he added, pumping the rag doll at her.

Reluctantly, she took it and looked at it.

"Neat, huh?"

She shook her head.

"I want my own," she said, and put it down.

"Now that's what we call ungrateful, Jennifer. When children are ungrateful, adults have to punish them. You don't want that, so you had better change your mind fast."

He stared at her.

She started to sob silently.

"Yeah, girls are harder than boys," he muttered. "All right. For now, I'll just leave you to yourself to think about your ingratitude."

He went to the door.

"You behave now," he said, and walked out, closing the door behind him. He locked it again, stood there thinking a moment and then, with the pajama top in his hands, returned to the dinghy.

He could see Sanchez pulling out with his two

tourist fishermen. The Mexican saw him as well and waved. He didn't wave back.

He was still in a bit of a sulk at Jennifer's ingratitude.

He calmed himself by recalling that she was a child and she didn't know, couldn't know, all that he had done for her already and would soon do for her.

He'd get that smile back on her face.

Or else, he thought.

The dark possibility that perhaps he had to begin with a new child faster than he had planned crossed his mind. He looked back at his boat as he pulled away and slowed up. Maybe it was a mistake to bring Jennifer along in his new life. He played with the idea of turning around and returning to the boat. It tempted him for a few moments and then he looked down at Jennifer's pajama top and thought, No, this will work.

It will be fine.

It's meant to be.

He headed for the dock to finish what he had begun.

Scott stepped out of the courthouse with his father and Taylor Stewart.

"I have to tell you," Stewart told them both, "that this isn't a result of my great lawyering as much as it is of the FBI's intent to find your daughter. You're out, but your phones are being tapped, including your cell phone for sure, and you'll be under constant surveillance, Scott. As your attorney, I have to advise you that if you have any more information as to the whereabouts of your daughter, you should bring it forward now. If it comes later as a result of any of this—"

"I didn't attack Megan and take my daughter," Scott insisted. "I'm being set up."

"You can't blame it on your wife. She didn't hit herself on the back of the head and put herself in the hospital," Stewart said. He waited for Scott to say something more and then turned to his father. "All right. I'll be in touch, Gordon."

"Right," Gordon Lester said.

They watched Taylor Stewart head toward his car.

"I can't believe we're standing here," Scott's father said. "That this is happening."

"You think I can? Do me a favor, Dad, switch cell phones with me."

"Why?"

"You just heard what Stewart said. My phone will be tapped."

"So? What do you have to hide?"

"I'm not hiding anything, but I need some room to maneuver. Please."

Hesitantly, his father gave him his cell phone. Scott handed him his and then headed away.

"Where are you going?"

He paused and turned back.

"To find my daughter, Dad. What I intended to do from the beginning of this mess."

"Scott . . ."

He kept walking.

"Don't get into any more trouble," his father shouted after him.

Scott got into his car and sat for a few moments. His father's remark felt like a sword to his heart.

From his earlier questions and his comments now, his father sounded as if he really suspected him. His own father! And he knew why. His father never thought he measured up to him. He always thought he was too weak or too soft, especially when it came to Megan. In his mind, this dastardly act would be something a whiner and a coward might do.

He turned and watched his father get into his car and drive off. Ironically, all this went far to convince him even more that Megan had been on solid ground with her criticisms. I was trying too hard to please my father, to be my father, he thought, and in the process, I've lost track of what is really important in my life. I've got to find a way to win that back. I will, he concluded, and started the engine.

But then he continued to sit there. It was all well and good to be determined, but where to begin? Who would attack his wife and want to take his daughter? Who put that woman up to calling the office and who put the rag doll in his car? He couldn't imagine anyone he knew to be capable of such a thing, and he certainly didn't have such a dedicated enemy. To be sure, there were people in the business community who didn't like him, probably mostly because they didn't like his father. But surely none of them would have any motive enough to come at him and his family this way.

The only really incongruous part of all this was the stranger who had come into Megan's life. It was important to know how and when. He had no time to rehire the private detective and wait for answers. He had to get them himself, he thought, and backed out of the parking spot. Twenty minutes later, he pulled into Tricia Morgan's driveway. Somehow, he had to get her to trust him enough with the truth.

He could see her car was there, but he had to ring the door buzzer three times to get her to come to open the door. She stood there looking at him, but not backing up to let him enter.

"What do you want, Scott?"

"I need a friend, Tricia, or at least the benefit of the doubt."

She didn't move.

"Look, I know I've screwed up, screwed up big-time, but you've known me for years, too. You must have at least some doubt of my being guilty of all this."

"Not from what I've been told."

"I'm being framed, Tricia, and the worst thing here is not my being framed. The worst thing is what might have happened or will happen to my daughter, to Megan's and my daughter."

"What do you want from me? I told the police all I knew."

He lowered his head. This was so hard. He had little respect for this woman, yet he needed her to have some respect for him, to look past his opinion of her, an opinion he did little to hide.

"I don't have any vicious enemies, at least not this vicious," he continued. "And certainly neither does Megan."

"So?"

"So I can't think of anyone who would do this to us."

"Except yourself?"

"This guy, this man she's been seeing, Steve whatever," he said, plowing on. "Who is he? How long has she been seeing him? What do you know about him?"

She smirked.

"I should have known that was where you were going. That way you can still blame stuff on Megan."

"No, no, that's not what I'm after, not at all."

She shook her head. He could see she was toying with simply closing the door in his face.

"What harm can it do now for you to tell me anything, Tricia?"

"Megan was not seeing Steve before she petitioned for divorce," she offered.

"Well, okay. Thanks for that. When did she begin to see him?"

Tricia looked away, pursing her lips.

"I mean how much do you know about this guy?"

"She met him at the Cage one night and he took her out to dinner. The night you saw him at the house was only the third time she met him, as far as I know."

Scott nodded, hoping for something more.

"He came to her aid at the bar the first night and punched someone."

"Punched someone?"

"Some creep who was bothering her. He's been supportive and concerned about her ever since. In fact," she added, putting her right hand on her hip, "he was the one who told her you hired private detectives to spy on her."

"Was he?"

"Yes. Okay?"

She started to close the door.

"Wait. Where can I find him?"

"All I know is his name is Steve Wallace. He's in construction work and lives with his mother in West LA. He tells great stories, but not that much about his personal life. At least he didn't to me."

"Do you have his address?"

"Of course not. He wasn't interested in me. He was interested in Megan. In fact, he sent her flowers almost as soon as she entered the hospital. He'd be the last person I'd suspect to hurt Megan. So you're going to have to look for some other patsy. If anything, he's tried to be her guardian angel," she said, and then slammed the door in his face.

CHAPTER FOURTEEN

"I need you on the case again," Scott told Bob Anderson the moment he answered. Scott had remained in Tricia Morgan's driveway to make the call.

"Mr. Lester?"

"Yes."

"You're all over the news. This is quite complicated now. I don't want to get in the middle of a police investigation, especially one involving the FBI."

"What I want you to do is quite simple and I'm not asking you to withhold any information you discover or anything you and I discuss or will discuss."

"What is this 'quite simple' thing?"

"I need you to locate a man. All I have is his name and that he's in construction, but he lives in Los Angeles, somewhere in West LA. Lives with his mother."

"A man in construction. You mean a contractor?"

"I'm not sure if he's a contractor. His name is Steve Wallace."

"A contractor at least has a contractor's license. It would be easier to locate him."

"I don't know."

"That's all you have?"

"He drives a yellow Corvette and a red pickup. He's about six feet one, one hundred and eighty pounds, I'd say. Light brown hair."

"This is quite a task, Mr. Lester. Do you have a license-plate number or at least a partial license-plate number?"

"No. Damn. I could have gotten that, but never thought to do so. I'm just not cut out for your kind of work or this kind of life."

"What year is the Corvette?"

"Looked like this year."

"Is there someone else who might know anything about him?"

Scott hesitated and then said, "My wife."

"Your wife? Oh. She's in the hospital, isn't she?"

"Yes."

"To be frank, Mr. Lester, I'd have thought you would hire me to help look for your daughter."

"That's why I need to know who this man is and where I can find him," Scott said, now not hiding his annoyance. "I didn't attack my wife and I didn't kidnap my own daughter."

"Well, this sort of assignment will take a while."

"I need the information tonight," Scott said. "I'm willing to triple your fee."

"But . . . Okay, when did you see this guy last?"

"I saw him in the hospital today. He was visiting my wife."

"Visiting . . . Well, if he attacked her and kidnapped her daughter, why would he be visiting her?"

"I don't know all the answers," Scott said, frustrated. "And I'm not asking you to do any more than locate this guy."

"Your wife won't tell you?"

"No. Do you think I'd be calling you if my wife would talk to me?"

"Do the police know about him?"

"I guess so. Megan should have told them. I mean, she might have told them about him. I can't say."

Anderson was quiet.

"There is something else," Scott realized.

"And that is?"

"My wife's girlfriend said he sent my wife flowers."

"In the hospital?"

"Yes."

"You know how many florists there are in Los Angeles?"

"Well, chances are he'd have used one in West LA, wouldn't he?"

Anderson sighed. Scott looked at his watch.

"Get me something within four hours and you've tripled your fee. Under two hours and I'll add a thousand-dollar bonus."

"She's at Cedars, right?" Anderson asked, his voice betraying his greed and interest now.

"Yes."

"Okay. I'll give it a shot."

"One other thing. According to my wife's girlfriend, this guy was in some sort of fight at the Cage in Beverly Hills recently. See if there's a police report."

"Oh, that could be something, Mr. Lester. You should have mentioned it first."

"I'm not exactly thinking clearly, Mr. Anderson."

"Understood. I'll get back to you."

Scott closed his cell phone and permitted himself to breathe again. A shelf of ominous-looking bruised clouds were sliding over the remaining blue sky. Shadows deepened and spread over the houses and the street behind him. He felt as if the world were closing in over him, felt like a man lying in a coffin but still alive. The lid was slowly being shut and no one could hear his screams and cries.

When he backed out of the driveway, he noticed the black automobile parked on the street because two men sat in the front, watching. Tricia would probably be getting a visit soon, he thought. They or another pair of detectives would want to know why he'd visited her, what he wanted. They might even think she was somehow in cahoots with him. That oughta make her feel really good about helping me at all, he thought, and drove off slowly. There was no sense in trying to lose them. That would only make him look more guilty anyway.

He couldn't get himself to return to the office. For now, he wanted to stay away from his father. He didn't want to go to his house either. What was he going to do? Drive around and around? Without really thinking about it, he found himself driving down his own street and stopping at his house. He saw the police tape across the front door. It was as if he had to see it to believe this wasn't all some nightmare. He had a great desire, a great need to go into the house, to seek comfort from its familiar surroundings, especially from his daughter's room, but when he looked at his rearview mirror, he saw the black automobile pull to the curb, the two men watching him. He imagined they were thinking the criminal always returns to the scene of his crime, maybe to cover up another clue.

Nothing I do will look innocent now, he thought. He felt so trapped. After he started his engine and pulled out, he decided to get something to eat. He had little appetite, but it was something to do, something to fill time while he waited and hoped Anderson would have something for him. His shadows were right behind him. Would they come into the restaurant, too, or just wait outside? What a lousy job they had, he thought, ironically feeling sorry for them.

Especially since I'm innocent.

Less than two hours later, his cell phone rang.

"I got you your address," Anderson said. "555 Brody Avenue, West Los Angeles. I was able to run some other data. Wallace did have a contractor's license, but it's expired. He's basically construction labor. There's an interesting detail however. I picked it up on a Google search actually."

"What's that?"

"Three years ago, Wallace's wife died in a boating accident. Fell off and drowned. He owns his own boat, a Cantiere di Lavagna Admiral 26, which is a good-sized yacht. It's in San Diego."

"Boating accident?"

"Yes. Maiden name was Julia Brooks. As I recall, she was about your wife's age at the time. That doesn't mean anything, I suppose. Just one of those interesting facts people like me pick up on. Routine investigation concluded it was an accident. They got caught in some bad weather.

"As to the incident at the Cage . . . Beverly Hills police do have a report, but Wallace wasn't mentioned. Apparently no one, not even your wife, could identify him. She might have been protecting him or she might not have known his name yet, I suppose. You can tell just so much from written reports. They're not exactly journalists."

"That's okay. I have what I need and you'll get your bonus," Scott said. "Thanks."

"You don't want me to do anything else, do a surveillance on this guy or anything?"

"I'll call you if I need anything more," Scott said.

He paid his restaurant check and started to get up, then stopped. The men following him hadn't come in, but he could see them across the street. Having them on his back was unnerving now. They could crimp his activity, stop him from doing much more. After all, there was no doubt in their minds that he was guilty.

An idea occurred to him. It would only do more to confirm their suspicions, but it made sense to him at the moment, and what was the risk? He couldn't change their minds about his guilt or innocence anyway. He rose and headed toward the restrooms in the rear, but once he was clearly out of their vision, he continued into the kitchen. The two chefs and their assistants looked up, surprised.

"Is there a rear entrance?" he asked. He knew there had to be one for deliveries.

No one spoke, but one of the assistants nodded his head to the left and Scott hurried to the door. It let out on a back street. He hurried down to the corner and turned right, making his way toward

Olympic Boulevard. He remembered a gas station nearby and went directly to it. Even before he reached it, he called for a taxicab. Ten minutes later, the taxi dropped him off in front of a rental-car office and he went in and rented a sedan.

He wasn't that familiar with the street address Anderson had given him, so he was lost for a while and then finally found it. Nearly a half hour later, he pulled up across from the Wallace house, a small one-story with that dull pink stucco that characterized most of the low- to middle-income homes in the area. He recognized the pickup truck and saw a 2000 Ford that had some rust stains and dents, but he saw no yellow Corvette in the driveway or on the street.

Now that I'm here, he thought, what the hell am I going to do?

Again, he was extra careful about his speed on the 405 Freeway. Except for his mother's stupid accident, everything had gone perfectly. Steve was always a believer in fate, in the idea that nothing is purely coincidental. All that had occurred involving Megan underscored this core belief. He saw patterns that made sense to him: He walks into a Beverly Hills hot spot for well-to-do men and women and finds himself directed immediately to Megan. The man who is annoying her provides an excellent opportunity for him to win her faith in him and eventually her love. Her difficult husband gives him the bigger opportunity by being so aggressive, hiring private detectives, barging in on her and threatening her.

It all was falling into place, just as some divine

design might. He had only one thing left to do: convince Megan it was all meant to be.

Yes, he was sorry about his mother, but maybe she would have been an obstacle, and fate knew that. Fate took her out of the picture, he decided. Later, he'd pretend to come upon her and then call the police and tell them he'd found her dead. He was away for a while and hadn't been in contact with her. Whatever. He wasn't worried about that anymore.

He glanced at Jennifer's pajama top and then ran his right hand over it gently. Once Megan sees this, he thought, she will be most cooperative and the rest will be easy. He could see the three of them together, planning their future. He'd work harder than hell to get them everything they wanted. He'd even put up with crummy jobs and obnoxious contractors. Every time something unpleasant occurred, he would simply think about Megan and Jennifer and overcome it.

His thoughts returned to the business at hand. A light drizzle had started. Sanchez had said there was some weather coming up from the south, but from what he had heard, it didn't promise to be too serious. He regretted that an increase in the wind would rock the boat a bit and imagined Jennifer might get a little seasick. Then again, maybe she won't, he thought. Maybe she was born to be on the sea, too.

The cloud cover had brought evening down faster. It seemed like a curtain falling all around him. Car lights were brighter, and at times during his trip the drizzle became more intense. He was riding in and out of the cloudbursts and had to adjust his speed accordingly. What more terrible thing could occur than his being in some sort of automobile accident now? By the time he exited the freeway for Cedars-Sinai Medical Center, however, the rain had all but stopped. In fact, off to the west, he could see a break in the clouds. That was promising. It was as good as a rainbow to him. Cheered, he drove on and finally pulled into the visitors' parking lot. With the pajama top under his arm, he hurried to the hospital's front entrance.

It wasn't until he was on Megan's floor that he realized there was a very good chance she wouldn't be alone. Her sister at least would still be there. When he walked by her room and glanced in, he saw that not only was her sister there, but Tricia Morgan and two other women were too. Megan didn't see him, but he had a good enough glimpse of her to conclude she was getting tired of her company. They wouldn't be there much longer. He had no choice, however. He had to go back to the lobby and watch the elevator, keeping himself as unnoticeable as possible. Nearly an hour later, Tricia and the two women stepped out of the elevator, and a good fifteen minutes later Megan's sister emerged. None of them saw him.

Now was his time, his chance. He watched her sister leave the hospital and then moved quickly to the elevator. Moments later, he was on her floor. He saw a nurse go into her room and he waited in the hallway. As soon as she left, he headed for the room. Megan had her eyes closed and was lying back on her pillow when he entered. She didn't hear him, but it wasn't long before she sensed he was there and opened her eyes.

It's no accident that she feels my presence, he thought. We're in tune with each other and will be forever.

For a moment she had no expression and then she realized who it was and gave him what he treasured: a small but warm smile.

"Oh, Steve. I didn't hear you come in. How long have you been standing there?"

He nodded. "Not long. That's all right. Do you have anything to wear?" he asked.

"Wear? What do you mean?"

"Wear. A dress, anything?"

She widened her smile.

"Why?"

"You're going somewhere," he said.

"Now?" She started to laugh.

"Yes and believe me, you're going to want to. You're going to want to very, very much."

She pushed herself up on her elbows.

"What is this?"

He took Jennifer's pajama top out from under his arm and handed it to her. She looked at it and then up at him quickly.

"This is Jennifer's."

"I know."

"How did you get it?"

"Do you have something to wear?"

"I have what I wore when they brought me here. It's in the closet," she said.

He went to the closet and took out her skirt and blouse.

"We'll get the rest of your clothes later," he said, turning back to her.

"What's going on, Steve? I don't understand.

How did you get this? Where do you want me to go?"

"I know exactly where Jennifer is," he said. "She won't be happy unless you come with me. You want to see her and comfort her, right?"

"Of course."

"Then trust me," he said, handing her the clothes. "I'll wait outside while you dress. Here are your shoes, too," he added, placing them by the bed. "We've got to move as quickly as we can."

"But . . . why don't we call the police?"

"Think of Jennifer. The police, guns, strangers. You don't want that, do you?"

She looked at him askance.

"Who took her? Was it Scott?"

"Everything will become so clear so quickly," he said. "Did I tell you more than once that I'd be your guardian angel or not? Haven't I been there for you? I'm here for you now. It's best if you get dressed and we leave without any fanfare. That will cause more commotion and more problems."

"I think I should call my sister," she said. "She can come along."

"No. She doesn't understand, couldn't understand, what you and I can do together. She'd only . . . create some confusion."

He looked at her sharply and then at the phone by her bed.

"I know what's best for us right now," he said, walked over to the phone, and ripped the wire out of the wall.

Her eyes nearly exploded.

"What are you doing?"

"I don't want you making any mistakes. I'll be

right outside the door. Hurry." He picked up the pajama top. "You want to see her right away, don't you? Well?"

Megan nodded, but felt her throat tighten. What was this?

He smiled, brushed her hair softly and then went to the door. He didn't close it completely, so she could see him standing guard.

Her guardian angel?

Or what?

She began to dress and couldn't help but feel a bit wobbly. Managing, however, she went to the door.

"What are we doing, Steve?" she asked, and he turned and smiled.

"You look just fine," he said. Then he took her arm. "We walk directly to the elevator as if nothing is unusual. It's perfect. Two of the nurses are tending to patients and the one at the counter is busy. Just walk."

"But where?"

"Don't ask questions right now," he ordered, his voice suddenly gruff.

He tugged her forward and she went along. She was feeling quite nauseous, not only from her condition, but from her tension and fear. He was correct about the nurses, however. No one noticed them go to the elevators and the elevator door opened almost immediately after he pushed the button. He practically pulled her into it.

She watched the doors close and then turned to him.

"What now, Steve?"

"Now? Now we go home," he said.

* * *

Scott got out of the rental car and slowly approached the front door. The house was totally dark, but maybe whoever was in the house was in the rear, in the only lit room or something, he thought, and then pushed the door buzzer. Tricia had said the man lived with his mother. Perhaps the Ford was hers. That could mean she would be home and could tell her where he was, at least. He waited and pushed the buzzer again. After the third time, he went to a front window and looked in.

It was dark everywhere inside, but lighting from the house next door threw enough illumination through side windows to outline some of the interior. He could see well enough down the hallway and into what looked to be the kitchen. He wasn't completely sure, but he thought he saw a woman's legs. She was lying on the floor. He waited to see if she would move, but she didn't. What was this? He remained there a while, listening for any sounds from inside. There were none.

He looked around. The neighborhood was very quiet—not a car nor a pedestrian. A slight drizzle had begun. The street took on a sheen, and from what he could see on the cross street, traffic was thinning out a bit. He was as good as a ghost . . . but what to do now?

He looked in the window again and strained to get a better view of the woman's legs, which still had not moved. He returned to the front door and tried the buzzer twice more with the same result. He knocked and called.

"Hello? Anyone home, please?"

There was no response.

He tried the front door, but it was locked, so he went around the left side of the house and came to what was a rear door. He tried this, but this door was locked, only not as securely, he thought. He rattled it and then, looking around first to be sure no one was watching, he hit the door with his left shoulder. He hit it three times before he heard the jamb crack. The door opened and no alarm sounded.

His heart was thumping. Here he could be caught breaking and entering, and on top of everything else, he'd look more like a lunatic than anything. He paused to be sure no one nearby had heard anything. His neck was wet from the light rain and also from his own nervous sweat.

What am I doing? he asked himself.

This is the only lead you have toward any explanation, he answered.

He entered the house.

"Hello?" he called. "Mrs. Wallace?"

He waited, heard nothing and moved through what was a small entryway and a back entrance to the kitchen. As quickly as he could, he found the light switch and flipped it. Then he stopped dead and froze like Lot's wife in the Bible. For a few long moments, all he could do was gape at the woman sprawled on the floor, a pool of blood around her head, the stream thinning out as it moved and stopped near her arm.

Except for a drip in the sink, there was no sound. If there was anyone else in the house, there was no sign he or she had heard him enter.

"Mrs. Wallace?"

He approached her and knelt beside her, taking her wrist into his hand. He didn't have to check for a pulse. One look at her glassy eyes told him she was dead. He put her hand down and looked closer at her head. The gash in her temple was ugly. He stood up slowly and listened. The house remained silent. Apparently, there was no one else there.

Of course, his first thought was to call the police. He had no idea what they would think, but this woman was dead. He wasn't sure how long, but it looked as if she'd been dead a while. He turned toward the wall phone and paused to look at a note on the table. Slowly, he lifted it to read it.

Would you please tell Mr. Lester that she wants her rag doll. He left it in his car and she's getting sick over it. Please.

It was as if the note were aflame, burning his fingers, and he dropped it to the table. He even took a step back. Those were the exact words Arlene Potter had quoted to the police, words meant to condemn him.

Who were these people? Why were they doing this?

Where's Jennifer?

He looked back at the dead woman and actually cried, "Where's my daughter?" Did he expect she would enjoy a resurrection, sit up and confess?

"Jennifer!" he screamed.

He went quickly through the rest of the house, turning on lights and looking for her. He opened closets, checked the bathroom, even pulled the shower curtain open to look at the tub. There was no evidence of her anywhere. Then he returned to the kitchen and reread the note as if he had to reconfirm what he was seeing was real.

He gazed at the dead woman.

How did she get that horrible gash in her head? Could he somehow, someway, be blamed for this, too?

He saw something else under the table. A wallet. He knelt down and picked it up. When he opened it, he felt the gasp in his chest as if he had developed a second mouth there.

Ed Marcus's wallet! They'd killed Ed Marcus, but here he was touching it. His prints were on it. He dropped it quickly.

He was certainly gun-shy when it came to the police. This woman didn't matter anymore anyway. She was dead. She couldn't tell him or the police anything about Jennifer or about Ed Marcus. But there was one thing he had to do. He had to call Megan to let her know what he had discovered. He had to get her to see he wasn't the monster she thought he was and that he was in pursuit of their daughter and her kidnapper, the man she apparently had trusted, who was obviously a murderer as well.

And what about this man and his mother? If neither he nor his father had yet received a ransom note, what was the point of attacking Megan and taking Jennifer? What were they dealing with here? Megan had to talk to him now, had to tell him more about this man.

He called the hospital and asked to be connected to her room. It rang and rang but she didn't pick up, so he hung up and called the hospital again, describing his inability to reach his wife. The operator connected him to the nurse's station on her floor.

"I've been trying to reach my wife," he said.

"Her phone rings but she doesn't answer. Is she all right?"

"She's fine. Let me check to see what's with her phone," the nurse said. "Hold on."

He waited what seemed like an eternity but was really only four or five minutes. When the nurse returned to the phone, he heard her note of panic.

"Your wife isn't in the room, Mr. Lester, and someone tore the phone out of the wall. I've called security and we're calling your wife's doctor."

"What? Oh, God," he said.

He hung up and spun around. For a few moments, he was unable to think, even to move. Fear and indecision planted him to the kitchen floor. The sight of the dead woman seemed to hollow out his heart. He took a deep breath and told himself to get a hold of himself. This was no time to have a panic attack, no time to be the son his father thought he was.

As calmly as he could, he reviewed the information Anderson had given him. One thing stuck in his mind: that reference to Wallace's wife, Julia, who had drowned, and her being Megan's age. Of course, it made no sense to dote on that coincidence. What was Wallace, a serial killer who only went after women of a specific age? But there was something about it, something else that could be a big lead.

The man had a boat, what Anderson had described as a yacht. People could live on yachts. That made the most sense right now, he thought. He went into what was clearly Steve Wallace's room and began a rigorous search of anything and everything. He was looking for one thing in particular and when he found some bills that gave him the dock information he sought, he charged out the same back door he had broken through and ran around to the front of the house.

The street was as quiet and deserted as before. The rain shower had stopped. It was as if all the houses had dead people in them. Maybe it was good that no one had seen him arrive and leave. Suddenly, though, a house door opened and closed. He heard a man and woman talking. They got into their car, backed out of their driveway and started away. He hoped neither of them had noticed his rental car. He had kept well in the shadows, so he felt confident they hadn't seen him.

It was only after he got into his car and started away, however, that he again realized his fingerprints were all over the place back there where a woman lay dead—on the wallet, the phone, everywhere.

Anyone would think he had killed her for revenge.

He almost wished he had.

CHAPTER FIFTEEN

Megan couldn't believe how exhausted she was by the time they reached Steve's yellow Corvette. He opened the door for her and then lowered the back of the seat so she could lie back. He returned to sounding soft and concerned, making sure she was comfortable and that she had her seat belt on. Then he hurried around, got in, started the engine and drove out of the parking lot. She kept her eyes closed and tried to get her bearings and drive down the nausea.

"Are you going to explain all this to me, Steve?"

"Oh sure. I knew from the very moment I set eyes on you, Megan, that you needed me," he said. "I certainly needed you," he added, turning to her and smiling. "You know, sometimes it just takes some people longer to find the one who they belong with. Many people, most in fact, make mistakes along the way. I did. My first wife was one big mistake. She had me fooled. I thought she wanted all the things I wanted.

"You want the same things I do, I'm sure," he said, turning to her as he sped toward the freeway entrance. "A good home, a family—the old American dream, white picket fence and all. I'm sorta old-fashioned when it comes to all that. I always saw myself coming home from a hard day's work, work I didn't mind, because it was bringing in the money I needed to provide well for my wife and kids, know what I mean?

"I know you know what I mean," he added before she could even think to respond.

"I don't understand. You said your wife was pregnant when she died."

"Did I? Well, I meant I wish she was pregnant maybe. Maybe then, she wouldn't have died."

"What?" Megan rubbed her forehead. "I'm so confused here, Steve. What does any of this have to do with Jennifer? How did you get her pajama top? Where is she?"

"She's waiting for us, Megan. She's safe. Don't worry about that."

"I don't understand," she said, starting to cry now. "Where is she? How did she get there?"

"You ever believe in fate, Megan, believe in destiny? I do. You ever hear a voice in your head, a voice you know comes from somewhere very powerful? Maybe it's the voice of God. Maybe it's the voice of fate, whatever. The point is, it's there inside you, talking to you, telling you what to do and when to do it, telling you how to take advantage of opportunities. Understand what I'm saying?"

"No, Steve. I don't understand anything you're telling me," Megan said. She watched them enter the freeway and speed up. "Where are we going exactly?"

"Exactly? San Diego. Remember my boat? We're going to my boat. Consider it a kind of honeymoon," he said. "No, not kind of, but really," he corrected.

"Honeymoon? What honeymoon? We can't be

going on a honeymoon. We're not married. Steve, please make sense. I'm very frightened and very confused. I don't want to go any farther until you explain. Stop the car, Steve."

"I don't like your tone of voice right now, Megan. I'm sure it's because you're still recuperating. You're just not thinking straight. Let's both calm down for a while. Don't ask any questions. Don't talk. Just close your eyes and rest. It will all become clearer soon enough."

"But—"

"Please. I don't want to talk for a while," he said. "I'm a little upset. I thought you'd be happier and have more trust in me. Well . . . maybe it takes a little getting used to, a little more time, but it will come."

He sped up and then quickly slowed down, remembering the risk associated with getting a speeding ticket. Megan was quiet. She embraced herself and tried desperately to keep from shivering, not from any cold air as much as from cold fear now running up and down her spine like an electric shock. What was she to do? Really, what could she do? Open the door and jump out at this speed? There was no way to call anyone for help now. How had this happened?

She looked at him. He was concentrating on his driving, chewing gum vigorously, the muscles in his jaw moving like creatures living under his skin. She closed her eyes. The pain and nausea were getting worse.

"I'm not feeling well, Steve," she said in a loud whisper.

He didn't respond.

"I think we should stop somewhere. I feel like I might throw up, Steve."

She didn't think he had heard her, but all of a sudden, he slammed the base of his palm against the dashboard.

"Damn it!" he cried, making her jump in the seat. "Jennifer is waiting for us, Megan. She's going to get frightened. The wind's up a bit."

"What?"

"I have the boat anchored away from the dock."

"Why? I don't understand what you're saying."

"Just get a hold of yourself, will ya? Jesus. You're really disappointing me, Julia."

"Julia?"

He looked at her.

"You're always thinking of yourself, damn it. Think of the family. Think of the family as a whole and not as separate people. My father never thought of his family as anything but a couple of burdens. You know, he once told me that if I hadn't been born, he'd have a good life. That's right. I was just a little boy, but I never forgot it because when he said it, I could see in his face that he was telling the truth, telling me what he really felt.

"How'd you like a father like that? Huh?"

She simply stared at him and then she began to dry-heave.

"Damn it!" he screamed again and pulled over to the side. Quickly, he reached across her and opened the door on her side. "Lean over and throw up if you have to," he said. "Don't throw up in the car."

She did. He didn't try to comfort her and he wasn't impressed with her being sick at all.

"You always get sick when I want to do something that's more like family. I wanted us to go to Disneyland, but you thought that was stupid. Why would two grown-ups go there? Right? What I wanted, see, was for you to see other couples with children, happy children, families enjoying being families, men and women realizing what they were made to be.

"You were afraid of that, weren't you? You knew once you saw it, you'd realize what a selfish bitch you were."

"Steve," she gasped. "I'm not Julia. You're confused. Look at me."

He said nothing. He sat there, panting like a dog, looking out the windshield at the passing automobiles. An idea occurred to her, a desperate idea, but one that she thought she had to follow. Slowly, she unbuckled her seat belt. She did it as quietly as she could. He was deep in his thoughts now and didn't see or hear her do it. When it was undone, she took a deep breath and then turned her body toward the open door and stepped out. Her movement caught him by surprise.

"Whaaa . . . ?"

She went around the rear of the car as quickly as she could and just managed to get her arms up to wave at the passing traffic, but the cars were going by so fast, their drivers couldn't have stopped if they wanted, and most didn't even see her before he rushed around to grab her and scoop her up and rush her back to the passenger's seat.

"Are you crazy? What are you doing? You want to cause an accident and bring attention to us or something? You know how long it would take us to get to Jennifer then?"

He pushed her firmly into the seat and buckled her seat belt, tightening it a bit. Then he slammed the door closed and stepped back, looking at her. She had her eyes closed and her head back. The activity effectively jolted him back to the present. He glanced at his watch and then quickly went around to get into the car and pull back onto the freeway. Now he would take the chance of getting a ticket, he thought, and sped up.

After a few minutes of weaving in and out to make better time, he looked over at her. She still had her eyes closed and now looked like she had passed out.

"I'm sorry, Megan," he said. "You just don't understand it all yet, but it's going to be all right. It's going to be fine. We'll be there soon and together, the three of us, together . . . forever."

He drove on, his confidence returning.

When they reached the dock, he pulled into a parking spot and poked Megan. She had fallen asleep.

"Where are we?" she asked.

"Almost home," he said. "We're getting out here. I have a dinghy moored just there," he said, pointing, and then pointed out to sea. "There's my boat. Beautiful, ain't it? Wait until you see how pretty it is inside and how modern, too."

The sky had cleared considerably with now only some puffs of clouds scattered toward the northeast. The sight of all the stars renewed him. If fate hadn't wanted this, the weather would have been as severe as it had gotten the day Julia died or had to die. Nature itself reconfirmed everything.

"C'mon," he said. "Jennifer's waiting."

He got out and went around to her side to open

the door and help her to her feet. She wobbled a bit, but gathered her strength as they made their way to his dinghy. She looked around for someone to call to, hoping beyond hope that maybe there would be a policeman about or some security personnel, but there was no one. Suddenly, a man appeared on the boat in the next slip. He was picking things up and closing and locking doors. The Spanish radio station he was listening to was quite loud. Shouting to him might be futile and who knew what reaction Steve might have to that. No, she had no choice but permit him to lead her forward and help her get into the dinghy.

As soon as she was seated, he untied it, started the small engine and aimed them toward his yacht.

The only thing that sustained her was the realization that soon she would have Jennifer in her arms again.

She couldn't even begin to imagine what would come after that.

Scott thought about calling his father at home. Primarily, he wanted to hammer down his innocence and make his father feel bad about even having any doubt about it, but he also wanted to show him that he was just as much a man of action as his father ever was. But then he realized his father would want him to go directly to the police and that all that time would be wasted explaining what he had done, how he had found things out and why he hadn't called them as soon as he had discovered a dead woman on the floor of her kitchen.

He was beyond this business between himself

and his father now anyway. He wasn't after his father's respect. Megan was missing. Why would she have left the hospital? It had to be that she had had no choice. What was the point of it all? He couldn't think of any reasonable motivation if a demand for money wasn't forthcoming. Unless . . . this guy thought he could get even more by kidnapping Megan, too.

The madness of what he was now attempting to do all by himself didn't occur to him until he was well into his drive to San Diego. For one thing, he had no weapon. He had seen this man, faced him. He looked strong, even vicious. Could he overpower him? What if he died trying? What would become of Megan and Jennifer? What would his father think of him then? He could almost hear the eulogy: *Just like my son to take things into his own incompetent hands and screw things up.*

These self-doubts were short-lived when he envisioned Jennifer in a state of abject terror. He had placed his wife and child in this jeopardy, he thought. If he hadn't been such a failure as a husband and a father, Megan would never have tried to cut him out of their lives, and she and Jennifer wouldn't be where they were now.

No, he wasn't going to run to his father for help, or to the police or anyone else for that matter. This wasn't simply an attempt to rescue his wife and child. It was an effort to rescue himself as well, rescue himself from all the inadequacies that had dominated his life and made him the sorry excuse for a man that he now believed he had become.

I'm not a James Bond or some cartoon character like Spider-Man, but I am a man and this is my responsibility, he told himself. He practically chanted it for another hour or so in the car and that chanting kept him strictly focused on what lay ahead. All hesitation was left behind, cowering in some dark shadow. In its place came his rage and indignation. It filled his veins with courage. He would do this thing.

What was it Tricia had told him in her doorway? The man was Megan's guardian angel?

Well that was what he would be now, what he should have been from the beginning.

He had to stop a number of times to get directions to the dock, and once he arrived, he had no idea how to find the exact slip. He looked about for some help, but saw no one until a man dropped something on his boat and then began to disembark. He hurried toward him.

"Excuse me," he shouted.

Sanchez Rosario turned and squinted. A man in a jacket and tie was jogging down the dock. When he reached him, he put his hands on his hips and gasped a few moments to catch his breath.

"*Qué pasa, amigo?*"

"I need help. *Habla inglés?*"

"Oh, yes. What help?"

"This slip number," he said, digging into his pocket. "*Dónde está?*"

"That's right there," Sanchez said, pointing.

"But the boat, yacht, whatever?"

"Oh, *si*. Mr. Wallace, he put his boat offshore. It was there," he said, pointing somewhere out in the ocean.

"Where is it?"

"Oh, he's gone off. Not long ago, I saw him get into his dinghy and go out to it."

"Did he have someone with him?"

"*Si*, he did. I think it was a woman," Sanchez added. "Maybe you can reach him on the radio or on a cell phone. Okay?"

"No," Scott said sharply. He looked at Sanchez's boat. "Can you take me to his yacht?"

"Take you?" Sanchez started to laugh. Scott reached into his pocket and drew out his wallet. He had six fifties, seven hundreds and six fives.

"I'll give you all this," he said.

Sanchez looked at the money, counted it mentally and then started to shake his head.

"I'll give you a thousand dollars more. Two thousand," he added when Sanchez just stared at him. "Here's my driver's license. I am a wealthy man. You hold onto the license and tell the police if I don't give you the money."

Sanchez looked at the license, the cash and Scott.

"You have a credit card?"

"Yes, sure," Scott said and took out his cards. "Whatever card you like."

"Okay. I take credit cards. I take people fishing." He plucked the Visa and Scott's license. "I'll write your license number on the card."

"Yes, yes, do whatever you want, only let's get started. How long ago did they leave?"

"He left about fifteen, maybe twenty minutes ago. I don't know if we can catch them. I can't guarantee—"

"I think you can do it," Scott said firmly. "Right?"

Scott put the money into his hand.

"Consider this a tip and charge another thousand dollars if you do catch up to the yacht."

Sanchez smiled. "If anyone can do it, I suppose I can," he said.

"Good. Let's go."

He started for Sanchez's boat.

"Why is this so important, senor?"

"My wife and daughter are on that boat," Scott said. "I think their lives are in danger."

Sanchez paused. "You should call the police."

"No time. Just get me to the boat," Scott said. "Hurry."

"Mr. Wallace, he did this? Took your wife and daughter?"

"Yes."

Sanchez nodded. "I can believe it," he said, and boarded the boat.

Scott waited until Sanchez got them underway.

"Why did you say you can believe it?"

Sanchez shrugged.

"My grandmother she had an expression: *el que mal hace, bien no espere.* Whoever does evil, do not expect something good. Mr. Wallace, he never trusts, never accepts a favor without waiting for the cost. He never expects something good, *comprende*?"

"Yes. Your grandmother is very wise."

"*Si.* She still lives and still teaches me."

"Someday I'd like to meet her," Scott said, and looked out into the darkness where his wife and his daughter waited for some miracle that he hoped he could bring them.

After Steve helped Megan board the boat, he tied up the dinghy and then led her slowly to the stateroom. She hadn't said a word. She was too terrified now to question anything he was doing. Her eyes widened when he took out keys to unlock the stateroom door.

"You locked her in there?"

"Just to make sure she didn't get hurt wandering about the boat," he said. "You know, a real father thinks about these things. A real father is always concerned about dangers for his children. I'm not saying he has to turn them into sissies, but he should be protective. My father practically told me to go out and play in traffic," he added, and opened the door.

Megan gasped.

The room was a mess, food wrappers everywhere. Jennifer, obviously in some state of shock, had her thumb in her mouth and was drooling. She was curled in a fetal position, but her whole body was shuddering as if she were experiencing an electric shock, and her eyes looked sewn shut.

"Jennifer!" Megan cried, and charged forward. She sat on the bed and lifted her, embracing her and holding her closely, rocking and kissing her forehead and cheeks. Jennifer's eyelids fluttered. "Oh, my darling, my baby, my Jennifer," Megan chanted through her own sobs.

"You guys get settled in," Steve said calmly from the doorway. "I'm getting underway."

Megan ignored him. She continued to stroke Jennifer's hair and kiss her cheeks, rocking her. Gradually, Jennifer started to come out of her tremors and her eyes remained opened.

"Mommy," she moaned.

"Shh, honey. I'm here."

"I want to go home," she said.

"Yes, honey. We will. As soon as we can."

Above, Steve got the yacht underway, but the wind had come up again and the waves were rougher, higher. He checked the weather report. It wasn't promising. The clear skies he had seen were a false hope. The storm that had ridden in from the southwest was still approaching. He had precious cargo now and he didn't want them to be unhappy. He didn't want to turn back, but he'd have to keep his speed down. Hopefully, they could reach Playas de Rosarito before it got too rough out here. Normally, it would be only two hours, but at this slower speed, it would take a little longer.

Once there, he would take them to great restaurants and shops and buy Jennifer something new to play with. As the weather improved, they would make their way farther down the coast on what he continued to believe would be his honeymoon. Sure, they were both upset right now. It was quite a sudden change, after all, but he remained confident that it would all turn out well, turn out just the way he had planned and dreamed it would. He flipped the radio dial to get some music and settled in comfortably.

Below, Megan could hear the music vaguely. She felt as if she had been dragged and dropped into a well of madness. She was swirling like someone caught up in a whirlpool. Her mind had to make a sharp turn from believing Scott had become some sort of monster to the realization that it was her so-called guardian angel who was the monster.

Jennifer rested her head on Megan's shoulder. She was falling asleep again, probably from emotional exhaustion. Who knew what he had put her through to get her here? Gently, Megan turned her and settled her back on the bed. She took deep breaths. What was she going to do? She was out at sea. She couldn't simply go up on the deck and start screaming for help. And what if she could somehow overpower Steve, something that looked as impossible as her flying to the moon? She didn't know how to navigate a yacht.

She buried her face in her hands. Think, think, she told herself, and concluded the only thing she could do was humor him, play to his madness. He was just crazy enough to buy it. Perhaps she could convince him that Jennifer needed medical attention and after that, he would bring them back ashore where she could get help.

The yacht was rocking quite a bit, however, and with her nausea and dizziness already started, it made it nearly impossible to stand, much less climb back up to the deck. But somehow she had to manage it. She steadied herself by holding her hand out and pressing against the stateroom wall. Then she left it and started to climb the short stairway. Twice she thought she was close to passing out and fought herself back to consciousness, but she worked her way up on her hands and knees and reached the deck. She saw Steve sitting comfortably in his captain's chair and also saw how alone they were out to sea. The clouds above turned it all into a world of darkness with only some lights visible here and there through the fog.

When she rose and made the turn to get to the bridge, she did see a smaller boat behind them. She couldn't tell how close it was and again thought

that if she started to scream, no one would hear her
with this wind and noise, except Steve, of course—
and there was no telling what he might do to her
and Jennifer then.

"Steve," she called. He seemed to be asleep.
"Steve!"

He opened his eyes and looked at her. His expression frightened her even more. He looked like
he didn't know who she was or how she had gotten on his boat. He rose and looked to the side as if
there were some clue in the ocean. When he looked
at her again, he seemed absolutely terrified. What
was going on in his wild, mad imagination now?
she wondered.

"You were just waiting out here all this time,
weren't you?" he said. "Biding your time, waiting
and hoping I would come by. I should have taken a
different route."

"What? Steve, what are you talking about? We
need your help now. Jennifer is very sick. We need
to get her to a doctor. You have to protect her, help
her. You said you would," she fired off as quickly
as she could. It was what she had rehearsed as she
made her way to the deck.

He stared, and then he smiled. She thought that
was good. She felt some relief until he spoke.

"Very clever, Julia. You always were smart. For
years you manipulated me pretty damn good, and
even now you're still trying to do it, pretending to
be her."

"No, Steve. I'm not Julia. I am Megan, Megan.
Jennifer's not well."

The rocking of the yacht, its rise and fall, was
turning her stomach into a yo-yo. She gasped, held

tightly to the railing and waited, hoping he would snap out of whatever dream he was having.

When she opened her eyes, she saw him starting toward her, but his expression had not changed.

"You're going back where you belong," he said.

"Oh, God."

She turned to flee but lost her footing and fell to the deck hard. It nearly took all the wind out of her. He stood looking down at her as she squirmed to get herself standing. She couldn't get any footing and opted instead to continue to crawl. Now she merely wanted to get back down to the stateroom. Maybe she could lock him out.

He didn't touch her. He stood over her, watching her struggle.

"Yeah," she heard him say. "You can't stand that I have a real family now, can you? You'd do anything to stop me, to ruin my life. You want revenge, don't you? For once, I fooled you, I manipulated you and got you to fall into the sea. It's too late for you, Julia. It's over. This vengeful resurrection won't work," he said, and seized her ankle.

She screamed.

My God, she thought, he'll throw me overboard, and Jennifer . . . My God!

She reached out to grasp the bottom of the railing near the stairway in hopes of keeping him from casting her off the yacht at least long enough for him to realize what he was doing, but her weakened hands and battered body were no match for his superior strength. Her fingers lost their grip and she felt her body being pulled and lifted.

I'm going to die, she thought.

And despite all her effort, she couldn't keep herself from losing consciousness.

"Okay," Sanchez said. "We found him. He's going slowly because of the wind and the waves."

"Get me close to him," Scott said.

Sanchez cut his engine as they pulled up alongside Steve Wallace's yacht.

"What now?" he asked Scott.

Yes, what now? Scott thought. He looked about desperately and spotted a pole with a large hook.

"What is this?" he asked.

"It's a gaff. We use it to hook heavy fish."

"I've got a pretty heavy fish to hook," Scott said and took it off the rack. "Okay. Call the Coast Guard," he said. "If something happens to me . . . don't lose sight of this yacht . . . just call the Coast Guard . . ."

He navigated himself to the side of the boat. The rocking and movement made it almost impossible, but he threw the gaff over the side of the yacht and then leaped up to grasp the rail and pull himself up and over. Sanchez watched in amazement and then quickly went to his radio.

Scott got to his feet, grabbed the gaff and made his way aft. He stopped dead when he saw Steve Wallace pulling Megan by her ankle and moving toward the side of the yacht. She looked unconscious, maybe already dead. There was no time to think, to plan to build his courage. He rushed forward, taking advantage of Wallace's turning his back to him and then he shouted, "You bastard," and swung the gaff so that the hook caught Steve Wallace on his right side, just above his hip bone. It sank in deeply enough so that when Scott tugged the handle, Wallace fell back, releasing Megan's ankle.

Scott rushed to Megan and knelt beside her, lifting her head to rest against him.

"Megan . . . Megan," he cried.

Her eyelids fluttered and then opened.

"Scott?"

Steve Wallace reached back and struggled to pull the gaff out of his side. The pain was excruciating, especially when he ripped the hook out, tearing more of his flesh. He worked his way to his feet and looked at them in disbelief. Then he lifted the gaff like an axe and charged forward. Scott pushed Megan to the side and like a football lineman, lowered his head and lunged at Steve Wallace's legs just as he swung the gaff. The hook caught on the side rail and Wallace fell forward hard, losing his grip on the pole.

Scott spun and leaped toward the pole, lifting it quickly as Steve Wallace began to push himself up and turn. This time Scott swung the gaff at his neck and caught him with the hook on the side, severing an artery. Blood spurted and Wallace reached up to grasp the hook, shock now settling in his face. He stumbled back against the railing. Without hesitation, Scott shot forward, seized Steve Wallace around his calves and lifted him up, pushing forward to send him over the side of the yacht.

He dropped into the sea.

As he sunk beneath the water, he turned and died, swearing that he saw Julia waiting there, floating and smiling.

Above, Scott fell to his knees and then embraced Megan.

"Jennifer," she whispered. "Below. Go . . . I'll be all right."

He rose and hurried down, finding the stateroom and seeing her on the bed. She was sitting up, crying.

"Daddy!"

"Jen," he cried, and embraced her, lifting her and kissing her cheeks. "Jen . . . Jen . . ."

She clung to his neck. He turned and carried her out and up to the deck where Megan waited. The three of them held each other for a long moment and then he pried Jennifer's arms away from his neck.

"Come on," he said. "Let's get you two into the salon. I've got to stop the yacht," he said. "The Coast Guard is coming."

He looked over the side at Sanchez.

"You got your fish, senor," he called. "The Coast Guard is on its way. Pull back on the throttle and stop the yacht. I'll tie up alongside and help you."

"*Si, muchas gracias,* Sanchez."

With tears of happiness streaking down his cheeks, Scott turned to the bridge. Less than an hour later, the Coast Guard pulled alongside and boarded. Megan and Jennifer were taken off by a second Coast Guard vessel to be brought to the hospital for an evaluation. Scott remained behind, answering questions and explaining as best he could how this had occurred, while the Coast Guard navigated Steve Wallace's yacht back to the dock in San Diego. He told them about finding Steve Wallace's mother dead on her kitchen floor and the note that provided her the dialogue for her call to his office.

"I left the note on the table. I have no idea right now why he was trying to kill Megan," he told them, "or even why he kidnapped our daughter."

He described how he had also found Ed Marcus's wallet, and who Ed Marcus had been.

"I left it back there as well. Please inform the police."

One of the Coast Guard officers contacted the FBI, who told him they would contact the Beverly Hills police.

"An agent is being sent to meet you here," the officer told Scott.

A third vessel had located Steve Wallace's body, the gaff still sunk in his neck.

"Call the FBI back and tell them to have the agent meet me at the hospital. I must see about my wife and daughter."

As soon as the Coast Guard boat arrived at the dock, Scott was ready to rush off to the hospital. But he did thank Sanchez before he left.

"You helped me save my family," he told him. "You deserve your bonus."

"I need no bonus, senor. My grandmother, she would tell me helping you save *su esposa* and *su hija* was bonus enough."

Scott thanked him again and swore he would make a trip someday to visit this grandmother. Then he raced to the hospital.

He found Megan and Jennifer in the same examination room at the hospital. Outside in the hallway, the doctor on duty told him that except for a few bruises, Megan looked to be okay.

"She'll still need time to recuperate from the original injury, but I see no reason to keep her in the hospital. Your daughter suffered terrible emotional shock, but she's fine otherwise. Let them rest a while and then get them home," he said. "I've given your daughter something to help her sleep."

Scott thanked him and went in to see Megan and Jennifer. While Jennifer sat on his lap with her head resting against his chest, he explained to Megan how he had come to board the yacht. She listened, but he could see she was too exhausted to really understand most of it.

He was called out to meet with the FBI and went through his story again. One of the agents spoke to Megan for a while and then they both told him they'd contact him tomorrow for further information.

Megan was still in a daze when he finally took her and Jennifer out to the rental car and started the trip back. They both slept almost all the way. He was still far too hyper to be tired, but he imagined that when he did hit the bed, he would be like someone under anesthesia.

After he pulled into the driveway of their Beverly Hills home, he picked up Jennifer and carried her, with Megan holding onto his arm. He fumbled for his key and got them inside.

"Let me get her into her bed and help you up the stairs, Megan."

"I can manage," she said.

He nodded and took Jennifer up. She was half asleep, but he helped her put on another pair of pajamas and got her under the blanket.

"Daddy!" she cried when he started away.

"I'll be right here, Jen. I promise. I won't go far."

She nodded and lowered her head to the pillow again. Then he went out to see about Megan. She was sitting on their bed, still looking quite dazed.

"You better get some sleep, Megan."

She looked at him and nodded.

"I'm sorry," he said. "This is really all my fault."

"Not all, but most of it," she told him and he smiled.

"Need any help?"

"I'm okay."

"All right. I promised Jennifer I'd hang around. If you don't mind . . ."

"Come to bed, Scott," she said. "For once, be where you should be when you should be there."

"Right," he said.

He thought about going down to call his father to tell him about it all.

"Call your father in the morning, Scott," she said and he laughed. "Yes, you're that obvious," she told him.

He nodded and got himself ready for bed. It was very late, after all, and tomorrow was soon enough for everything that had to be done.

And if ever there had been any doubt before, there was none now.

There was a great deal to be done.

CHAPTER SIXTEEN

Jennifer was up before them in the morning. Neither had heard her come in, but both felt her crawl onto the bed and set herself comfortably between them. Megan kissed her right cheek and Scott kissed her left.

"I'm hungry," she said, and they both laughed.

"Hopefully, in her mind it was just like watching some scary television show," Scott said, sitting up.

"Tell you what, Jen. Why don't you come down to the kitchen with me and help me make breakfast to bring up to Mommy.

"I make a wicked cheese omelet, if you remember," he told Megan.

"I remember, although it comes under the heading of ancient history."

"Well then, let's go back in time." He clapped his hands, rose and went into the bathroom to wash up.

"Is Daddy staying here?" Jennifer asked Megan.

"He is for now," she said. "How are you, darling?"

"Why did that man do all that to us, Mommy?"

"Believe it or not," Megan said, "because he was lonely and wanted a family. He was in a lot of pain."

"Loneliness hurts?"

"Yes, it does, honey, but don't you worry," Megan told her, embracing her and kissing her. "You won't ever be lonely."

As soon as Scott emerged from the bathroom, Jennifer jumped off the bed and followed him out and down the stairs to the kitchen. She seized his hand in the hallway and held it so tightly, it was as if she would never let go.

Megan closed her eyes and opened them as soon as she lay back again. She was afraid of the images that wanted to haunt her. How do I win this battle? she wondered. She recalled something Scott had told her when they were first dating.

"Whenever I fall into a depression or get sad for any reason, I follow Joseph Campbell's advice and follow the bliss."

"What does that mean?"

"Think of a happy moment, a happy time. It doesn't have to be pure ecstasy, but a time when you were very happy."

She would do that now. Or at least, she would try, she thought.

Scott did make a great omelet. She didn't think she could eat it all, plus the toast and jam and little sausages, but she did. In fact, all three of them ate a good-sized breakfast. While he was gathering the dishes to take downstairs, the door buzzer rang.

"Your father?"

"No, I haven't called him yet," Scott said.

"Oh?"

"More important things to do first," he told her, and went down to see who it was.

It was Detectives Parker and Foto from the Beverly Hills police. They had another detective with them, who covered West LA, Detective Wilson. He had been investigating Steve Wallace's mother's death. Scott took them all into the living room.

"You should have called us as soon as you made the discovery of Wallace's mother's body," Parker told him as soon as they were all seated.

"I had more important business to attend to than a woman who was beyond any help and who looked to be party to this horror. You guys shouldn't jump on the easiest way to solve a case," he countered. His father would have liked that one, he thought—and then thought, forget his father. He liked it.

Parker looked as if he'd wilted.

"Your wife told the Coast Guard something about Wallace's first wife," Foto said.

"Yes, I did," Megan said. She appeared in the doorway. She was wearing a robe.

"I didn't want you disturbed, Megan," Scott said.

"Too late for that," she said dryly. She walked in and sat on the heavily cushioned easy chair. "He originally told me she died in a boating accident, but I believe he caused her to fall overboard and drown. Maybe he even threw her overboard, as he tried to throw me."

"We ran his file," Foto said. "It was a hard case to investigate. Her body was never recovered, so we couldn't look for trauma or anything underhanded."

"How did his mother die?"

"Forensics found tissue and blood on the side of the table. Did he push her? Was that an accident? We can't tell," Detective Wilson said.

"Do you know any motive for all this?" Parker asked Megan. "There never was a demand for money, correct?"

"He wasn't interested in money," she replied.

"Then what was he interested in?" Foto asked.

"He was looking for a new family or his first family. What I read between the lines was his wife didn't want children."

"He did all this to have a family?" Foto asked. "We have tons of creeps out there trying to dump theirs."

No one laughed.

Least of all, Scott. He looked down at the floor.

"My husband saved our lives," Megan said. "I'm sorry I implied anything that would lead you to believe he was guilty of this horrible thing. If you have any doubt . . ."

"Oh no, Mrs. Lester. We're just here to tie up some loose ends. Unless you have any more to add, we'll get out of your hair for now."

"No—for*ever*, I hope," Megan said. "No offense. You're probably all good guys."

They all smiled, even Scott.

He walked them to the door. Parker turned to him after he stepped out.

"I wouldn't say this in public, Mr. Lester, but off the record, good job. If you ever want to change professions . . ."

Scott laughed.

"Thanks. I'll stay in the dirtier business of making money, but not the same way as before, believe me."

Parker nodded. "I do," he said.

Scott watched them leave. He turned when he heard Megan behind him.

"You should call your father," she said. "The news media isn't going to be much farther behind."

"Right."

"Go to your office. I want to shower and dress and get Jennifer up and about. We're not going to lie about like invalids. That would be the worst thing."

"Absolutely right. In fact, a change of scenery might be just what the doctor ordered," he said.

She didn't respond. He watched her walk off and then he went to the den to call his father. Scott didn't permit any questions. He told him basically to shut up and listen. At the end of the conversation, Scott told him that he would indeed be the one to go to London now.

"Good idea. You should get away."

Scott looked toward the stairway.

"We're all getting away. Tell Arlene to buy three first-class tickets. Keep the return open-ended. We might do some more traveling."

"We?"

"Yes, we," he said firmly.

"Are you sure about this?"

"As sure as I am about a number of new things, Dad. We'll have one of our private executive sessions when I return."

"Now look, you've been through quite a traumatic time. You need to step back and be sure that you're thinking things out logically, clearly and—"

"You can be confident, Dad. For the first time in a long time, I am."

He hung up and slowly climbed the stairs. Megan, in a robe, with her hair wrapped in a towel, stepped out of the bathroom and paused when she realized he was standing there.

"What?" she asked.

"I want to ask you for a favor. It's a very big one and if you refuse, I won't argue. I'll accept it and walk away."

"What is it, Scott?"

"I want you to imagine I have a big eraser in my hand, a magic eraser." He held up his right fist.

She smiled.

"Yes, and . . . ?"

"And I want you to let me try to erase all my mistakes, all the errors I've made with you and Jennifer these past years. Then I want you to stand with me on some European shore and throw the eraser into the sea."

She held her smile.

"Why European?"

"I've got to go . . . *We've* got to go to London for a business meeting. A short one," he quickly added. "And then take in some theater, some touring—Jennifer's old enough to appreciate a lot of it—and then when that's done, go to that dream place where we spent our honeymoon."

"Capri?"

"Where else? I want to go to the same restaurants, if they are there, and I want to sail around the island and have lunch and swim in the colorful water, walk the narrow beautiful streets to look at the shops and hear the music, but most of all to dream of the future again. To top it off, I want us to restate our vows in that little church."

"The Church of San Costanzo, where we watched that young Italian couple marry?"

"*Si, il mio amore.*"

"That's a long time for you to be away from home and the business, Scott. What about your father?"

"We'll send him postcards."

She laughed.

"Look. Someone has to live the life he lost," he said. "After all, what's a son for?"

She continued to stare at him, unmoving. Her hesitation wilted his hope.

"I know you have good reason not to believe me. I haven't exactly given you any—"

"Shut up, you idiot," she said. "You won me back with the magic eraser."

He smiled, crossed the bedroom and embraced her. They kissed as if it were the first time. Once again, he started to roll off a litany of apologies, but she put her fingers on his lips.

"Get that eraser started," she whispered, but not as softly as she thought.

"What eraser?" Jennifer asked from the doorway.

They both laughed.

"You can't see it, Jen," Scott told her. "But you'll know it's there."

Back in San Diego at his favorite breakfast hangout, Sanchez Rosario was holding court describing his exciting adventure. His fellow fishermen and friends were in rapt attention hearing the details about this gringo who had the courage to attack so formidable an enemy on his own turf.

"And with no real plan and no real weapon," he emphasized. "I told him to call the police, but he insisted he had to do this himself."

"Was he loco?" another fisherman with a boat nearby asked. "I've seen this man Wallace. He looked like he could eat a shark alive."

"And he had the temperament of a scorpion."

"You say the gringo looked like a banker?" another inquired with a note of skepticism.

"Worse, like an accountant."

They all laughed and then the other fisherman asked, "How did you know it would work out well, Sanchez? You could have been in trouble, too, if not. I wouldn't have gone after him like that."

Sanchez smiled. "You don't listen to my grandmother."

"*Si.* Why would that matter?"

"It's like my grandmother says," Sanchez told them. "*Donde hay amor, no hay temor.* Where there is love, there is no fear. This is great strength, strength you don't know yourself is in you," he said.

His friends all nodded.

"And of course," Sanchez said, not willing to be too modest, "he had me with him."

That brought the most laughter.

Weeks later, thousands of miles apart, he and Scott would stand looking at different bodies of water. Scott would have Jennifer holding his left hand and Megan holding his right, but both he and Sanchez would think the same thought. It was what made him want to return to the shore and look out quietly. It was indeed the magic eraser.

It's the sea, they both thought, the sea that has the power to restore us.

And always will.

ANDRÉ LE GALLO

"A tale of intrigue too frightening to believe—and too believable to ignore. But you had better believe it, because Le Gallo is the real thing."
—Porter Goss, former Director of the CIA, from his introduction

A radical Muslim group has dedicated itself to the restoration of the Caliphate, a global Muslim empire, and will stop at nothing, including assassination and terrorism, to reach its goal. Steve Church is just a US businessman in Paris. He never expected to be recruited by the CIA as an undercover operative. But now, with his life on the line and with a beautiful woman as part of his cover, Steve is on his way to North Africa—and the terrorists' Saharan headquarters—in a whirlwind adventure that will change the politics of the Middle East.

"No one can talk the talk better than a man who really walked the walk for us. Now Le Gallo's in from the cold and at his typewriter, putting us on a hot trail that still balances fact and fiction."
—Barry A. Goodfield, Director of the Goodfield Foundation

The Caliphate

ISBN 13: 978-0-8439-6305-2

To order a book or to request a catalog call:
1-800-481-9191
Our books are also available at your local bookstore, or you can check out our Web site **www.dorchesterpub.com** where you can look up your favorite authors, read excerpts, glance at our discussion forum, and check out our digital content. Many of our books are now available as e-books!

✂ # ☐ **YES!**

Sign me up for the Leisure Thriller Book Club and send my FREE BOOKS! If I choose to stay in the club, I will pay only $4.25* each month, a savings of $3.74!

NAME: _____

ADDRESS: _____

TELEPHONE: _____

EMAIL: _____

☐ I want to pay by credit card.

☐ **VISA**   ☐ **MasterCard.**   ☐ **DISCOVER**

ACCOUNT #: _____

EXPIRATION DATE: _____

SIGNATURE: _____

Mail this page along with $2.00 shipping and handling to:
Leisure Thriller Book Club
PO Box 6640
Wayne, PA 19087
Or fax (must include credit card information) to:
610-995-9274

You can also sign up online at **www.dorchesterpub.com**.
*Plus $2.00 for shipping. Offer open to residents of the U.S. and Canada only.
Canadian residents please call 1-800-481-9191 for pricing information.
If under 18, a parent or guardian must sign. Terms, prices and conditions subject to
change. Subscription subject to acceptance. Dorchester Publishing reserves the right
to reject any order or cancel any subscription.